Love Comes At Twilight

A Love Story for Seniors

By
KAY MEHL MILLER
With
AL FRANCIS

Love Comes at Twilight: A Love Story for Seniors

ISBN: 1495304213
ISBN 13: 9781495304217

kaymill@aol.com
Cover photo
Michael Palmer

Authors' photo by
Phyllis Steinman Caplan Nesbitt

Printed in the United States of America
First Printing 2014

Address all inquiries to:
kaymill@aol.com

Love Comes at Twilight: A Love Story for Seniors /Kay Mehl Miller
1. Love story 2. Elders 3. Seniors 4. Fiction

Love is our true destiny.
We do not find the meaning of life by ourselves alone—
We find it with another.

Thomas Merton, *Love and Living*

ACKNOWLEDGEMENTS

First of all, thanks to you, dear readers, for choosing my book. I am delighted when you find meaning and enjoyment in my works. That you are anonymous, for the most part, doesn't make you any the less appreciated; your participation is vital.

The late Karen Batchelor was the capable editor of my last book *Living With the Stranger in Me: An Exploration of* Aging. She started to edit *Love Comes at Twilight*, but was unable to finish. I am grateful for Karen's initial observations as I am to Jeanine Dahlquist, a first reader. Jeanine enjoyed the late-life romance in the book along with the humor, the determination to live life fully and the strength shown by still independent seniors successfully coping with challenging situations in aging.

As I was writing the story, my critique group colleagues Jonathan and Osha Hayden focused on an entertaining tale with all the necessary elements of good writing. Thanks to them, I gave my very best.

Katy Byrne, a fellow writer, was the book editor. As we worked together, I saw wisdom in her ideas and adopted many of them. She is a great editor. She respected my voice as author while helping me with pacing and details that enhance visual aspects of the text.

Arlene Miller, known as the grammar diva in our Redwood Writers Club, proofread the manuscript, catching typos, errant words and odd twists of grammar. She professionally polished the manuscript.

Of course, there are those, too, who read the manuscript and wrote endorsements. Their names and credentials are on the cover. My thanks go to them for their time and effort.

Last of all, my deep gratitude goes to my very special friend Al Francis whose name appears on the cover with mine. Both of us recognize that life, love, and talent are gifts from God.

Kay Mehl Miller
Santa Rosa, CA
January 13, 2014

Chapter One

*H*ow had it happened? Love is not supposed to come in teenage proportions to someone in her seventy-eighth year, especially with someone in his eighty first! Then, too, Ellis was already married— though Carol could easily accept that being married to someone with Alzheimer's was truly a lonely business leading him to seek intimacy elsewhere.

Intimacy. That's what she missed most about Mario's passing. Not sexual intimacy, for that was over long before he died. She missed the everyday "Good mornings." The surety of his physical being, though worn and frail, had the capacity to invoke in her the feeling of belonging. With his death, she felt lost—as if she no longer belonged, not to him, not to a family, not to the world. She was a widow, a word she considered ugly, for it implied she was a remnant of death.

She shuddered. Hopefully the lingering pall of sorrow that had plagued her for so long was beginning to retreat. She crossed her fingers. She was in love, wasn't she? Oh, my God, she hadn't felt such excitement in years! Just the mere thought of Ellis sent her back fifty years. She felt like a giddy twenty-year-old, seriously infatuated, but this time armed with the blessed knowledge of flowing hot bodily juices. Not that either of them contained much in the way of hot juices at their ages! *Well, that remains to be seen*, she defiantly thought. She chuckled aloud.

Still, Ellis was thousands of miles away. They had met playing bridge online. She was unlikely to ever meet him in person. Would emails and phone calls be enough?

Her mood shifted as she thought of how much her status had changed. People think that grief is all about missing the partner, but Carol knew better. Grieving is mostly about no longer being who you thought you were. Grieving is feeling so alone that you can hardly stand to come home at night to a house empty of the energy once felt there. Grieving is bewailing the fate that brought fullness to life and then stripped it away, leaving you isolated.

Applying her lipstick, she did what she knew worked best: prepared herself to go out into the world to be distracted again. Home was a trap for her right now. Better to be with people. Besides, she did have a life to attend to. Today was women's group meeting. Yesterday had been AA and Wii bowling. Monday was basically a free day. Sunday, of course, was church, and sandwiched into niches of the week were meetings of her writers and publishing clubs, opportunities for readings at open mics, church council meetings, theater or concerts with friends, Bible study, and bridge club. Would all these busy comings and goings be enough? Perhaps she'd get an answer today with her women friends.

She checked that the doors were locked and the stove was off before she left. Sometimes she came home hours later and found she had forgotten to close one of the sliding doors to the patio or had left one burner on.

It was a short drive to Stella's house, but, as usual, she was ten minutes late.

"We were about to call you," Sophie gently scolded. Sophie was the mother hen of the group. Keeping track of everyone was an obsession with her. She needed to know how all were faring. Having been orphaned early in life and farmed out to one too many foster families, she instinctively held fast to those dear to her.

"Sorry, on the computer again and time got away from me." Carol joined the ladies in the kitchen and poured herself a cup of coffee.

"I well know how that goes," Sophie admitted. "If I want to be on time for anything, I dare not turn the machine on."

Jennifer, the newest member of the group, laughed. "Isn't it funny how all these technological inventions are supposed to save us time and end up using all the time we save?" She had met the other group members in the hospital while visiting with Sophie, who was in recovery from hip surgery.

The ladies took their coffee into Stella's living room. Evelyn, the oldest member of the group, wasn't there that day. Nearing her ninety-eighth birthday, she was beginning to fade. Her friends were concerned, but also realistic. After all, even Evelyn herself, though an avowed atheist, would look skyward and moan, "When, God? When?" She seemed ready to go, but then would be distracted by the next new thing to consider—her daughter or grandchildren going on a trip, Carol writing something new, or a new movie she'd heard about and wanted to see.

Stella tried to quietly sit down with her coffee, but in reaching for the armrest on the chair to balance herself, she exposed damage to her upper right arm.

Sophie noticed and was immediately alert. "Oh my, Stella! What happened to your arm? That's a big bruise, and it looks swollen. Is it broken?"

"No," Stella said flatly. "I fell again. Hit my arm against the dresser as I went down."

"You've got to use your walker," Dana chided. Dana's husband had died of Parkinson's, the disease that was ruthlessly threatening Stella with monstrous consequences that, for the past twenty years, she had fought to defang. A walker was a reluctant concession, and even then she had fallen using the walker.

Dana, biting her lips, tried to keep her words gentle, but the scolding intent was obvious. "Use your walker inside the house as well as outside."

Stella had heard this advice ad nauseam. She did try to use her walker in the house, though it was often in her way or it wasn't where she needed it.

"I don't understand," Jennifer said. "You seem to be falling so much."

"It's the Parkinson's," Stella sighed. "Some of us fall backwards because of it. I never know when it's going to happen. One minute I'm fine. The next, I'm down."

"Well, I still think the walker would help," Dana persisted.

"Here's what I think," Carol interjected, sensing a serious scold and hurt feelings about to surface. "You should get yourself a big inflatable suit and wear it at all times. Then when you fall, you'll bounce." She bent her arms and, hunching her shoulders, did a sitting bounce, looking more like a chicken fluffing its feathers than a bouncing ball.

Stella laughed as did the rest of the women. "That's exactly what I'd like to do, believe me." She settled back in her chair and looked gratefully at Carol.

It was time to bring up her news. Carol wasn't sure how she was going to tell them, but she knew she would tell them. They had been a group for fifteen years now, beginning as a bridge club that met once a week in a Monte Verde Village facility clubhouse. They brought their lunches and took a noon break to eat and talk. Being feisty older women who wanted more out of life than playing card games in retirement, the bridge playing ceased, but the group meetings survived.

At first, they shared their frustrations about living in a community designed for seniors while still feeling young, at least in spirit. In Carol's case, she had moved to Monte Verde when she was 58, barely old enough to qualify as a resident. Most of the women in the group, except for Evelyn, had moved in when they were also fairly young, and so they talked a lot about getting used to a place where gray hairs were the norm. As the years went by, the women in the group who colored their hair eventually gave in to nature's gray (though none of them admitted to being *gray*; they were *silver haired*) and settled down to the idea that, yes, they were aging, though they all agreed aging is a bitch.

Both Carol and Dana had recently lost husbands; Sophie's partner died before she moved to Monte Verde. Stella's husband had his own failing health to consider as he helped her manage her Parkinson's. Jennifer, at first, had not spoken much about her mate, except that they lived different lives in the same house. The group knew revelations would come in time and did not press for details. Those revelations came all at once after a scary domestic incident, which appeared to be settled now. At least Jennifer seemed less fearful, more resigned to her situation, if not happy with her marriage.

The women chatted on about Stella's injury until they decided she had done all she could to make sure she wasn't more seriously injured. Satisfied, Sophie turned to Carol and asked, "What's happening with you?"

Carol took a deep breath. Her face lit up and her eyes sparkled as she began to speak. "You know for the past four months or so I've been playing bridge online with a certain tall Texan."

"Yes." Sophie nodded uncertainly. "You've told us how cleverly he managed to get his email address to you even when the online game host blocked yours from the "friend's" message you sent him.

Carol blushed. "Yes, he actually sent me a roasted chicken recipe and told me to take the first letter of each ingredient, put them in formation, and I'd have his email address. We've been corresponding ever since; yesterday he called me."

"How did he get your phone number, not that I don't already know," Dana teased.

"Yes, I sent it to him."

"And?" Stella asked.

"He's got the most charming Southern drawl," Carol muttered, feeling heat rise in her body. "I get so lost in hearing it that I sometimes forget to listen to the words."

"So when is he coming to see you?" Dana was practical. Carol paused, thinking of Dana's experience in seeing a gentleman friend of her own. Her mind flashed details of her friend's fast-track romance; for a long moment Carol was caught in reverie. Frank came into Dana's life when she met him at a December holiday party sponsored by their local bank. He sat next to her on folding chairs and made her laugh at the silliness of hors d'oeuvres. "How can a dab of chicken on top a slice of cucumber on a bitty piece of white bread trigger such an ear-splitting belch?" was his way of introducing himself, for he had unexpectedly burped loudly in her ear. "Oh, and, by the way, pardon me," he said, clearly pleased she found his explanation for bad behavior amusing. "I had meant to say hello first."

Although it wasn't exactly love at first sight, the novel male attention and Dana's natural gregariousness created more than a friendship between them. Soon, too soon for Dana, they were living together. Feeling crowded in her own home, she packed up his things, threw them in the car, and took Frank back to living with his daughter. He howled in protest: "But we work so well together!" And cajoled: "You know I help with expenses. Two live more cheaply than one." Finally, he warned, "I'll be back. You wait and see." Dana knew better. Frank, without a driver's license because of serious sight problems, needed her to drive, and that circumstance put her in the catbird's seat. She could call the shots on picking him up or inviting him for overnight or weekend visits, and, most satisfying of all, when to take him home.

Frank's excessive attention became uncomfortable. She wanted companionship; he wanted sex. Dana was reluctant. It was only two years since her beloved David's death. "How can I?" she asked the group. "I'm still grieving. I'd feel guilty. Besides, it's been so long I'm not sure I'd know what to do anymore."

"It's okay to wait until you're ready," Sophie advised.

"Yes, I guess. It's just that it feels so good to hug and kiss someone once more."

Evelyn had made it to the group that particular day. As a retired school counselor, her interest sparked at quandaries others expressed, though she had reached a life stage where it was hard to hold on to fresh information. "Tell me," she said, "just who is this Frank?"

Dana had told the story many times before. Patiently, she answered. "Oh, Evelyn, he just kind of barged right into my life. We had such a good time talking in the bank that when he asked me to dinner, I asked what time he wanted me to pick him up."

"Now he wants sex?" The women laughed nervously. Because Evelyn also had a hearing problem, her questions required a now-expected, but painfully time-consuming, repetition of explanations that were sometimes interrupted by embarrassed hilarity. It was one of those aging things, Carol decided—something akin to not being able to hold your pee and pretending you did. Brought up to be habitually polite and proper, Evelyn ignored the laughter.

"That's about the size of it," Dana said with a broad smile.

"And you don't want sex?" This time the laughter was stifled, even though it was felt to an even greater degree. The women knew that, if given a life as long as Evelyn's, all of them would, at some point, experience similar perceptual difficulties. What now was funny to them in Evelyn was dreadful to contemplate in their own lives.

"No, it's not that, Evelyn," Dana said, still smiling. "It's just that I feel strange approaching it. I feel shy, intimidated even. How do we even start?"

"It seems to me," Evelyn said, warming to the idea of being useful to someone else, "you could talk it over and make some sort of plan."

"Maybe."

"Or," Carol interjected, "you could tell him that you need time to get acclimated to the idea. Suggest that you would be willing just to lie down on a bed next to him and cuddle a little. If he agrees to that, you just let things take their course."

"Sounds like a good plan," Evelyn agreed. Dana nodded as the other women murmured approval. Carol smiled as she remembered Dana coming to the next meeting with a glow of satisfaction that announced the strategy had worked. Dana's voice interrupted Carol's reverie and startled her.

"So?" Dana stared at Carol, wondering where her friend had gone, but eager for an answer, asked again, "when will he come to visit?" Carol considered the question. It was coming from someone who knew what it was to have an interested gentleman come into her life at a time when loneliness was an unrelenting burden. She breathed as if coming up for air. "Probably never. Ellis has a serious lung infection on top of emphysema. His health problems make traveling problematic." She paused, and then added, "at least for now."

"Perhaps that's a blessing in disguise," Sophie interjected. "You don't want another old man to take care of, do you?"

"He has assured me that would never happen." Carol felt awkward and defensive.

"So he *has* talked about coming to see you?" Sophie crowed, pleased at her own insight.

"Yes, but it is light-hearted banter. I'm not sure he really means it."

"Well, I say enjoy his friendship for now, and don't put any unrealistic expectations on yourself or him," Stella soothed, hoping to avoid conflict between the two women she wanted to keep as friends.

Wise words, Carol thought. She still didn't have the nerve to tell the group that she believed she was in love with him, or at least with the potential of him, especially when she perceived implied criticism coming from Sophie. "I feel like a giddy schoolgirl," was all she could muster.

Sophie raised her eyebrows. "Somewhat like Dana did when she talked to us about sex with Frank?"

Dana laughed. "We don't have any problems now. He is remarkably virile for a man nearing his nineties, I'll have you know." Her smile was wickedly provocative. At 71, she coquettishly felt like flaunting her new knowledge. "It's all still there!"

"Oh, Dana," Sophie scolded, "don't say it again. I was more than mildly surprised the first time you told us he could get an erection at his age and keep it."

"He doesn't consider himself old," Dana countered. "He's only 17 years older than me." She laughed again. "He always wants to go places, and *he* doesn't like to use *his* walker, either." She gave Stella a meaningful glance and sighed. "Sometimes, I'll admit, he seems so frail to me, but then it is I who am wearing out with all the driving I need to do."

"The things we have to get used to in order to have a life!" Jennifer observed. "None of the established rules seem to apply anymore, do they?"

"You've got that right," Carol said, thinking that even though Ellis's wife was not really there for him, she was nevertheless his wife. On the other hand, even AARP endorsed outside relationships for spouses of those with Alzheimer's. Did the old feminist saying "you've come a long way, baby" apply to senior women seizing uncertain opportunities? And what of the feminist values of sisterhood and banding together? Didn't she owe something to his wife? God, she didn't even know her name. She'd ask him next time they talked. She needed to know much more and, yet, she was very reluctant to disturb the cozy relationship she felt with him now. What if he didn't want her anymore? *Like that would happen*, she reminded herself. *He's thrilled that someone like me would love him. He doesn't realize how much I love and need him.*

"And so, where are we meeting next week?" Carol heard Sophie ask. It was time to stand up and go through the ritual they had casually adopted. They stood close in a circle, arms entwined, and affirmed, "So we be. Friends to the end." *True, so true,* Carol thought. *Where would we be without one another?*

Chapter Two

The unlikely romance started last September with an innocent plan to help Ellis deal with the sorrow of losing a wife to Alzheimer's. Carol imagined him lonely and isolated, living with a loved one whose mind no longer made room for him, and she felt compassion. She offered to chat with him privately in the Internet bridge game room.

At first, he didn't respond to her offer. The typed, polite "thank you" with no follow-up piqued her a little, though she couldn't say why. She chalked it up to feeling unduly rejected, for she was formally trained in helping people with problems. Surely he saw her credentials in her player's profile! Then, again, she felt weird about even thinking those kinds of thought. *Show-off*, she scolded herself. Where was this unsettling need for attention coming from? Was she afraid no one, particularly men, would ever really see her again?

Her new book, *A Journey in Time: Age, Loss, and Opportunity,* had just been published. On the Gameville "Friends" page, she wrote a private message to Peggy, a bridge-playing friend, alerting her to the book's publication: **Haven't had a chance to play bridge with you lately, though I did notice you were in the game rooms today. I chatted with Bonnie briefly, and friended a gentleman from Texas, who plays under the name Roadrunner. I am happy with my decision to play bridge on Gameville. It took me so long to decide to do so—I feared making** mistakes. Well, now I make mistakes and simply laugh about them.

Later, in the game room with Ellis, she chatted with Bonnie about her book. Ellis quietly noted the conversation, and the next day sent a private message to Carol: **Last night after dinner I went to Barnes and Noble and ordered your book. I will be going to my place in the country on Tuesday for a week of R&R and trailer repairs, not to mention the fresh air. I hope your book will arrive before I leave, for the peace and quiet of the country life is conducive to reading and reflection. I also plan to practice my culinary arts. Perhaps I will "see" you on Gameville before Tuesday, but if not, please take care. Thank you again for the kindness you've shown to a total stranger—a rare quality indeed.**

Carol was so thrilled that Ellis had actually bought her book and wanted to read it that she gave no thought to his remark on practicing culinary arts. If she had thought about it, she'd have realized that people seldom practice culinary arts when cooking for one. Lonely dinners more often were canned soup with crackers and cheese. Lost in the celebration of her own experience, she wrote back immediately.

Thank you so much for ordering my book. I am delighted that you want to read it. As for being nice to a stranger, you felt more like a friend at the bridge table. I wanted to lend you some support.

You should receive the book before you go to the country. If Barnes and Noble took your order, they should get it promptly from their distributors. I hope you enjoy it.

Have a good rest. I'll see you in the rooms, maybe, before you go, but certainly after you return.

When Ellis answered her the next day, Carol was overjoyed that she had sparked the interest of an intelligent man with a bent for philosophy and clearly stated opinions. Here was a man made for conversation, someone who emphasized ideas and probably disliked small talk as much as she did. However, the reference to "one" in his message, instead of the more personal "I," gave her pause. She viewed him with a writer's eye, thinking his prose a little stiff and formal, but nevertheless, fused with content that boded well for establishing a friendship between them. Yes, at least a friendship. Additionally, he had almost immediately dropped the "one" business. She sighed. Must she analyze everything? The answer, of course, was yes.

Ellis had written: **One must, in order to survive, reinvent oneself as one transitions through life, or wither and die emotionally. I do not participate in Facebook, Google, Twitter or any other of the myriad forms of "social" gatherings on the Web. It all seems rather desperate to me and possibly invasive. One can have one million "Friends," but what is to happen when the computer is turned off and the loneliness returns? I think millions are deprived of intimacy and are searching madly for ways to find it.**

I am wondering, with your experience and background, if you have ever considered writing on the dynamics of all these kinds of happenings. There is a great disconnect between the natural world and the sterile world in which we have been urbanized, standardized, mesmerized, categorized, organized, and Sanforised. If we did not know of other worlds, we most likely would think the one we live in is normal and all there is to life. How very, very sad. I view the world in which I find myself now as totally unacceptable; in order to navigate life, one must appreciate the paradoxical nature of it all, or otherwise become

rudderless and tossed about on a very unforgiving angry sea. You, from what I read so far of your book, have "been there, done that," and have the T-shirt to prove it.

Re-inventing the self after life leads you in a new direction. Of course, he would know something about that with a disengaged wife. Carol's heart went out to him. Sensing that this Gameville message was his way of making a significant disclosure to her, she decided to send him her email address in her next message.

Yes, I've been to those lonely places. My book does speak of this. After Mario died, I felt so lost—-angry too—in a world designed for couples. You will read in my book how I began to rebuild my life by going to church. I don't even know why I decided to go, except the church I picked was one where Mario attended a group designed especially for men who had lost their wives, had wives with dementia or Alzheimer's, or, as in Mario's case, were anxious about their own future. Anyhow, in that church I started playing bridge with their card club, and then volunteered to be on an advisory committee to the pastor. Soon, the pastor and I were teaching a Bible Class in theodicy. I began to feel real again until I'd leave that comforting space to come home and face a cold, empty loneliness.

The worse part about it, as you must know, is not having someone in the house to talk with you—that's the intimacy that I miss. I'm recovering now. I still get lonely, but I can handle my feelings better now that I've stepped back into the world.

I agree with you about technology. My fellow writers are advising me to get on Facebook, Linked In, Twitter, and all the other nonsense that is out there. I haven't yielded yet. I like the idea of selling my book the old-fashioned way—talking to people and letting them pass it on. What I see in all this exchanging of mostly useless information (besides selling) is a longing to connect to another human being. I guess I'm lucky. I am not afraid to approach people and start talking. That's the kind of connection I like best.

If you'd like to talk with me about your world now—your unacceptable world—I'd be happy to listen and respond. My email is Caroling2560@aol.com. I knew a happy couple, years ago when I lived in Hawaii, who had their normal life interrupted when she got Alzheimer's. He had to put her in a home. After a while, he began to appear in public with another woman, and all his friends were glad for him. He just wasn't meant to live alone.

As for me, I'm having a good time now being independent. I haven't sought a new relationship except very early in my grieving.

See you at bridge. Carol Bradley

Carol was pleased that she had added the caveat of not looking for a new relationship and had stressed her independent nature. After all, she really didn't know him, though he had signed his recent messages with his full name, Ellis Thompson. A little caution was surely in order. She chuckled to herself. *Old gal, what are you getting yourself into now?*

The reply to her message made Carol laugh out loud. How good it was to laugh once more, to revel in excitement. Possibilities were looming.

He next messaged her: **Dear Carol, Thank you for attempting to send along your email address. The first part was successful, but the last part, showing your Internet provider, was unintelligible. My guess is Gameville is protecting** your privacy and security by not providing your Internet provider. Alas, I cannot email you, unless you are a good detective. I am going to give you my address in an unconventional way. See if you can decipher this and thus email me:

Energetically a chicken ran across the road,
Light and feathery it was.
Lean and lanky roosters are not fit for the table.
It was not a frying chicken,
So a nice fat hen is most preferable
Tightly stuffed and roasted with
1 bay leaf,
9 Carefully selected stalks of celery
3 diced carrots
1 clove of fresh garlic, baked
@ 325 degrees for
A time until the juices run clear
Or the bird is nicely browned
Lightly all over
.Complete the dinner with mashed potatoes
Complimentary relish tray
Olives and
Mustard greens to give it touch of Texas.
Don't you just adore spy work?"

"I love it," she wrote in her first actual email to him. "Can you see the broad grin of pleasure on my face?" She jumped up from her computer chair and did a little victory dance. She had attracted the attention of a man with wit, humor, and a literary brain. At this point, the body didn't matter. In fact, she had no desire to even see a photograph of him. Here was a chance to build a fantasy with a man who might be her match.

There had been other men after Mario's death. One very sweet younger man, whose education after public school consisted of Army classes in electronics, responded enthusiastically, taking her to see the new production of *The Wiz* in San Francisco. Both enjoyed being together, but the physical attraction just wasn't there, though she hoped it would be; she missed so much having a man envelop her with hungry arms and loving hands. She was so vulnerable that, even knowing there was no chance of them coupling, she still schemed to make it happen. They did get as far as holding hands, but then, unexpectedly, he moved to the East Coast and out of her life.

The first few years of her mourning for Mario brought troublesome confusion. Her longing to be loved triggered a reckless disregard of whatever her sensible mind advised. She kept eyeing men she'd meet, starting conversations even. Often, just when things were getting interesting, a woman would plop down next to her and sweetly introduce herself as the wife or girlfriend. Carol, mortified, would hastily excuse herself, furious at Mario for dying and feeling wretched for being so needy. Even when she discovered an available man at some casual gathering, her sensible mind prevailed, urging caution, *extreme* caution. *What about extreme loneliness?* she wanted to scream. But that was then.

Carol let out a huge sigh and then slowly smiled, realizing that life was offering her a unique opportunity. This new man, Ellis, might easily become a very interesting part of her life. Conveniently, *he was thousands of miles away in Texas!* He had no face, no body, and no spoken voice at this point. His attributes lay in his intellect, his adroitness in writing, and his competence at playing bridge. She was free to fantasize—to make of him what she would—and to never have to answer for her behavior. This could be fun.

And so fantasize she did—at her next full-body massage. Lying there naked on Judy's table, she imagined him making tender love to her. The pleasurable strokes, the waves of anticipation, and the fiery desire were all in her mind; Judy's hands were professional, as usual, uninvolved in the fantasy. The massage had relaxed Carol to the point that she could disappear into a sweet inner world where Ellis artfully used the free rein he had been given.

Happy? Oh, yes, Carol was immeasurably happy. Here in her late seventies, she was reawakening to sexual pleasure. It had been so long, so very long. *Hope springs eternal*, she thought, laughing gleefully to herself. It was as if she had stolen back her youth, but this time seasoned with the experience of age. Could there be such life after life, and could such a life be satisfying without a physical presence? She didn't know, but she was going to find out. Definitely.

Chapter Three

On Sunday, an email from Ellis awaited Carol when she got home from her writer's club meeting. Having returned from his country place, he was reading her book on aging. He wrote: **After the first few pages, I began to realize that I am a sojourner with you on a journey that the two of us know all too well. Moreover, I understand that I am about to look rather deeply into your mind and soul. You can be assured I will not take this experience lightly.**

His words were sensual. Deliberately so? Or was he simply a passionate man, willing to be seen as such? A touch of old-fashioned thinking showed in his use of the word "sojourner." She liked that. His feet appeared firmly planted in the present and his mind able to reach judiciously into the past to appreciate time and values embedded there, character traits that made her feel safe.

She laughed as she read his intention to give her some of his history to assure her that he was not "Attila the Hun." As if Attila would be interested in a woman her age! Well, maybe so if Attila thought there was money in it for him. She supposed predators might use Gameville to stalk victims, yet she couldn't imagine one patient enough to play hours of bridge with her.

Carol's fear was that his old-fashioned manner might be an indication of conservative religious and political views. The last thing she'd ever want in a relationship was a fanatic who would not understand or accept her gay son. She'd prefer Attila!

Ellis Thompson, informally "El" as he signed his last email, was 81 years old. He had worked as a scientist in the oil industry, thus the Texas residency, she supposed. He was a Southerner, born and raised in Louisiana and educated in schools there. As a matter of curiosity, she Googled his name and found his picture in a college yearbook. The fading image was much too small for her to get any sense of what he looked like then. No matter what technique she tried, she was unable to resize the image. Frustrated, she scowled and gave up.

Reading her book and learning some of her history might seem a convenient shortcut for El, but the book wasn't the real Carol. If the relationship flourished, El would get to truly know her, all the secret parts of her, even those she kept from her closest confidents. Her book focused on aging—her aging. Writing it was a joyous experience, for she felt herself coming alive once more as she told the story of rebuilding her life. The power of her own words to heal and give her hope had been a surprise, one she fervently wished for her readers. Carol loved writing. She loved seeing words gather and group themselves as she typed. She enjoyed puzzling over just how to tell a certain part of the story, while looking for just the right word to convey the meaning she trusted to grow out of a collection of words—her words, but, mysteriously, not always her meaning. She truly understood what many authors had learned: "I write to see what I think."

Since joining The First Lutheran Church of Santa Bella, she had grown in her faith; she was only seeking comfort when she first walked through the doors, but she soon found herself involved, particularly in assisting the young pastor, Colum O'Neill, in teaching the class on theodicy. Meeting weekly to make and discuss lesson plans provided intellectual stimulation for both of them. Fresh from the seminary, but not a youngster (he was 30 when he was called to serve), Colum enjoyed helping Carol understand the theological underpinning of the church.

As a writer, she well understood the muse who took over her flying fingers on the computer keyboard, making rich with meaning the words coming out of her. With Colum's help and her willingness to trust her strengthened faith, she began to recognize the mysterious workings of the Holy Spirit in creating meaning out of the texts they were studying—not that she could ever say so publicly. She wasn't that comfortable yet.

Enough of this reflection, she thought. Typing a quick email to El, she told him of a fresh sorrow. **I just lost a very important friend to me. He was my first publisher and gave me advice on the new book. He was killed in an automobile accident two weeks ago It is doubly reassuring to know that new friends come, not to take the place of old, but to teach us that life does go on and that we need to respond to joy when it is offered to us.**

More later, I'm sure. Carol

Yes, she was glad to have El in her life. Losing Bob Clarkson had been hard. In addition to her first book, Bob had published Mario's work, a memoir of his travels as a young man during the Great Depression. She sighed. Another tie to her late husband severed. Suddenly, Carol was tired and depressed. *How can someone be so happy one minute and depressed the next? Answer, Ms. Psychologist*, she chided herself. *You're supposed to know the answers!*

No matter how hard she fought against it, she was still grieving. Grief would take its own time, unresponsive to the control that Carol had in managing her life. She knew, intellectually, that she was depressed when she talked to her friends in the women's group. "Life has no meaning," she declared one day. "We make it up. We create meaning as we do the things we do. Only then, do we know what those activities mean to us."

"Well, maybe," Sophie said, correctly assessing Carol's mood. "Right now, you feel that way. However, I hope life has some meaning other than the ones my poor brain creates from the things I do. When Kyle puts his little hand in mind, and I feel that absolute trust he has in his nana, that's all the meaning to life I need."

"Of course, an experience like that one is meaningful," Carol agreed. "Without you and Nathan getting married and creating a family, your grandson would not exist today."

"I don't know. That reasoning seems a little broad to me. If I had married someone other than Nathan, I still might have created a family and still have a Kyle of my own."

Carol sighed. "I didn't mean to say that there is no meaning in life, only that we seem to create whatever meaning there is. I usually don't think about life in those terms, but since Mario died, I find myself thinking what *is* it all about, anyway?"

"I know," Dana interjected softly. "Believe me, I know. "I really miss David. There's a big hole in my life now where there was once a person who gave my life meaning. Even the years I spent taking care of him provided a reason for my living. Now, I'm not so sure."

"But you have a big, supportive family," Stella said. "Surely, your family gives meaning to you as much as Sophie's grandchildren do to her life."

"Goes without saying," Dana agreed, "yet, losing a spouse is so traumatic, so jarring to your being. We were married fifty years! Remember when he first died, and I said I felt a sharp pain in my gut every time I thought of him? It's as if part of me were cut out and taken away with him. As the rawness softens, there's always that knowing hole inside. That space that used to be filled with love, joy, and purpose in being together as husband and wife is empty. I cannot fill emptiness with memories. Memories are past events to me now, or if I do reminisce, I tend to feel bitter. It's then that I question the purpose of life."

Evelyn let out a big sigh. "My Saul has been gone thirty years now, and I still miss him. I have a big loving family, also, but it isn't enough. Having someone who loves you, protects you, sleeps beside you every night, argues with you, even yells at you now and then— that gives meaning to being alive."

Carol leaned forward, eager to share an insight. "Colum says there is an alternative Adam and Eve creation story in which God took Adam, split him in half, and made one half female and the other male. The idea is that neither person is satisfied until united with the other."

"Who's Colum?" Evelyn asked, confused again.

"You know. He's my pastor," Carol explained. "Do you suppose it is as simple as that? Perhaps it does take a special person, a mate of whatever gender, to complete us."

"Interesting," Jennifer mused. "I'm not really into Biblical myths, but the metaphor is certainly striking."

Carol felt better. "It's always good to talk out problems with you, my friends," she told the group just before they finished the session. "What would we do without one another?"

Once home, Carol thought how fortunate she was to have friends to share her aging. The women, so different in many ways, were remarkably similar in outlook and feelings. She reviewed what she knew about them and made notes on her computer, thinking that someday she'd write about them.

Sophie, married at 21, lived with Nathan for 53 years before his heart attack. The loss was still fresh after six years; she could not bear talking about it. Nathan, seven years older than she, had been a doting, attentive husband, though inclined to introversion.

Sophie, on the other hand, thrived on relationships. Her numerous girlfriends vied for her attention; she generously gave time to them, prompting mild complaints from Nathan, that he seldom saw her. With Nathan gone, Sophie felt as devastated as the rest of the widows in the group, but was unwilling to show her grief.

Until her illness began to erode parts of her life, Stella was very active with her church and her neighbors. She started a block party in her neighborhood and a monthly luncheon for the neighborhood women. Stella, 73, and Ralph, her 77-year-old second husband of thirty years, visited family in Monterey and on the East Coast and still, despite her Parkinson's, managed trips overseas, though not as many as they used to take.

Dana was the practical member of the group. Whenever a problem arose for someone, it was usually Dana who had a solution that cut through emotional morass and helplessness. Her advice began with the words, "Why don't you . . ." and ended with a definite solution. More often than not, her suggestions provided just enough direction for the owner of the problem to puzzle out her own resolution. Brought up in a big city, Dana was street smart. She seldom trusted what she was hearing, a trait that came in handy in caring for her husband during the fifteen years of his illness when she had to make decisions based on sound research and common sense. She had two grown children, two grandchildren, and the knack of attracting many good friends. She was generous with her time and offers to help, but also knew how to guard against making sacrifices that cut into taking care of herself.

Jennifer, at eighty, was a bundle of energy. Her second marriage of twenty years was a bitter disappointment. She and Peter shared a house, but not a bedroom. They seldom ate together and rarely spoke. Jennifer had not yet aired her problems with the group, so Carol didn't quite know what to make of the situation. A socially conscious woman, Jennifer turned her interest in theatrical dancing into teaching local school children to express themselves through movement and poetry. Her own son and daughter were not close to her, and she seldom saw her two grandsons; her daughter-in-law was unwilling to share them, a situation that pained Jennifer.

Evelyn, ninety-seven, the oldest group member, lost her husband to a stroke in his late fifties. She was close to her daughter and her son and their children. When her first great-grandson was born, the group thought a jubilant and shining Evelyn might jump for joy, but she sensibly just beamed her pleasure. An intelligent woman, who had a long career in counseling and working with children, Evelyn was now so frail she seldom attended group. She wanted to come to group, just as she wanted to still volunteer in the many charitable organizations that had been her life's work after retirement, but her body just wouldn't let her.

There had been other members of the group. One of them, Irene, a woman who loved being fashionably thin, was insecure about her lack of education; she yearned to go to college, a dream crushed by an early marriage during World War II. When dementia set in, Irene panicked. "Oh, I hate this; I hate this," she'd moan. "I can't remember anything!" She left the group and ultimately died. Her loss saddened everyone, though what seemed worse was the long period Irene endured in a nursing home with no memory at all of who she was or had been. Even coherent speech was taken from her. In the end, her friends could not bear to visit her.

Then there was she. Carol had survived three relationships, two of which ended in divorce. Her first husband, Harold, fathered their two sons, Patrick and Paul. When he was 24, her younger son, Paul, told her, but not his father, "I'm gay." After the shock, shame, and self-blame, a newly aware Carol became an activist, marching in Pride parades, serving on committees, and writing columns advocating for gay rights. Patrick, always a loner, joined an obscure religious group and married a foreign woman who rejected a relationship with Carol. Carol had no idea why. What had she done? Eventually, Patrick's wife convinced her husband to cut ties with his mother, thus denying Carol access to two grandchildren and her only great-grandchild. She hadn't spoken to Patrick or his family for eighteen years now. If Carol had stayed with Harold, they would have been married fifty-four years. *How does time pile up like that?* The marriage lasted sixteen years, as did her second marriage—to Edwin, a man ten years younger than she. No children were involved in that marriage, but with Mario, twenty-three years older than she, came two grown children, four grandchildren, and two great grandchildren.

Carol shook her head and grinned. *And they say men are womanizers!*

Her past, with all the drinking and carousing, had its part in making Carol who she was. She was smart enough to know that her alcoholism during their formative years must have done damage to her sons. She was sorry about that. Although successfully recovered since they were in their early teens, Carol was left with enough guilt to distort her feelings about what she deserved out of life. Nevertheless, she was not a quitter; she used her experiences in helping other people understand and solve problems. In her writings, she openly examined her shortcomings. Being around recovered alcoholics in meetings, she realized that, for the most part, she and the others were sensitive and intelligent souls felled by alcohol. Life could resume and be better, she learned. Impulsively, she returned to school for two post-graduate degrees and became a therapist late in life, mostly, she admitted to herself, *to see what makes me tick!*

Carol leaned back in her computer chair, strangely satisfied despite the rough spots of life. She signed off her server and shut down the machine. Bed would feel good to her tonight.

Chapter Four

*E*llis was awed. Here he was, 81years old—realistically viewed as past his prime, to say the least— and a woman of exceptional interest to him, a published writer, no less, was unexpectedly thrust into his life. He had read enough of Carol's book to be stunned by her honesty, and though she was writing about women's issues, he, too, could identify with her feelings. Her words practically leaped from the pages into his psyche to trigger his own deeply felt response; but then, wasn't that what good writing was supposed to do?

What next? Carol was politely interested in him at the Gameville website bridge table when he mentioned that his wife has Alzheimer's; she even offered to lend a sympathetic ear should he want to talk about the latest addition to Joanne's many health issues. He was tired of the messy sham his marriage had become, angry that he'd stayed in the marriage only to feel trapped now by obligation. On reflection, it seemed bad mannered to talk about his wife in the chat room, so he hadn't acted on Carol's offer. That's what he told himself, but the truth was, he was mildly uncomfortable with the idea. What had possessed him to mention his wife's affliction in the first place? Still, Carol's immediate compassion aroused sufficient interest for him to buy her book. That she had written to thank him was gratifying. He didn't expect that, but it happened.

There was something about all this that seemed a bit magical.

Beth called from the active living area of the trailer. "I've got supper on the table. You coming to eat?" They were in their third day of a ten-day stay at the trailer site, a hundred miles into the country from the senior residency high-rise condos where he lived with his wife in Houston. Once a month he'd flee from the polluted hot area of the city to the peace and quiet of what he liked to call his country place.

"Be right there," he answered. Beth cooked occasionally, though he was the one who relished cooking. Soups were his specialty. Today, however, he was relaxing on the queen bed in back, reading Carol's book. He was unusually tired lately and a bit short of breath. He hoped the respite from the city would clear his weakened lungs. Like many of his generation who were Marlborough men, he had paid for the macho image with emphysema. Modern medicines kept him reasonably comfortable, though he was prone to sudden coughing and, during the winter months, especially, was plagued by phlegm, which definitely clashed with his image of himself as a dapper fellow. He was Southerner enough to refer to himself as "boy," but careful not to offend others with the term. He liked to think of himself as a perpetual thirty-five-year-old in an old man's body. *Mature*, that is, he reminded himself. *Not old. Never old.*

He put down the book, swung his six-foot frame off the bed as if he truly were a lad of thirty-five, but used deliberate caution to place his feet on the floor. He walked carefully through the bathroom into the dining area of the 40-foot park trailer. Beth had made an iceberg salad with a ketchup and mayonnaise dressing, a perfect accompaniment to the spaghetti and tomato sauce she was serving. He sat with her at the table, bowed his head as she said grace, and began to eat.

"So what do we need to do tomorrow?" she asked. "Is Ramon coming to mow the pasture? Or are we going to La Grange to shop for that robe you forgot to bring?"

He laughed. "Now, Beth, you know I can't stay dressed *all day long every* day. I need that robe. Grrr . . . I'm so mad at myself for forgetting to bring mine from the condo. I think we do need to go. I'll give Ramon a call tonight and ask him to delay a day or two."

"As you wish," she agreed. They ate in silence then. Beth was not much of a conversationalist, partly because she had physical problems. She ate slowly to avoid heartburn, a condition that routinely plagued her when she ate acidic foods. She believed if she ate deliberately, her body would strike a natural balance between digestive juices and the food she fed it. Ellis was skeptical, but didn't contradict her. He knew better. They had been friends for years—lovers, at one time— but ardor cooled when neither of them felt able to fulfill the emotional needs of the other. Beth was too private, too much of an introvert for him. He wanted more passion in life than she was willing to give. Even now, he thought, *I need passion*, especially now. He and Beth were comfortable friends; she was willing to accompany him to the country as helpmate, and he appreciated that kindness. Secretly, he suspected she was concerned with him being alone in the isolated location. Joanne had no such concern for his well-being. Even before Alzheimer's, she would never consider sleeping in his country trailer home—too uncomfortable, he suspected. No, Joanne was content to have Beth with him and apparently not at all interested in what another woman in his life might mean to him.

The pain of losing his marriage years ago still haunted him. Joanne at first made a good home for him and their two sons while working in the public library. He had a cushy job with a Texas oil company, exploring potential well sites. They had it all: big house, swimming pool, comfortable income, friends, parties, and good times together. He viewed their marriage as working fine, even though his job kept him away from home, sometimes for months at a time. She took an early retirement at age fifty-five when mysterious pains began to change her life. Doctors were baffled as she complained about her arms hurting, then her shoulders and her legs. There were no visible signs of disease, yet suddenly there were pains—shooting pains, stabbing pains—all over her body. She couldn't bear to be touched. She couldn't sleep. It took five long years for a doctor to finally say the word: fibromyalgia. By then, Joanne was clinging to her side of the bed, Ellis to his.

The disease made them both crazy. Ellis missed sex. The few times he attempted to reach for her, he was rebuffed by yelps of pain. He wanted desperately for her to recover; he longed to find a way to fix the problem. He was a solution guy and had no patience for problems that couldn't be solved. He sometimes thought he was the problem, for she seemed perfectly capable of going to lunch with her friends and being reasonably pain free then. She wouldn't talk to him about this contradiction. He wondered now whether Alzheimer's, unwelcome and unrecognized, had its beginning then; they had so many problems, and her refusal to communicate was baffling.

There was the guilt too. Looking back, he knew his most serious drinking coincided with the onset of Joanne's physical problems. When she first began to complain, he tried to analyze her problems, but she didn't want that help. She wanted him to hear her, to understand how much she was hurting; he just didn't get it. You have a pain, you take a pill, and if that doesn't work, you go to the doctor. The more she talked about her pains, without wanting to do something constructive about them, the more frustrated he got. When he was frustrated, he drank, and when he drank, he got drunk. The booze gave him courage. *Why not? She doesn't appreciate me. Has no use for me other than being a money machine. Why not?* Impulsively, he reached for his car keys. There was a bar he knew about where single girls looked for interesting guys. He still was an interesting guy, probably more so since his dark hair had started to show salt and pepper.

As the years passed, the drinking and carousing increased. Joanne's pain turned into diagnoses of arthritis, migraines, irritable bowel syndrome, female urethral syndrome, and vulvar vestibulitis. There were surgeries too. As arthritis eroded cartilage in her joints, hip and knee replacements were necessary. The mountain of drugs Joanne used did not alleviate her pain, but did give her a chance to manage it.

Ellis spent less time at home. When not out in oil fields, he was out in greener pastures, looking for love he didn't feel at home. His drinking fed the illusion he was adored by the bar ladies who clustered around him; the reality came the next morning, waking up early in some sad hotel room next to a drunken woman whose name he didn't know, his head still reeling from the booze, and a sour taste in his mouth.

Work came to a halt when he retired at sixty-two, but there were still years of hopeless drinking ahead. He couldn't stand being in the house with Joanne. The booze and womanizing did him in one night when he and his current femme fatale were stopped by a Texas state trooper who noticed Ellis fishtailing his Caddy convertible across two lanes of the US 59 Eastex Freeway. The charge was driving under the influence of alcohol for him; for her it was a taxi ride back home. Ellis sheepishly and gratefully paid the fare before being handcuffed and driven away in the police car to sober up overnight in a jail cell.

The irony was he had been careful not to drink too much that night. He didn't know that he had lost his tolerance for alcohol until a few months into the AA program to which he surrendered after the humiliation of a hefty fine and the threat of jail time should he offend once more. In AA meetings, he learned he could no longer predict which drink it was that pushed him into utter and complete drunkenness. Being caught was deeply shameful; telling Joanne was worse. He couldn't, he just couldn't face telling her about the woman he'd placed in their car or where they had been just before the trooper stopped them. Not that the expensive hotel room had been worth the effort. Booze and age—he was 66 at the time—made his sexual performance embarrassingly farcical. It was none of his wife's business anyway, he told himself, still angry with her hands-off, no intimacy attitude that was now the hallmark of their marriage.

He had to tell her about the DUI, however. She looked at him coldly, but said nothing. She had been in Alanon for a year, he found out later. When he finally understood the twelve steps of AA and Alanon, he was convinced she had been unable to absorb much of the concept. She didn't blame or scold, but treated him with indifference, which annoyed him. Nevertheless, he kept his anger in check. They never talked about his drinking and its effect on her. Conversation settled into a routine of checking on one another's schedules simply to decide where they needed to work together to put up a front for their families. Mostly, they went their own ways with a minimum of explanation of planned absences. They carried cell phones for emergencies.

After sobering up, Ellis realized he was truly alone and, if he were to have any meaning to life, he'd have to build a new one. He went back to the church he and Joanne had attended early in their marriage and began leading a Bible study group and serving on the church council. Busy with religious duties and service work in AA, he spent most of the weeknights out. In AA and in church, he made new friends. The distractions soothed him; he began to feel as if he had a life once more. Some of the distractions turned into brief affairs with AA women, and once, even with a lady at church; however, none were particularly stimulating. He wanted more out of life. He enjoyed being around smart women; he liked going to the theater and to classical concerts. Though there were women who had similar tastes, they all seemed to be unavailable to him—most were in stable marriages. Such women would accept his flirtatious teasing, but then ward off any serious attention with a discouraging "Oh, go on, you. I know what you're up to." He could get only so close. He was lonely and learned to live with the feeling.

In his seventies, Ellis settled down. Convinced that he had missed an opportunity to leave Joanne and was now beyond intimacy with another woman, he made his peace with a wife who was increasingly helpless and dependent on him. Church became burdensome at some point, so he dropped his affiliation, but kept his strong belief in God and his conviction that he was forgiven and loved by his Higher Power. He began to work with Christian ministries, driving seniors to doctors' appointments and delivering meals to the needy. He attended fewer AA meetings as he aged; he felt he had absorbed the principles of the program; he relied on his conscious contact with God to keep him sober.

Joanne began to show signs of serious dementia early in her seventies. At first he was impatient with her, believing she was deliberately forgetting plans they had made or carelessly misplacing her clothes and jewelry, or writing checks for the wrong amount or to the wrong payee. She didn't cook anymore. Planning dinner seemed beyond her grasp. She preferred eating out, and they did so every night, except for special occasions when Ellis would cook a meal for the gathered family.

Joanne was both lost and mysteriously capable: she dressed and groomed herself; she called friends to meet them for lunch; she spent time at the library where she had worked, and she was capable of driving herself wherever she went, as long as the place was familiar. Routine seemed to be her ally. Though he worried about leaving her alone, he knew there were people in the condo building who would look in on her and call him or one of the boys if needed. He didn't want the responsibility of taking her independence from her, not yet. Ellis sighed.

Since they had finished dinner, Ellis cleared the table and did the dishes while Beth watched television. "Want to take a short walk?" he asked Beth. "The moon is full tonight. Should be pretty."

"No, I don't think so," Beth replied. "I'm interested in this program now. You go ahead."

Ellis swung open the trailer door, walking the short distance to the chain link fence and unlocking the padlock. He walked down the country road, intending to walk briskly, but was stopped by shortness of breath. Nothing new, he told himself, but changed his mind, anyway, and reversed his course. Back in the trailer, he told Beth, "I'm just a little tired tonight. I'm going to lie down."

"Be there soon," she promised. He shut the bedroom door to tune out the noise of the television, lay down on the bed, and picked up Carol's book.

Chapter Five

*H*ome again from his retreat, Ellis couldn't wait to write to Carol: **My computer is making strange noises and may be about to crash. I don't know how long I can stay online. Aside from that, breathing issues have surfaced for me once again—groan. I'm off to my doctor tomorrow and fervently hope she can keep me upright.**

I really like your book. Your candor is amazing. Not many women, I suspect, would be so forthcoming in looking at the processes of their own aging. Bravo! You tell it like it is.

If **I can stay online regularly, I will keep you posted on the status of my computer as well as my own health. I wouldn't want you to think I have fallen off the edge of the earth if you do not hear from me for a while.**

To Carol's surprise, the irksome anxiety she felt when no emails from Ellis appeared in her inbox was easily replaced by satisfying calmness when one appeared. Apparently, there was no computer at the trailer. Recognizing that the Internet was their sole source of communication, a fresh worry assailed her: *if his home computer crashed, I'd be completely cut off from him!*

She typed nervously **I hope your computer gets stable and you as well! Please don't fall off the edge of anything; I'd surely miss your emails. I'm sorry to hear of your** breathing problems. I, too, have issues with breathing. I was diagnosed with emphysema twenty- eight years after I quit smoking. What a downer. I really thought I'd escape consequences, but don't we all? Did you smoke as well? My emphysema is moderate and doesn't usually slow me down. I may never need oxygen, my doctor told me. Oh well, I guess we are destined to develop *something* as we age.

I think of you often, though I'm very busy lately. Not only have I had the book to manage, but a friend from the Midwest is coming to visit. It's probably a good thing for me to take some down time with him. We will go to the ocean, to the Academy of Sciences in San Francisco, to my Bible class, and to church.

Thanks for your generous comments on my book. I'm glad you like it.

Carol deliberately shared her health status with Ellis. It was important that he know she was ailing too, and didn't mind that he had ailments. They were building a friendship, maybe something more. Carol grinned, mildly embarrassed at the thought. It was early in the relationship, but she couldn't help it; she dreamed of more. *This is no time for little girl coyness,* she told herself. It was a good thing Will was coming to visit. He'll provide a welcome distraction. Still, she found herself wishing it were Ellis that would tour her turf with her. She broke her mood by shaking her head. *Too early*, she thought, *really too early*. She had been corresponding with him for only a month.

Will came bouncing in from his cross-country drive to California from Nebraska, his boyish smile crinkling his face. She was genuinely happy to see him. They had known one another for thirty-seven years, having met in early sobriety in Hawaii. A twenty-five-year-old seaman in the Navy then, he was now sixty-two, but still seemed twenty-five to her.

"Howdy," he greeted her, looking like an old-fashioned farmer with his blue denim jacket and red baseball cap. "Got a cup of coffee for an old friend?"

"Of course, my dear, come in and make yourself at home." She gave him a quick hug and a huge smile. They talked frequently by phone over the years, for his stint in the Viet Nam War had left him with posttraumatic stress; he often turned to her for comfort and re-assurance. He was a sensitive man struggling to cope with complex feelings in a world full of pressures and problems.

"You look wonderful," she told him. He had aged well, losing the protective surplus of weight he once carried. His now-gray hair was thin, but there was still enough of it to suggest the youth he once was. "I haven't seen you in, what? Twenty-five years? Maybe more? You never met Mario, did you?"

"No, I didn't." Will lowered his head in a gesture of apology. "I did read his book, though. I keep it on my night table and pick it up to reread parts now and then."

"Yes, I'm not surprised. Mario was a really good storyteller. Supper's ready. Want to eat?"

The next few days were spent peacefully. Will was a considerate guest. Never married and used to living alone, he preferred explor-ing the town of Santa Bella on his own, leaving Carol time to follow her own interests before he returned to eat with her at supper time. At odd moments during the day, she'd go online and play a hand or two of bridge, looking for El, but not finding him. *Hmm. Must be busy*, she thought.

After searching through all the antique shops in town, looking for treasure to sell in Nebraska, Will usually brought home a treat for her—chocolate candy or fruit and, once, a half-gallon of her favorite chocolate ice cream. Ten days flew by, filled with talk; outings to the ocean, San Francisco, and church; and long drives through rolling hills brilliant with autumn vineyards. She didn't have much time to spend at the bridge tables or to think about El. When she did finally log in after Will left for home, there was no sign of Ellis. Surely, if his computer had crashed, it was back up by now.

"Where's Roadrunner?" she finally asked Bonnie in the game room chat.

"Don't know," Bonnie replied. "Haven't seen him lately."

"That's strange. He used to play bridge nearly every day."

"I know, "Bonnie typed. "I can't remember when he was here last."

His absence perturbed Carol. She looked forward to resuming their meetings at bridge. Most of the time, when she played, he was partnered with someone else; the few times they had partnered, the games were nondescript, preventing her from displaying her competence at the game, which she hoped would spark his interest in playing with her. Now he wasn't even there.

Annoyed, she deliberately signed into a rated game, hoping to improve her bridge standing. The code she had been assigned signified "beginner." *I am not a beginner,* she huffed. She had played the game since she was twelve. Because each player in the rated game had to approve her presence at the table and all were strangers to her, Carol felt nervous. She was used to social niceties of "Hi" and "Welcome" in the less formal settings, so she felt a little rattled by the silent, business-like start in the immediate deal of the hand; her brain hadn't yet registered which person was her partner. *If only, she had taken time to think!*

When the first player passed, Carol mistook the next bid of two spades for a strong bid from her partner, and, since she had an exceptional hand, she decided to jump in spades but, still rattled, she accidentally hit the six-no-trump tab as her bid. When she realized her partner hadn't bid at all—that the spades bid was an opponent's bid and that the strength lay in *their* hands— she knew she had made a horrible mistake. She tried apologetically to explain, but her partner steamed—now *her* prize rating would fall from advanced to intermediate level, as they were sure to go down six or more tricks. She gave Carol a cyber-tongue-lashing.

"What were you thinking?" the woman typed. "If you don't know how to play bridge, you shouldn't have come into our game!"

Ouch! Carol was stung. Mortified, she played the miserable hand, but left the game as soon as the last card hit the table, knowing that her injured partner would boot her out anyway. So much for being a good bridge player! She was grateful El had not been in that room!

Later, she confessed her error to her friends in the group.

Sophie gave her a wan smile. *Was there a touch of satisfaction at Carol's comeuppance?* "It's only a game. Even if it were a rated game, *I* would not have scolded you as sharply as that woman did," Sophie said sweetly. "She was rude. She didn't even know you."

"Nor does she care to know me," Carol added, still angry, still embarrassed.

"The point is," Stella said, "you are playing with strangers. No one knows whether you or anyone else at the table is handicapped. I assume everyone who plays is about our age—younger people these days seem to prefer video games to cards. When you are in a virtual room with older bridge players, most anything can be happening and no one sees it—neuropathy in the fingers, for instance."

"No, I'm pretty sure mine was in my brain," Carol quipped. Stella's sympathetic excuse was making made her feel better.

"Nevertheless," Stella persisted, "people who play together in online bridge rooms should be polite."

"By whose decree?" Dana inquired, innocently. "Pardon me, friend, but you did make a major mistake."

"I know." Carol blushed. "It's just that I didn't expect that kind of treatment. I know one thing it's taught me. I have to think before I click. Sometimes, I think I know what I'm doing, but my brain is a beat or two behind. You suppose the brain really does slow down as we age? I know we lose brain cells, but I expected the ones left to work as usual."

"Who knows?" Jennifer answered. "One day we are bright and sassy, and the next we are looking for our car keys in the refrigerator. "I think making mistakes as you did is natural at our age."

"Maybe the woman who hollered at you—did she use capital letters, by the way?—is losing her grip on reality as well," Sophie offered.

Carol just shook her head wearily.

"Are you still playing with that guy, the Roadrunner?" Stella asked

"Yes." Carol answered too quickly. "Well, no, actually. I haven't seen him in the online rooms since before Will came. That was two weeks ago."

"Strange," Stella commented. "I thought you said he was a regular. You'd see him nearly every day."

"El *is* a regular. We were emailing besides, and I haven't had an email from him since Will was here either." Carol covered her mouth in sudden alarm.

"Oh, that is not good, Honey," Sophie said.

"Don't say it," Carol pleaded. She couldn't stand the idea that El may have dropped in his tracks, and she'd never know. "Maybe he had to go out of town."

"Hmm, I suppose," Sophie said, "but you'd think he'd have access to a computer in that event."

"Yes, I guess so, but don't forget I wasn't online much either when Will was visiting. Besides, when I go somewhere, I relish being away from the computer, don't you?"

The women agreed. Carol was relieved to stop talking about Ellis's absence, but she still felt stood up. She didn't say that to the group, however. That afternoon when she logged onto bridge once more, she simply played with her bridge friends and ignored the fact that Ellis was not there.

A month passed. Carol was used to El's absence now. She had made up a story for herself. He had decided to stop emailing Carol since he was married. She thought that decision a callous one given the promise of sincere connection in their emails, but when she felt rejected, she could be a realist. Maybe his wife didn't have Alzheimer's after all. In her mind, if he had second thoughts, he was too cautious a man anyway. *More likely a coward*, she thought. The least he could have done was to tell her! Carol was more hurt than angry. How dare he stop without saying goodbye! He knew her well enough just from reading the book and seemed to like her. Why would he stop writing?

Okay, old gal, she sighed, *this one got away. It just wasn't meant to be, darn it. It's so crazy to care so much about someone I've never really met.*

Then, one day, unexpectedly, he showed up in one of the rooms. After playing for a while and before leaving the room, he typed in the chat space that he had been ill, but was recovering.

Carol clasped her hands to her cheeks, gasped, and then clicked on a fresh email and started typing, tears of relief sparkling in her eyes. **Hi El, I hope you continue to feel better. I was worried about you, so it was really, *really* good to see you and play with you at bridge today. Life isn't over until it's over, is it? Send me an email. I'm a good correspondent. Carol**

That night, she slept poorly, wondering whether she'd overdone her enthusiasm and might put him off. After all, though he had announced the reason for his absence at the bridge table, he hadn't emailed her. Her answer came the next day. **Just to update you as to where I have been. The first week in October was spent in a hospital here in Houston. My lungs are challenged because of my former smoking years. I was admitted for shortness of breath and overall malaise.**

After many tests and constant pushing and poking on my body, "they" told me they suspected I had TB. Well, now, a month later, "they" tell me that I do not have TB and I am not contagious; I have some kind of resistant bacterial lung infection. I am now under the care of three bright and caring women doctors located close to where I live.

I lost 10 pounds in the hospital. Frankly, I felt like warmed-over death and haven't wanted to do anything except lie down and rest all day. I must be somewhat better since I'm up and at the computer today. To get some of my weight back, I'm stuffing my face with high-calorie food and Ensure. I think I am making some headway; my skin is not so wrinkled now.

I will be under treatment for about a year or until the lung fluid tests come back negative. So, dear heart, that drawn-out experience is the sum and substance of this Texan. I deeply appreciate your concern for me. Everything has a season, so the Bible says, and this seems to be the season for El to take care of himself.

I enjoyed playing bridge with you yesterday; I consider it good therapy in many different ways, not the least of which is interaction with another human being. I have sensed all along that you are an exceptional woman. It's a pleasure to know you. Funny how these things happen,

isn't it? I am thrilled, and consider it a blessing that you want us to correspond.

Carol was relieved. El was back and enthusiastically so. She didn't fully comprehend his medical complexities. Her own lung problem gave her so little trouble she couldn't imagine him having such a complicated incident with his. Losing ten pounds just by spending time in the hospital was incredible: he must not have eaten anything while he was there!

You may have noticed that most of the people I value in my life are women. I have never had many close male friends. By my choice my doctors are female. It's not that men don't have abilities, they do, but women bring a more relaxed attitude to their abilities. One thing, for sure, women listen. I'm remembering from a movie I once saw, lines that describe the way I feel about most men: "Men, for the most part, are a sorry lot, and that's why I like to hang out with girls."

Well, my dear, enough of this babble. I hope I didn't bend your ear for too long. Write when time permits. What are you doing these days? Have you started another book yet? I would love to know.

Take care. El

A jubilant Carol felt renewed. The "dear heart," in the email stood out. It might have been a Texas colloquialism, but he had used it—maybe as a signal that he cared for her? Now that she knew that his absence hadn't been a rejection of her, all was forgiven. After all, he had called her an exceptional woman and cryptically noted, "It's funny how these things happen." *What had happened?* Carol wondered exactly what was in his mind when he wrote that. *No matter, I'm not waiting to find out. This time I'm going to just tell him how I feel.*

She wrote: **I am delighted to hear from you and to know that, even though you've walked through hell the past month, you are back here on earth.** *Especially with me.* **Lung disease is serious; I'm glad to know that yours didn't turn into TB. My emphysema, as I've told you, is from smoking. If I had continued to smoke, I would be long dead with no books to my name. So far, I've been able to basically ignore the condition except for dutifully taking my meds. We all have something to contend with.**

Yes, life does surprise us—a Texan bridge player landed in mine. I find that, since Mario died, my biggest hurdle is dealing with my loneliness. I miss the intimacy that my close friend and spouse provided. So, I am grateful that a little male energy was tossed my way. I cherish my women friends, but I feel enlivened by attentive males like you. Must be biological, don't you think? *Is this clear enough, dear heart?*

My Mario, too, preferred the company of women. He would tell me that after he died, he was coming back as a ruthless femme fatale. I haven't seen her yet.

You know more about me than I do about you. Tell me some things about yourself. Did you grow up in Texas? What interests did you have as a child, and did they lead you to your life's work? Do you have children? I hope so, because children can be very comforting when we face hard times in life.

I have been stuck in doing things to promote my book. Though these activities are interesting, they feel more like work than writing does. I haven't had time to write much. I am also busy with affairs of my church. I am currently council president, so I have a lot of correspondence and organizing tasks. Like most churches these days, we are continuously in a financial bind. Our church is small, our members are mostly old, and so holding on does get difficult.

Do recover nicely, my friend. We'll keep corresponding as the mood strikes us. You have my best wishes. Carol. Was she too polite? This wandering back and forth between her hints of longing for him and expressions of social niceties was frustrating. She felt unreal and loathed the feeling.

Ellis answered by giving her a brief sketch of his life as a lonely rebellious child who felt unwanted by parents so busy with their own lives and interests that, other than to see he minded his Ps and Qs, they generally ignored him. He told her he excelled in college, was the president of his fraternity, and belonged to several honor societies. After college he served a stint in the Navy during the Vietnam War but, fortunately, not at the front. When his enlistment ended, he was offered a job in a petroleum lab, which led to his long career in petroleum exploration with oil companies in Texas and a settled life in Houston with his wife Joanne and two sons George and Henry. After retirement, they sold their house and moved into a condominium more suited to an aging couple, though he admitted he often missed his house and garden.

By the bye, he wrote in ending the email, I can see that you are a very accomplished bridge player. It's a pleasure to play across from you.

It was obvious that each of them was indulging in word play, testing, she supposed, whether the interest in one another was genuine. For her part, it was, but she still wasn't quite sure about Ellis. It troubled her that, though she had offered him support in dealing with his wife's Alzheimer's, he had not mentioned the disease. Other than sterile facts about his family, he had yet to reveal just what was

45

going on in their household. Oh well, she thought, he *did* just get home from the hospital, and he *does* have a serious lung infection. He must be interested in her, she concluded because, otherwise, with so many concerns about his health, he certainly would not have continued with their connection. Maybe it was just awkward to talk about his wife; she had mixed feelings herself about bringing up his wife. Carol had to admit that she was enjoying the prospect of attracting a desirable man. To be brutally honest, she felt her concern with his wife's condition, at this point at least, was really to affirm the Alzheimer's so she could be comfortable with the idea of coming into his life looking for more than being friends with him.

"*Truth hurts,*" she confided in Pastor Colum, who assured her that he didn't judge her.

"But I covet a wife's husband," she blurted out.

Colum smiled. "I believe the commandment says, 'You shall not covet your neighbor's wife.'"

"Yes, it does." Carol brightened. "This is one time when I'll not dispute being left out by the sexist language in the Bible."

"Well," Colum quipped, "certainly if that's what the commandment meant, it should have been written that way." Colum was from a much younger generation than Carol. His ease with the Bible and culture showed an exposure to feminist views in his seminary studies. He liked Carol and wanted to support her. She had assured him that El and she were developing a friendship that would most likely stay on the Internet because of his health and hers. There was a remote chance of them ever meeting. What harm could come of two lonely, isolated people reaching out for a little intimacy in life? Besides, these were two elderly people. He couldn't help but know that most of his generation considered the elderly dead to any carnal emotion. Certainly, in those over seventy no hormones pinged, let alone raged!

Carol was surprised when Ellis next sent her an email saying how much he loved poetry along with a copy from the Internet of Robert Frost's "Stopping by the Woods on a Snowy Evening." He said the poem was a favorite of his. **It touches me deeply**, he wrote. She had the same feeling. The last lines, "But I have promises to keep and miles to go before I sleep," seemed a message to her to take heart— their relationship would develop in time.

This is very strange, she thought. *It's as if we are caught up in some kind of movie or something. Someone's making this up. Yes*, she concluded, *I am!* Suddenly, she didn't care. *A very special man has come into my life, and I'm going to see what happens.*

She sent him a link to Carl Sandburg's "Honey and Salt," one of her favorites, adding a quote from the poem:

"Is there any way of measuring love?
Yes but not till long afterward
when the beat of your heart has gone
many miles, far into the big numbers."
Ok, my friend. We'll talk soon. Hugs, Carol
It was their very first Internet hug.

Chapter Six

Can it be that this woman is truly attracted to me? Leaning back in his computer chair, Ellis shook his head in disbelief. *I'm 80 years old, for heaven's sake! I know how I feel, but, come on, I'm not even in her league. She's smart. She has a Ph.D., and she has written two books. What is there about me that could possibly interest her?*

"Huh!" he laughed out loud. *You lucked out, fellow. Big time! Really strange, though, the love poem, that is. What is she thinking?* "Hmm." *We probably do get to know love's value only after going "many miles, far into the big numbers." Is she talking about us or is she just doing an intellectual exercise here—Frost and Sandberg in parallel? Or is she simply making a comment on our similar taste in poems?* He sat back, tapping a finger on his cheek. *But then,* he noted, gleefully, *she did add "hugs!"* He smiled, undeniably pleased with that addition. *Let's hope we both have miles to go before we sleep.*

He wrestled with answering her beguiling email. To comment on a love poem might open the path to an involvement deeper than he was able to offer—his health was so uncertain. Was it fair to either of them to move in that direction? That was a question he didn't want to answer just yet. He decided to ignore the love poem and discuss his admiration for Mark Twain instead, continuing the literary theme, but moving it to a subject less charged.

Ellis wrote that, along with his humor, he enjoyed Twain's benevolent cynicism. **I would never rank myself alongside this** man, but I do brand myself in the same fraternity as Mr. Twain. I think he cared about people and his beloved country so much that the only way he could cope with the self-serving nature of most people was to poke fun at all elements of our society. No venue, group, or segment of our country escaped his penetrating eye and pen. He was a fearless, freestanding man, unafraid to speak his piece and expose the true nature of many men and institutions.

Back came her reply. She, too, had moved away from the subject of love. **Such a heavy load of events and tasks for me today that I need to escape to a place with some semblance of sanity for a moment or two. Are you that place, my friend?** The extent of her involvement with people and activities amazed him. Being a place for her to find some peace of mind thrilled him.

Most disturbing is serious illness in my friends or their families. An old friend from college sent me an email detailing her son-in-law's rapid decline; he's been fighting brain tumors. Friend Evelyn, at 97, lay on her floor with a cracked pelvis yesterday until neighbors stopped by to check on her and called the ambulance. Also, a rather new friend I made in church is dying; I'm dreading a phone call.

Sooo . . . (Deep breath!) There are tasks to be done: a budget to tackle in tonight's church council meeting where we'll have pizza to eat and, hopefully, share some laughter to soothe some of the sadness.

We go on, don't we?

We most certainly do, he thought, touched by her willingness to lay aside heavy burdens. He was tempted to stop reading at this point and write an immediate return email, but he decided to read on instead.

I thought of you last night as I sat in the audience of the Santa Bella Symphony. A living composer, David Carlson (b 1952) collaborated with a poet to produce a piece called *The Promise of Time: Three Songs for Soprano and Orchestra*, based on the lifespan of a woman. From the blossoms of spring and summer, through the tumult of middle age and autumn, and into the hourglass of finality, the piece was soaring with passion and longing. "Change: change is all." It was powerful. We read the words as the soprano sang and the orchestra raced through tumbling emotions. I found that, like most good works, I would need to hear this one a few more times before I could connect more fully with it. I felt as if I simply rode the tide this first time which, perhaps, served the composer's purpose.

The second piece featured master violinist Tedi Pavrami playing Sibelius *Concerto in D Minor*. (I'm copying from the program. I am not really conversant in classical music—I just happen to like it.) This youngster is so talented. Violin is not my favorite instrument, yet Pavrami's playing captivated me. I thought of how Sibelius, despite his insecurities and his tendency to drink too much, was able to write such amazing music—music that lives on long after he has left us. Maybe the universe truly is founded on musical notes—vibrating strings, as it were; our composers echo eternal life with their works.

By intermission I was spent, so I drove home and forfeited the third piece, another Sibelius. It was getting late; I had had a long day.

Why think of you while I'm sitting alone enjoying music? Because, I suppose, you pay attention to me. I wondered if you, too, like classical music.

He chuckled with pleasure. He was tempted to explore this happy, unexpected connection, but, since there was more to her email, he read on.

Mark Twain is a favorite of mine too. I taught his *Huckleberry Finn* to my seventh graders in Hawaii. What a talent! I haven't read his "Bible." It's a bit thick for me and, as you know, I'm not really a cynic, though sometimes I can't help but be cynical in our crazy world. I wonder sometimes if there is any hope for our leaders! Caught up in their own self-importance and their need to be reelected, they neglect our country's best interests, and we all suffer. Come on folks, we can't take a penny with us! The only thing that endures is love. Why do we need to be taught that over and over again? *Ah, there! She said the love word.* Ellis was heartened despite his reservations about his health.

Well, I guess I'll get back to the tasks on hand. Thanks for being here. It's such a relief to stop all my busyness and let my spirit be refreshed. Your friend, Carol.

Ellis let go of his heavy concerns. He couldn't hold onto worry with his heart dancing in ecstasy. *She likes classical music!* He adored classical music. Joanne did not. She went to Jones Hall with him the year they purchased season's tickets to the Houston Symphony, but didn't comment on the music. Mostly, she talked about how uncomfortable the seats were, or, when the orchestra played a modern piece, she told him how she utterly hated hearing dissonant chords. Joanne had no patience for anything she didn't instantly understand. He could see her point since he too preferred the familiar, and slightly resented pieces he felt primarily of interest to trained musicians; but, unlike Joanne, he'd listen to try to find some redemption in the pieces, if only for his basic love for music. Music, so many times in his lonely existence, had carried him through days when he felt he couldn't stand another evening living in the same house with her, sharing the same bed, yet having no intimacy. God, why hadn't he divorced her when he could? *The price of pride!* He sighed. *More likely alcoholism,* he admitted

Joanne came into the den just then. "Okay if I turn on the television?"

He denied her little, happy that some part of her mind could relate to the movies they watched on TV. "Go ahead," he agreed.

"Catching up on emails?"

He was surprised she noticed. "Yes." That was all he said. She settled down to watch the movie.

"*Casablanca* is on. We didn't see it, did we?"

We saw it yesterday, he wanted to say, but knew that if he gave her that answer, she would argue, telling him they had never seen the movie and blame him for a faulty memory.

He temporized. He wanted to go back to his emailing rather than to argue with her. "Go ahead and turn it on. I'll watch it again some other day. The sound won't bother me." The "again" was so satisfying. She wouldn't realize that he was actually affirming they had seen the movie—many times, in fact. *Casablanca* was a favorite of his. He wondered what she thought; her mind was a mystery to him now. Not much made sense anymore.

Gratefully, he turned to his computer and wrote to Carol. **I developed a love for classical music when I was nine years old, back in the days of 78 RPM records that had to be treated with kid gloves—else they could be broken or hopelessly scratched. I had a record player that played one record at a time through the speaker on the Philco radio in the living room. I started then to take piano lessons a few blocks from where we lived. My parents bought a lovely piano for me—something larger than a spinet. I took lessons,**

playing classical music for nine years, but after a while I began to realize that I did not have the talent to be the concert pianist I wished to be, so I dropped out and didn't study the instrument again.

He thought of how good it would be to play once more. There was always a piano until they moved into the condo and found the instrument too big to fit their limited space, so he gave it to Henry. *Besides*, he thought, *my fingers tips are getting numb. I would stumble on the keys anyway.* He went back to typing, ignoring the lack of feeling on the computer keys. Sometimes, it was difficult to keep typing, but he was determined.

This does not mean that my dedication and love for classical music diminished in any way—to the contrary, I was then, and still am today, passionate about this music. I sang in church choirs for years and was exposed to some of the best religious music within Christendom. One thing that you need to know about me—I am a total romantic and approach classical music and just about everything else in my life with passion.

He wondered what she'd think about that statement! Had he overstepped? Maybe he hoped she'd feel drawn to filling some of the loneliness in his life. He wasn't sure how this relationship would develop or what paths he might want to take. Truthfully, he wasn't even sure if he wanted the challenge of uncertain paths. All he knew was that he, paradoxically, felt incredibly happy. He liked this energetic woman. Maybe he was borrowing life from her. Right now, he was still taking pills for the cursed lung infection and not at all sure he would recover. Constant coughing and congestion plagued him. What would she think of a worn body like his? Still losing weight, he was now down twenty pounds from his normal 150 and worried he'd appear skeletal to her.

She had told him in an earlier email that she too was dealing with loneliness and had practically invited him to pay attention to her! **I'm glad a Texas bridge player landed in my life,** she had written. He decided to ignore his infirmities and typed: **I wish people would stop getting sick and dying. Oh, I know that statement is ridiculous, but I still cannot get used to the idea that life is far more temporal than I ever imagined! I am an earthbound human and suffer emotionally from the thought of permanent separation from those I love. Intellectually I get it—from an emotional standpoint I am hung up. You see the realities of this come into sharper focus because I have lived this long and consider mortality with a different mindset than I did when I was younger. Time is sterile and waits for no one. That is why living in the here and now is so important to me. My credo these days is: if not now, when?**

I am usually pretty "up" most of the time, yet I do have my pensive moments, such as today with too much time on my hands. I do not think life events are random or happenstance. I have seen so clearly that God has a way of taking the mundane things in life and turning them into something beautiful. I have too many examples in my life to think otherwise. You and I meet at the cyber bridge table and find value in the meeting. Why did it happen? It seems magical to me, and, since I operate more and more on a feeling level, I go with it. I am a risk taker. I see clearly that nothing of value takes place without taking risks. I believe in the old adage: it is far better to have loved and lost rather than not loved at all. He surprised himself by talking love, after all.

Well now, I guess I'm sending out an invitation. He smiled, decisively, as he reread his own words. *Okay, might as well go for it all.* The keys on the computer keyboard made the anemic "clicking" that no self-respecting typewriter would have made in its day. He typed boldly: **Improvement in my health seems agonizingly slow to me; I need to be patient since the bacteria is described as "stubborn." I do not have any appointments this week, so I'll just be a slug and rest. I was greatly relieved to hear from the doctors that what I have is not communicable. It frees me up to move around if I feel like it and, at the least, go out for dinner in the evening.**

With a final flourish, he added: **I know now that I would miss you if I thought you were not there. . . E**

Shutting down his computer, El prepared for bed. Joanne had fallen asleep while the movie played. When he shut off the television, she woke with a start. "Is it time for breakfast?"

"No, mam," he said, gently. "Time for bed."

She gave him a look that told him she was confused about her confusion; then she pursed her lips, trying to do some serious thinking. "We will go out to eat, won't we?" she asked expectantly.

"Yes, of course," he agreed. "Right now, though, I want you to lie down and rest for a while. Okay?" She was already in her pajamas, as it was her habit to change her clothes after their evening restaurant meal. Because Ellis had wearied of making supper for both of them, they now ate out nearly every night.

"I do feel tired. Maybe I do need more sleep," she said, moving toward the bedroom.

"You go ahead," he said. "I want to do my breathing exercises and then I'll be right in."

He was grateful she was still able to take care of her hygiene and dressing. He knew that when she climbed into bed, she'd fall asleep immediately. At least, that is a blessing, he thought, and reached for his breathing exercise tubes.

Chapter Seven

*Y*ou like to write too, don't you? Your choice of words delights me, Carol wrote back to Ellis. **We are having wonderful conversations here**. She was feeling good: last night's council meeting had gone well, she had enjoyed her breakfast, and El's email gave her hope—they had a lot in common.

I am glad you like classical music, she typed. **I wasn't raised to appreciate it.** Books, not music, were emphasized in her home. She remembered fondly the year her mother read *Alice in Wonderland* to her little sister and her as all three of them snuggled under a homemade feather quilt in the early morning light. **It took eight years to get electricity to the house where I was born. I can't remember when the radio was brought in, but that modern marvel was as popular as iPhones are now. We shivered in dread when *Inner Sanctum* came on. Remember that weird music and creaky door? Or that maniacal laugh spewing its terror directly at you right after that slow bass-voiced, "Who knows what evil lurks in the hearts of men. The Shadow knows." It's a miracle we ever slept after listening to shows like that. No wonder I thought ghosts were in the attic!**

Speaking of technology, I read in the paper today that using an iPad is helping Alzheimer patients in exercising their brains and hopefully recovering some memory

power. Might be something to check out with your wife's doctor. Thinking for a moment of Ellis coping with his wife's dementia, Carol gave thanks she was spared that difficult circumstance in caring for Mario. **I developed an interest in classical music when my son Paul started to play the oboe in high school. Soon I was buying season tickets for the Honolulu Symphony Orchestra. (We were Hawaiian residents at the time.) Though I have much to learn, I find the music itself brings out the best in me. Music jars me sometimes and stirs me to action. At other times, I feel my soul singing along.**

You play the piano. How nice. I took piano lessons as a child, but that endeavor lasted only long enough to play some hymns (badly) for Sunday school. And you sing too! I'm impressed. I like to sing myself. She felt as if she were rushing to fill him in on facts about her life. She didn't know why. She had an impulse to delete what she had written, but didn't. *Oh, well, let it be.*

Yes, we are both passionate people. *That "yes" needs a joyous exclamation point,* she told herself. She was tired of the mundane. She longed to really feel alive again. **I think that's why we enjoy emailing one another and discovering things we like about each other. We are bound to bump into some negatives sometime, but I have a feeling those won't really matter**. She was on a roll, a bit worried, but ready to take a leap of faith.

So, you are a Christian! I am too. Our cyberspace meeting seems magical to you. I agree. My view is that God gives us precious people as we need them, and asks us to spread the joy around a bit. I'm spreading a little of mine to you, and think I feel a lot coming back to me. *If that statement was too bold, he'd just have to deal with it.*

I, too, am a risk taker. You can see that side of both of us in the way we play bridge. We quickly measure the reward and its worth and then go for it. I didn't used to be this way but, lately, I have developed a knack for taking more risks in the whole of my life.

Enough of passion, precious people, and risk taking!

Council went well last night. We made a budget and approved it. Early last week, our pledges were only at $44,000, but the stewardship chair, the pastor, and I put out the word, and by last night, the pledges had risen to $90,000, giving us hope that we will make our goal of $128,000 in promised funds. All this high finance from a gal who just wants to write; I was an English major in college!

The pizza was great! Especially the chicken garlic. Yum. We had a wonderful conversation as we ate.

Don't miss me, my dear. I'll be here as long as you are. We've got a lot of bridge to play. But today, I need to eat lunch, and then go get a mammogram; maybe sometime this afternoon, I'll get back to bridge.

Today I am wearing a device to monitor my oxygen levels. A respiratory technician came to the house just before breakfast and fitted her with the oximeter. So far, the levels look fine to me (consistently in the 90s, a good reading), but sleeping will tell the story. I'll know the results by November 28. It would surprise me greatly if I needed oxygen during the night. Intuitively, I feel that I don't. Not yet. Hugs, Carol

She took a deep breath, ran the spell check, and reread the email for errors. The oximeter hadn't hindered her typing much.

Her son Paul would celebrate Thanksgiving with her. With the holiday just a week away, a 20-pound turkey was thawing in the refrigerator. She chuckled at buying an oversized bird for just the two of them. There was something about the largesse of Thanksgiving that prompted devil-may-care extravagance. She planned to send a generous portion of the turkey home with Paul to share with Joseph, who'd declined her invitation because he and Paul were having difficulties in their domestic partnership.

She got up and opened the refrigerator to see what she wanted for lunch. She wasn't really hungry, but felt the urge to eat anyway. She used food to try to fill the hole in her life left by Mario's illness and death. Thank God, she no longer craved alcohol. Over the years together, she had put on extra pounds and was now ashamed of the 220-pound readout on the scale.

"I'm *not* dieting again," she told her doctor. "I've lost 50 pounds three times in my life and, after three years, all of the weight and more comes back."

"It might make you feel better if you lose just a little weight," he said gently.

She frowned at the memory of the conversation. She heard the kindness in the doctor's voice. If he had scolded her about her weight, it would have been easy to resist his suggestion. Reluctantly, she accepted the obvious; she couldn't walk any distance without getting short of breath and had given up all semblance of exercise beyond normal walking to and from the car. What would El think of the extra poundage? She knew he was tall and thin and probably fussy about the way he looks. Would he want to be seen with her? Well, no matter. She wasn't *about* to start losing weight during the holidays. There were pumpkin pies to eat!

She found some leftover chicken and made a sandwich. Thinking about losing weight drove her to put extra mayonnaise on the bread and add two slices of cheddar besides—just to show her independence! With lunch, she had a glass of water and her noon supply of calcium tablets. She was using natural supplements to guard against osteoporosis since her last scan had shown some bone loss. An extra cushion of weight came in handy whenever she fell, which thankfully wasn't often—just when she did something stupid like overreaching or not paying attention to where she was stepping.

After lunch, she turned off the computer, got dressed, and headed out for her mammogram appointment. It was a beautiful fall day. She was thankful the rains had not yet started, though she dare not say that aloud. Californians looked askance at any grumbling about inclement weather. People in her town blessed rain and snow forecasts, for draught was an ever-present and wicked enemy. "We need the rain," was a constant rebuke to such complaints. Carol, sun-lover that she was, had to agree. The growing population in California was thirsty.

The oximeter proved no barrier to Carol in getting her mammogram. She wore it in the testing room. Either the equipment was getting better or the fact that her breasts were less dense made the experience less painful than when she was young.

The next day, the technician from the respiratory services lab came to her house and took the oximeter for analysis. Even though it hadn't been any trouble, she was glad to be rid of it. *Her oxygen levels at night would be fine*, she told herself.

Two days later, while playing bridge, El wrote in the chat that he was going out for Chinese that night. "I think I shall make crab cakes tonight," she teased, sensing that he was tired of restaurant food.

"Oh my, that sounds wonderful!" he typed.

"You could come for dinner," she wrote.

"I'll be right there," he answered. Crossing space via Internet carried only the imagination, not the body, unfortunately. *I wonder what it would be like to meet him,* she mused.

He sent her an email after bridge: **There must be something wrong with me! My mind has been in overdrive since you** told me you were having crab cakes tonight. I suppose the only way I'll be able to put this desire for these delicious morsels out of my mind is to go to bed. With my luck, I'll dream about them. It's no good for me to make any attempts at enjoying them vicariously because—forgive the phrase—I am a "hands on" kind of guy. Sigh . . . Oh well . . . sigh . . . Groan. Sleep well, E

Hands on! She caught her breath and shivered. *That rascal knows exactly what he is doing.* Later, she again lay on Judy's massage table and imagined El's sweet insistent caressing. Judy, as professional as ever and still unaware her hands were the touchstone for Carol's fantasy lovemaking, interpreted the satisfied sigh that escaped Carol's lips as a release resulting from the massage. In a way, it was.

That next morning she wrote to El: **Well, my dear, I didn't get around to making the crab cakes. I had a massage late in the afternoon and while lying on the table, comfortably covered with only a sheet, I thought of you and thought of you and thought of you . . . No wonder your mind was in overdrive. Later, I slept well. Very well. C.**

With a grin, she hit the "send" button. *Oh well, another risk taken.*

Chapter Eight

"Oh God," Ellis groaned. Carol lying on the massage table with only a sheet covering her body raised more than the level of his imagination. *What is this? Am I a fifteen-year-old still?*

"Yep!" he said aloud, grinning from ear to ear. The beast within had been reawakened—and through crab cakes, no less. Never again would he think of crab cakes as a simple delicacy. No siree!

He wrote to her in a tempered style, sensing he needed to tread gently. He wasn't really sure what her intentions were—she was incredibly open in her email. **I guess the crab cakes will be on your agenda at some point in time. I'd love to have the recipe if you'd share it with me.**

Sometimes when my body and muscles won't cooperate, I have considered having a massage, but I am an essentially private person; anyone who touches my body must be gentle and invited in by me. I am selective, although I have found love can be pretty irresistible at times.

I must tell you that it is very flattering that you would think of me. I am sure they were sweet thoughts.

Thanks for sharing! He considered adding the phrase, but didn't. Such a remark might dispel the magic of sharing her fantasy and embarrass her. He didn't want to do that—ever. There was, however, a smoldering anger in him, not directed at Carol, but, if he were not careful, it might slip out and *seem* directed at her.

Why was he so angry now that something so wonderful had come into his life? *Well, look at me, God! Just a little over a month out of the hospital and I'm so weak I can hardly stay upright. Yet here I am flirting with the idea that an unbelievably interesting woman might be interested in more than my bridge playing. Have I lost my mind?*

His wife had dutifully visited him in the hospital, brought there by their son George. Henry, the younger son, hadn't made it, nor had their spouses. Both mother and son wore masks before they were allowed into his isolation room. Ellis saw little understanding and no compassion in Joanne's brown eyes. Managing her many illnesses had robbed her of interest in others and particularly in him. That was over for years—eighteen *long* years, he thought, maybe more.

When Joanne no longer tolerated sexual intimacy, insisting his touch was too painful, he'd considered divorce, but turned to alcohol instead, drinking up years of potential opportunity for permanent release. After his recovery, ennui set in. They were reasonably comfortable, living separate lives under a common roof. Besides, by then he had begun to reinvent himself. He actually liked the idea of a private life, a place similar to a Walter Mitty fantasy world—only his world wasn't fantasy. In his world was the trailer in La Grange. He also volunteered and liked the work of driving the needy to their appointments. Besides Beth, there were a few remaining female friends, admittedly a bit fragile with age, but still interesting women to talk with on the telephone. Because of his age and reluctance to start a marriage-type relationship with a new woman, he was convinced that *this is as good as life gets.*

That day in the hospital room, Joanne seemed more interested in leaving for dinner with George than in talking to her husband. She didn't even ask how he felt, though George had. Sitting silently in the bedside chair, glancing now and then at George, Joanne barely looked in Ellis's direction. When they left, she didn't say goodbye, but gave the foot of the bed a tap with her open hand—a kind of "well that's done" gesture.

Being sick and helpless in a sterile, lonely hospital bed had made Ellis realize that he had settled for less than he deserved. Carol's book was on his mind as he thought of the email he had written to her. Here was a woman who had recreated her life as he had, and she did a good job of it. Maybe Joanne had done the same thing; only her life had turned into pain and suffering, a nightmarish Never-Never Land. No wonder he was angry. Years of smoldering anger were fully stoked now. Tantalizing possibilities beckoned, but present circumstances made them *im*possibilities. Even if he did want to consider a romantic connection with Carol, how could such an affair be remotely attainable? He couldn't abandon a wife stricken with Alzheimer's; despite his many faults, Ellis still viewed himself as an honorable man who kept commitments. Carol was 1,552 miles away—he'd measured the distance on Google maps. To travel in his present condition would probably kill him or present him exactly as he was—a very ill, very skinny man.

Joanne came into the study where Ellis sat brooding at his computer. She was dressed to go out. "I'm having lunch with Hilda and Floyd," she announced and then looked at him with pleading eyes. "I can't seem to remember where I said I'd meet them. Did I tell you?"

"Yes," he sighed, aware of her increasing and unwelcome need of him. He swung around in his chair so his body blocked her view of the computer, not that she'd care, anyway. "You said you were going to Oriental Gardens."

"Oh, that's in the neighborhood, isn't it?"

He turned to his desk and switched off the monitor. Picking up pencil and paper, he drew a large map for her, outlining the route from their garage space to the restaurant, and then carefully explained the route, tracing with the pencil each turn on the map. It wasn't very complicated. He was pretty sure she could manage the short drive she took nearly every week.

She nodded her head as if thinking.

"Will you be all right? he asked.

"Of course. Why not?" she replied, testily. "I know where I'm going. You really didn't have to go to so much trouble."

"That's okay," he said quietly. He fought the impulse to grit his teeth; he wanted to say so much more, but knew it would accomplish nothing. He could so easily have started an argument with her, so sensitive were his feelings just now. "Have a nice time," he said instead.

He was glad she still had friends from her work at the library. Though most of her favorite friends had drifted away, Hilda and Floyd had not. Both of them were as needy as Joanne. Hilda tended to drink too much after losing her husband, while Floyd was a permanent bachelor, unable to confront his sexual attraction to men. They made a strange and sad trio. Ellis felt sorrow for his wife's diminished life. He wondered how much she could understand of what was happening to her.

After Joanne left, El spent the day listening to music, eating his own lunch, taking his medications, and resting. Joanne returned and escaped to her bedroom to read. He shrugged; she had been reading the same book every day for the past month.

The next day, an email came from Carol. **My recipe for crab cakes is on the refrigerated can of crab I buy from Costco. If you can't find the crab with its recipe, I'll copy it down for you. Oh, by the way, I may make the crab cakes tonight.** He imagined the tease in her voice. Ellis smiled. *Sure you will!*

The results of the oximeter tests came in earlier than I expected. I am low on oxygen at night; therefore my doctor has ordered some. I will use it when I sleep. Apparently,

I don't need oxygen during the day. The therapist says oxygen should do wonders for me. I will no longer wake up tired, she says, and my memory should improve. Older folks worry about memory lapses, but many of these losses are related to oxygen deprivation, I was told. Who really knows? I guess she does. We'll see.

So she needs oxygen, Ellis thought. *We both have our health trials and tribulations. Maybe I need to be a little more patient with myself. She seems to take things in stride.* He read on.

I hope you don't think me too naughty thinking of you while having a massage. (Or, maybe, I do!) Very definitely the thoughts were—*joyful*, let's say. You should see the smile on my face as I write. *I'll bet they were*, Ellis thought.

Life is short. If we can find a little pleasure here and there in one another, why not?

Have a good day, my friend. I may see you at the tables later.

This is getting pretty interesting. El rubbed his chin, thinking of Beth. Seven years now since Charlie died. How long it has taken her to come to grips with *that* loss! Charlie and Ellis met years ago on an oil-drilling job. He, foreman on that particular project, impressed Ellis with the way he handled his men. Later, they shared a beer, and before long, the families were meeting socially. A solid friendship grew over the years.

When Ellis needed a retreat from his family problems, Charlie was the one who suggested Ellis put a trailer on a piece of land he and Beth owned in La Grange. The trailer was a popular spot for Charlie and Beth too, who took their children with them whenever they wanted respite from the job or Houston.

The day Charlie died, Beth sobbed while Ellis held her. He felt responsible for her, not only out of a sense of friendship, but because he liked Charlie—unusual given that he didn't get close to most men. Only a month after Charlie's death, Ellis took Beth to the trailer with him, which was a mistake. The place aroused such memories in her that she couldn't stop crying. Ellis held her then, soothing, comforting, patting her back, saying, "It's all right. It's all right."

Her grip on him tightened. She reached up and pulled his face toward her. Her lips met his with a hunger he'd never forget. He kissed her back. She led him into the bedroom then—her crying had become forlorn squeaks of the hurt and pain of loss. He didn't know what to do with such grief, but lay with her on the queen-sized mattress, cradling her body to him as he would a hurting child. She finally fell asleep, lying on his chest while he lightly stroked the arm she had stretched over his shoulder. He felt so sorry for her.

He awoke to the sensation of being kissed once more and instinctively tightened his arms around Beth. She had undressed. Her skin was sensuous to his touch. Her kiss told him she wanted him. He said a silent prayer as he took off his clothes and, lying next to her on the bed, drew her close.

The sex wasn't satisfying to him. He kept thinking of Charlie so newly gone, yet curiously present—at least it felt that way to him. He didn't know what Beth felt. When they were done, she simply rolled over and, like a child, softly sobbed herself to sleep. The whole experience unnerved him.

He was determined not to go through such grief with Carol. He wasn't sure he could completely trust her seductiveness, and so he wrote: **It seems to me that feelings and emotions are beginning to stir within you since Mario's death. I am convinced that no two people will experience the grief process equally. Someone I am close to lost her husband suddenly, and after seven years, she is finally beginning to enjoy life once again.** It had taken more lovemaking and some awkward talks, particularly at the end of their affair, but he and Beth were simply friends again.

If reasonably intelligent people were asked the question "If you could have anything you wanted in this world what would that be?" some might answer money, influence, an expensive home with servants, power, more money, security—and so forth. Yet, what these people really want is something that may have eluded them all their lives. That something is intimacy. Intimacy, yoked with love, is what makes the world go around. I want intimacy in my life, and so do you.

What were the odds Carol and he would meet with nearly identical needs? *Astronomical!* They were strangers playing bridge the *only* day he had ever publicly admitted he was lonely. Moreover, he had felt compelled to explain himself by telling everyone there his wife has Alzheimer's. *Surely, the hand of God is in this venture.* He wondered if she had prayed for a mate as he had prayed for some relief from his stunted existence.

He positioned his hands on the computer keyboard. **For me, there are four essential elements in intimacy: spiritual, emotional, intellectual, and physical. Each element is vital to a healthy emotional life. Remove one, and we poor humans are incomplete.** *I sound like some psychology professor! But that's what I believe, gal,* he imagined telling her.

Despite the fact that we are older, all those longings that raced in us when we were younger are still with us now—in some ways they are even more intense and urgent. So, as I've said before, and this is my credo: if not now, when?

Just what was he saying? Was he inviting her to be a greater part of his troubled life?

We need to share life with friends but, especially, we need to share life with a particular significant person who satisfies our physical needs and brings out in us those innermost thoughts and feelings that make us who we are. He was sweating now from the exertion of sharing himself with her at this level.

I have had to reinvent my life; you have done the same. None of us knows where tomorrow will lead us, but I know that when love comes our way, it will not be because we sought it out, but because that love was a gift from God. There is sweetness about being blindsided by love. Passion is fanned once again; the idea that another human being loves us for who we are is intoxicating.

I'd better leave her some wiggle-room just in case her intentions aren't really what I hope they are.

I wish us well; it is my hope that you will be able to find contentment in your writing and relationships. Is there someone of interest on your radar screen right now? I know that you will be open to letting things happen. *Ha! That probability is pretty obvious, I think.* Ellis laughed.

Perhaps someone at church? Someone in the writing community? Or, maybe, simply someone out of the blue? *Maybe me?*

Meanwhile, I am here for you, and I invite you to come out and play. More later. E. xoxoxoxox

The old-fashioned symbols for kisses and hugs expressed a kind of love for her. *Maybe the real kind.* That thought was intoxicating indeed.

Chapter Nine

Dear El, I love the phrase, "Come out and play."
Remember when we were children, and we'd pester
parents of our friends: "Can Frances come out and play?"

Carol's heart was racing happily. *And now, you—you, my special
friend, have asked me to play! No parent here. Oh, yes, I'd love to play!* It
had been so long since she'd felt this way. She wanted to dance and
sing out loud. *I'd better be careful here or I'll be hopping a jet to Houston,
dragging my oxygen generator behind me. God! None of this is real, is it?*

She shivered, hit suddenly with a wave of caution. Wary now of
her excitement, Carol retreated to the safety of her intellect. **Play is
important to a child's development, it is said. I believe that
play is necessary at all stages of life. In a sense, that's what
you and I have been doing all along. We've delighted one
another with our intellectual antics, have touched on our
spiritual lives, and have shared some light emotional moments, but we've only physically touched in our imaginations. The reason our exchange is so magical is that we are
experiencing all the joys without the hard work of actually being in a physical relationship. We are playing.**

That should set a boundary, she mused. She hoped she wasn't setting up an obstacle to further dialogue, but she wanted him to recognize she wasn't in the business of breaking up marriages. To say so
outright seemed presumptuous and rude. But, and she hoped he'd

realize this as well, neither was she in the business of breaking up interesting, budding friendships!

You suggest that I might find intimacy with someone local. I talked about that possibility in my book, but even as I wrote, I realized that I don't want anyone living with me anymore. I'm not willing to make the sacrifices a committed relationship takes. Friendship? Now, that's a different story; I have a wide circle of friends, mostly female, and have room for more.

Oh, yes, I do have room for you, Mr. Thompson. Please take my hints that way. Carol hated being so needy, but then her attraction to the sweet attention Ellis was giving her was irresistible. What was she saying to him? Come here? Go away? She wanted to be honest with him, but how could she make clear her desires when her own feelings were so confused?

I do miss the intimacy of just one person sitting and watching television with me or sharing a meal or cuddling in bed; but the price is too high. I cherish my independence.

She grimaced. *Was she actually telling him there was no chance of her ever being involved in a physical meeting?* She had done it again, hadn't she? She'd set another boundary. Her heart told her to go for it; her mind kept putting up stop signs. Why was this unrelenting urge to follow her heart so hard to heed?

Of course, like most humans, I am conflicted. At times, I long for someone to be here. The constant drone of loneliness in this house is maddening. My house is just that—a house, not a home. She could feel grief welling, flooding out her heart's plea.

Home had died with Mario. The house she lived in now was lifeless too. Carol hadn't expected that consequence. It was bad enough that the love of her life had vanished. Why had the coziness of home been taken as well? She cleansed herself with a huge sigh and resumed her writing.

My good friend Will spent ten days with me in early October. I've known him for 38 years. We were newcomers together in AA in Hawaii. Will left the Navy there and headed home to Nebraska after discovering he had a mental health issue. We have never been physically intimate.

No, I haven't slept with anyone since Mario died. Not that I haven't wanted to. There just hasn't been anyone stable or exciting enough for me to risk starting a relationship. She permitted herself to think: *'Til you.* The thought of sleeping with Ellis certainly had occurred to her more than once. *Could it be* I'm *not even stable enough?*

After Will left, I felt an incredible longing for him to be back. It had been so nice to have someone else in the house with me—someone to eat a meal with, someone with whom to jump in the car and drive down to feel the breeze off the ocean. On the other hand, if Will had stayed longer, I would have begun to feel that I *had* to do things for him, rather than wanting to do things for him.

Ambivalence. It seemed that particular mood was the bane of her existence lately. She was tired of it. Tired of grieving. Tired of being so uncertain about what she wanted. Tired of being so damned needy.

So you see, I thank God for you. You are intellectually my equal. (Does that sound egotistical? Of course it does!) You are adventuresome, you are a good bridge player, you are wise and caring, and you are fun to talk to. I feel appreciated by you. All I know is that I smile a lot when I think of you. So, I send you a measure of love equal to the one you sent me. Hugs, Carol

She pressed the "send" button quickly before her mind registered "delete." *What did she mean by a measure of love equal to the one you sent me?* What measure of love had he sent, after all? A few hugs and kisses like kids send one other in elementary school—an "X" here and "O" there? *Never mind*, she told herself. It was time to check in with her girlfriends. She got dressed and drove to Sophie's house.

The women were discussing politics when she arrived. Dana had served a term on the Monte Verde Village council and was outraged that a new council was considering building a six-figure theater arts building. "Our facilities were *just* updated," she argued to no one in particular. "At our age, why do we need a fancy music hall? None of us is starting careers."

"Pardon?" Carol interrupted, her antenna tuned to dismissiveness.

"Oh, *you*! You are definitely the exception," Dana said, still certain of her point. "You've had a career in writing. You just have a new platform, that's all, since you moved from writing about gay issues to issues of aging.

"Oh yeah, *that* career." Carol laughed. "But I'm supposed to be retired."

"Retired, yes, but not dead," Jennifer added. "All the volunteering I've done since quitting work amounts to a job in itself. Maybe a job and a half! However, I enjoy doing the work. Those elementary kids love learning new dance steps."

"And I bet *you'd* use a new theater arts building," Stella said to Jennifer.

"Darn tooting. I'd turn our village play-reading group into a repertory group. I'd do the directing."

"Talk about new careers!" Sophie interjected.

"Okay, okay," Dana gave in. "There's value in such a place, but where are we getting the money?"

"Oh, *please!*" Sophie shook her head. "You know there are wealthy people all around us. They remodel their homes twice a year! They need someplace else to put their money. The Monte Verde Village Council will get the money all right."

"Most likely they'll raise dues," Dana said. "There are people here barely making it, you know. People whose only pension is social security."

"Yeah, yeah, we hear that all the time," Sophie flatly declared. "If folks are so poor, why live in a place with two golf courses, three swimming pools, and a pair of champion tennis courts?"

"Why not?" Carol asked. "Many of us are house poor. We have assets, but not income."

"Don't tell me you live on social security alone?" Sophie challenged.

"No, I don't, but I've damned little income besides. A teacher's pension based on a 1970s economy hardly covers twenty-first century bills! Sure, I have some modest investments, but the shenanigans on Wall Street shaved at least thirty percent off their value. Now, I'm stuck holding them until they go up again—if ever!"

"I hear you, sister," Jennifer said. "If I had something substantial beyond my social security, I wouldn't be living with Peter." It was the first time in group she had said her husband's name.

Carol gently confronted the situation. "What is making you so unhappy with him, may I ask?"

Jennifer stared at Carol, her face stark with desperation. "I hate to burden others with my problems," she began. Then, hiding her face with her hands, she whispered, "I just can't take much more."

"What's happening? We want to know," Sophie softly interjected while the others murmured assent. "That's what group is all about. Lending support to one another."

"I'm ashamed to tell you," Jennifer began. "I thought I was too smart a woman to get involved with a man who can't handle his liquor." Her eyes filled with tears.

"Oh, Honey," Stella reached over to hold Jennifer's hand, "you're not alone. We've all been in impossible situations."

Carol, sensing that Jennifer might shut down, interrupted. "Please, go ahead. Tell us what happened."

"He . . . he," Jennifer inhaled deeply, trying to find the breath to continue. "He started drinking and got out his gun. He threatened to kill me."

Stella and Dana gasped, but Carol, shifting to a professional presence, pressed on, "And then?"

"He pointed the gun at me. I told him to go ahead and shoot—I'm so tired of his threats. He's been like this since we married. I don't know what to do."

"You're here, Sweetie," Dana said gently, suppressing the anger she was feeling. "Obviously, he hasn't shot you yet, thank the Lord!"

"No." Jennifer was on the edge of an emotional meltdown. "He shot a hole in the ceiling."

"Good God!" Stella exclaimed. "How did you get away?"

"We were in his bedroom. I walked out. I had gone there to ask him a question about a bill I was paying. I called the police, but by the time they got there, he had spread out gun-cleaning equipment on the bed and told them he accidentally fired the gun while cleaning it. He pointed to the hole in the ceiling. He has a permit for the gun." She punched a fist in a sofa pillow. "Stupid! Stupid! Stupid!" she shouted. "Why do they give gun permits to alcoholics with anger issues?"

The group was silent. Jennifer's news was sobering. Each woman had experienced abuse in her earlier days, but nothing as life-threatening as Jennifer's experience.

"They took him to jail," Jennifer continued, leaning forward, tears in her eyes. "They charged him with discharging a firearm in a residential section of town. Apparently *that* is against the law. Can you imagine? They didn't seem to want to believe my story—that he had aimed the gun at me. Oh, he's such a smooth talker." Jennifer's tears were drying now; her face was contorted with the sting of injustice. "I'm sure they must have smelled the alcohol on his breath, but they didn't even do a blood test. His lawyer says he will get him off since it was an accidental discharge of a weapon. He's bragging about it to me!"

"Oh, Jennifer!" Sophie's voice expressed the horror and sympathy everyone was feeling. The women spent the rest of group time discussing courses of action for Jennifer and looking up community assistance in Sophie's senior resource manual. None of them said it, but all of them thought it: *What would such a man do to friends helping his wife?* Despite feeling helpless and vulnerable themselves, all were staunch in their commitment to Jennifer.

By the time she left for home, Carol was exhausted. After lunch, she turned on her computer and found a puzzling email from Ellis. *Not a word about my reply to his "come out and play" invitation.* Ellis had written a lengthy account of a long-ago visit to California, instead. **During my 43-year career in the oil business I was with a company who placed me in charge of a drilling program and geological evaluation of wells to be drilled in the Sacramento Basin. I traveled extensively to Los Angeles, San Francisco, and Bakersfield where the partner oil companies were located. It didn't take long for me to fall in love with the area. When time permitted, I would steal away to Carmel, soak up the art galleries, eat delicious food, and drive to Big Sur to find my rock overlooking the ocean.**

The email was a travelogue, an attempt to keep her interested in him, but at arms' length. *What happened, Mr. Thompson? Did we get a little beyond ourselves? More enthusiastic than we should be at this point?*

In the grove of redwoods at Henry Cowell State Park near Santa Cruz, there is a narrow-gauge logging train that steams up the mountain and returns in an hour. I've ridden it many times in the five years I flew back and forth to your lovely state and mixed pleasure with business.

Carol's frustrated breath came out in a rush. After going through such an emotional roller coaster with Jennifer this morning, maybe it was just as well that Ellis had decided to put a damper on their correspondence. She read on, not really much interested.

Being in this fairyland of artists—Clint Eastwood's Hog's Breath Inn, and Anton & Michel's French Restaurant—was sensory overload. I spent a number of days and nights in Ojai doing business with a geologist, a wild Bohemian, and stayed at the Ojai Valley Lodge and Country Club. Yes, I was living high off the hog. I have tons of memories of northern California. I feel sorrow that I will not be able to once more soak up the cool air and lovely sights once afforded me. E

Okay, if that's the way it's going to be, Mr. T., I can be restrained as well.

Carol sat forward in her computer chair and gripped the keys. **So, you loved our state. Great! My first love in states is Hawaii, since I lived there for 23 years and felt a deep attachment to the place and the people.**

When I was a Navy wife, we were stationed for a brief time in Monterey and lived in the forest on the 17 Mile Drive. Used to be the Bing Crosby Tournament was the big happening on the lovely and famous golf course there. We visited Carmel and even thought about living there, but couldn't find the right place for a young family. I do remember Big Sur and how lovely it is there.

I've been to Southern California. Went to a women's conference once, which was wonderful. My second husband and I stayed with friends in San Diego. We, of course, visited the zoo. I did spend some quality time with my best friend when her mother lived in a retirement village near Laguna Beach. I remember running and diving into the water at Laguna Beach, thinking the ocean would be the same as in Hawaii. I came up breathless, shocked, and shaking with cold, but miraculously alive.

Now, *Texas*. There's a state I haven't really visited. We just drove through it—and drove through it—and drove through it—on the way to California. I found it utterly boring. However, I have never been to any of your cities. I'm sure I'd find all kinds of things to like about them. C.

Chapter Ten

*E*llis felt too tired, too congested, and too stressed by his constant coughing to attend his grandson's wedding. His family braved the unusually cold and nippy November Texas day to pick up Joanne and sympathize with Ellis, telling him, "Rest and feel better, Dad. You're not fully recovered from your hospital stay."

Alone at last, Ellis savored reprieve from the struggle of putting up with Joanne. He hated to admit he felt such relief; it seemed insensitive even to think of his wife as a burden, but she was. He wanted to run to his trailer retreat with Beth, but health problems kept him chained at home.

Lying down on the bed, he tried to read and fell asleep. Later, he got up. Feeling bored, he decided to play bridge online. Carol joined the table as his partner, giving an instant and welcome boost to his mood. They played and chatted with their opponents about nothing more than the weather and plans for the upcoming holidays. Carol bid a doubtful slam, and both of their opponents, unexpectedly, left the room, leaving computer robots to play their hands. He sat back to watch Carol play the hand, but, before she was finished, he left too.

Later, he realized she must have felt abandoned, so he wrote a quick email to her: **Sorry about having to leave the table so abruptly, but my family returned from my grandson's wedding and made me a part of the celebration. Today was not** one of my better days, so I had stayed home to take care of myself. I loved playing with you.

If you are having a crab cake, please take a bite for me too. xoxoxooxxox E

She answered right away. **Thanks, El. It's so thoughtful of you to let me know why you left. There I was, glowing with success in making that difficult hand and, suddenly, there was no one there to crow with me. I stayed anyway, all by myself. "We"—you and I—bid another hand and won the rubber!**

It's too bad you missed the wedding, but I'm glad that if you had to, at least you spent the day with us online playing bridge. I loved playing with you, too.

I'm heating up my crab cake now. Later, my friend. A quick hug, Carol

He was relieved she had answered so quickly. He chuckled, wondering whether her visions of crab cakes were the same as his, though he quickly repressed the thought. He didn't want to do or say anything to scare her off, sensing that he came close to doing just that in recent emails when he told her he was there for her and invited her out to play. After all, they were only in their third month of knowing one another,

He let out a surprisingly deep sigh. The reality was clear—he had fallen in love with her while reading her book. In her writing he found the woman he'd always wanted: strong, yet a little vulnerable; smart, but not absorbed in her own intelligence; and independent, but willing to listen to another viewpoint. She was lonely—that was obvious. She had told him she missed intimacy, and he, a self-confessed romantic, pictured himself filling that void in her life—being her rescue knight in shining armor. Ellis smiled, and then struggled to catch his breath as a sudden coughing fit ensued. When it was over, he wiped his face with a handkerchief and shook his head. *Some knight, eh? More like Don Quixote. Not old, though. Never old,* he reminded himself. *Okay, if I'm not old, and I'm still breathing, despite this damned infection in my lungs, I'm going to continue my quest. I'm alive! I'm in love! And I'm going to let her know it—eventually, that is.*

He put his fingers on the keys: **As I read your book, I feel as if I am walking along with you in your journey of self-discovery. I confess that, at times, your experiences bring tears to my eyes. I, too, have traveled much of this same road. Amazing that we never met along this path. I suffered from drinking, also, and although I think occasionally about a glass of wine or beer, I know better than to retrace those steps; they nearly led to my complete demise. I have never done drugs, but I've sampled other dubious offerings of life, which, I must say, I mostly enjoyed.**

Dubious offerings. Hmm. I'm not entirely sure she'll interpret that one correctly. Oh, well, it will give her something to think about.

My marriage died 30 years ago. What remains is still characterized by respect, kindness, and civility since honor and duty were programmed into my being early on. However, living with someone who has become a stranger is difficult. I am unsure if my code of honor and duty is a blessing or a curse. Life today is what it is. I, like you, have set out to reinvent myself.

The reinvention came with kickback, especially when El first started to go regularly to the country with Beth. George, particularly, was outraged: El needed always to be near enough to take care of any needs Joanne might have. *Like I'm going to sacrifice myself for her?* He patiently, but firmly, told George: "Look, I see that your mother's safe when I'm gone, but that's all I'm willing to do. I'll be damned if I'll make her life more important than mine. Look at me, son. I'm a finite creature too. I'm going to live while I still have a chance to live." He was aware that his answer seemed harsh, but he also knew that taking care of Joanne, after her long indifference to their marriage, would kill him.

He wasn't sure George approved of his answer, but he didn't care.

Pensively, he typed: **I praise God for caring for me and carrying me in grace to this point in my life. In you I have discovered a comrade in arms and, perhaps, even more surprising, maybe a soul mate. You *are* a very rare find, dear heart. E**

Carol clasped her cheeks. Her mouth opened in amazement as she shook her head. *This is pretty heady stuff*! His words excited her. She was drawn to his desire for her, but she was disturbed that he had a wife. The actuality of a wife, chronically ill and possibly unable to contend with an affair her husband might be having with her, was a consideration doubly disquieting for Carol. *Why, if his marriage died thirty years ago, had he not divorced her?* Carol still didn't know the wife's name. Something kept her from asking El. *Yeah, I don't want her to be real*, she admitted.

She reread Ellis's email. She knew, from personal experience, and from her long association with stories AA members told, exactly what Ellis meant by "the dubious offerings" in life. Empty, self-seeking affairs were thankfully behind her now—she hoped over for him, as well. His honest statement about wanting a drink now and then unnerved her. She wondered if he actually *took* a drink now and then. Dismayed at her distrust, she frowned. She didn't know whether he had undergone treatment for alcoholism or not—his drinking sounded serious enough. *I just couldn't put up with a practicing alcoholic*, she told herself. *No, not "couldn't;" I **would not** put up with that!*

Ambiguity again! This friendship shouldn't be all that difficult. *I'll just write and tell him what's on my mind.*

She stretched hands over the keys: **Thank you, my dear El, for sharing all of this with me. I am honored to be considered your soul mate. It is indeed rare to find the compatibility we seem to share. And, yes, we taste the heights of delight in our conversations. We are gifts to one another. At our ages, I think it is best to think of our relationship in that way. We can continue to write one another until one of us runs out of life, I suppose. I hope that circumstance is far down the road.** Inanely, she thought of the poem "The Road Not Taken," as if she might regret what she was saying now. She hurried past the thought, however.

It is a wonder we didn't meet during my drinking days. I particularly liked drinking with men, and they liked drinking with me. You sound just like the type that attracts me. But I'm glad we didn't meet in those days. I like this clear-eyed view I have of you with nothing about which to feel ashamed. I've been sober a long, long time; I do not drink at all. In fact, I know that were I to drink, I would be back in the terrible troubles I had before—or dead from drinking. I'm thinking you do not qualify as an alcoholic, at least not the type of alcoholic I was. *Am I hoping he is not an alcoholic at all, just a heavy drinker that decided to quit drinking? Will he stay quit?*

On the positive side, we who like alcohol (or liked, in my case), seem to be sensitive, intelligent souls. I sense those qualities in you. *I can't ask him about whether he is or is not alcoholic. I might insult him. He might stop writing me.*

I'm glad you are honoring your commitment while also reinventing your life. It seems that I'm a part of that life now. We can have some great times together online. Let's take it one day at a time.

Know, my dear that I'm growing quite fond of you. Hugs, Carol.

There, Mr. Thompson, you have my ambiguity wrapped prettily in my interest in you.

Ellis noticed the ambiguity. He wanted so much to clear her mind of it, to share with her all he was feeling, yet he was experiencing ambiguity as well. His health wasn't up to par. No matter what he ate, he was still losing weight. *Maybe she's right. We should just enjoy our conversations online and consider them a gift from God.* He hoped he wouldn't run out of life too soon either. He felt fortunate to have Carol in his life. The thought of her brought him such joy.

He also noticed that Carol had spent some time explaining her alcoholism, differentiating her experience from his; even suggesting that he might not be alcoholic. Despite his time in AA, he had never really liked to use the term "alcoholic." Perhaps it was his upbringing as a proper Southern gentleman that excluded the idea that he could ever be an alcoholic. Yet, he had qualified through his drinking and the antics that came with it. He liked the idea that the only requirement for membership in AA is a desire to stop drinking, which he had, though it had taken some time in AA for him to curtail his drinking. Rather than leave the groups, he stuck with the hard work in seeking sobriety and was glad he did. AA, coupled with his church experience, gave him a strong belief in God's care for him. With what he was going through with Joanne at the time, he needed to believe that someone cared for him; human power didn't fill the bill. God did. *And still does,* he gratefully acknowledged.

Carol wrote a blog on her website, announcing to the world that she had found an interesting male companion while playing bridge on the Internet. **He's a match for me in age, in intellect, in our various interests, but he's a thousand miles away with an established family, definitely out of reach, except as a** special friend. **You see, he is lonely too, because his wife has Alzheimer's**.

Impulsively, she sent the copy to Ellis. He replied by sending her Robert Herrick's poem "Delight in Disorder" and declared that he, like the poet, enjoyed the mystery of women. **I value women and always have. I like the way they think, their sensitivity, their sense of fairness, devotion to family, the way they walk, the way they talk, the way they smell, and last, but not least, the effects they have on me. I have always thought that Eve really got a bum rap and that the story in Genesis was written by some male. Actually, I think Adam and the snake colluded because all Adam wished to do was seduce the woman. I have told this little ditty to some of my more literal Christian friends. You should have seen the looks on their faces. My wicked nature surfaces; my escape clause is always: "The devil made me do it."**

Despite her worrisome misgivings, Carol couldn't help but smile. She decided to stay the course. She loved the way El fed her information about himself through his stories. *So he isn't a right-wing conservation Christian, thank you God. He likes poetry, even writes it.* She reread Herrick's poem and wrote to him: **What lovely thoughts in which to wake! Good morning to you too, sweet man. I open my computer each morning to read a daily devotional from Luther Seminary; then I look at my email. Like dessert, I save the best for last: yours.**

I like Herrick's poem. I never could present a perfect image myself, especially in the house. I'm forever trying to clear my dining room table, not of dishes, but of papers: mail, scattered notes to myself, books, receipts—they all collect until I do a sweep. My computer desk is littered with paper as well: more notes, business cards, pens, last

week's symphony program, mailing labels that I've yet to put away. . .

The more I try to order things, the less success I have. So I live with a certain amount of clutter. The living room is fairly neat, except where I've left cloth bags full of books— books from church council, copies of *A Journey In Time*, book holders, pens, pencils, notepaper—on the couch. All is fixable when I expect company, but a certain amount of clutter reminds me that I am human—that there are other more creative things to do than put things in their places. So I relate to your poem. Isn't Herrick the fellow who advises us to gather our rosebuds while we may?

You are a little devilish poking innocent fun at people too literal in their interpretation of the Bible. Have you ever closely read that passage in Genesis? It says in one Biblical version, "And the man said: the woman whom thou gave to be with me, she gave me of the tree, and I did eat." You see, Adam did not blame the woman, really—he blamed God for giving him the woman! I like your idea of Adam colluding with the snake. It would certainly be in character.

Send me some of your own verses, my friend, if you care to share. I'd love to see how you write poetry. Not that your feelings about women are not already poetry. You paint a word portrait of ideal women yet, certainly, some of the women are real, or the ideal would never occur to you or anyone else. She was curious about his experiences with other women. He had hinted enough about the importance of women in his life.

I hope you are feeling better. I look forward to hearing some good news, I hope, after you see your doctor tomorrow. I'm off to play bridge with people offline today. Hugs, Carol

Chapter Eleven

*C*arol wanted to tell her friends about her conflicted feelings toward El. She really liked him but, as yet, she didn't quite trust that their embryonic relationship would go anywhere.

The group was meeting at Jennifer's house. Peter, her husband, was off somewhere—Jennifer didn't know where. "He's so moody and uncommunicative."

"Are you all right?" Sophie asked.

"Yes, sure," Jennifer said, sarcasm tingeing her tone, "if you consider being unhappy *all right*."

"I'm sorry." Sophie laid her hand over Jennifer's and looked her in the eye.

"Well, there's nothing to be done about it." Jennifer was resigned. "He won't go to court until after the holidays. Probably sometime in January. "I'll be damned if he's going to chase me out of this house. I put my money in this place as well as he did; certainly I have more sweat equity in it."

"But the gun business?" Stella let the question hang in the air.

"I know. That is scary," Jennifer admitted. "After the police took Peter to jail, I picked up his gun and hid it."

"You hid it? Why didn't you give it to the police?" Dana wanted to know.

"They didn't want to take it. Can you believe that? They said he had a legal permit. They weren't concerned about me. Probably thought I was some hysterical woman. He hadn't hit me. I wasn't visibly injured. There was no argument that led up to the discharging of the weapon. They bought his story about the gun going off while cleaning even though no one in his right mind does gun-cleaning on a bed!"

"They did charge him with something, didn't they?" Dana asked.

"Yes, discharging a firearm in a residential area."

"Then they need the gun for evidence," Dana concluded.

Jennifer sighed. "I think they took him off to jail and charged him just to cover their backsides because I was so upset. They took photos of the hole in the ceiling and the paraphernalia on the bed."

"Where did you hide the gun?" Carol asked.

A small, wicked smile crinkled Jennifer's worried face. "I put it in my closet at the bottom of a box of panty liners."

"Perfect!"

"If I know nothing else about that man, I do know he wants nothing to do with panty liners." An eruption of laughter broke the tension. Each woman appreciated survival strategy.

"Still," Sophie warned, "you might want to get that thing out of the house."

"Where?" Jennifer asked. "I did try to take it in to the police, but they wouldn't accept it—told me I wasn't the owner. He is." Jennifer gritted her teeth, shook her head, and spat out an angry grunt.

"Another example of the law protecting the guilty," Sophie declared. "I'm all for capitalism, but it does tend to protect property over people."

"Well, you take care, Honey." Stella spoke to Jennifer, softly and offered help. "If you see him drinking, get out the house. Come to me. I've got an extra bedroom."

"Thanks, friend. I don't want to bring trouble to your door. I'm okay for now. I'll keep you all posted." Jennifer signaled an end to the discussion. "Let someone else check in."

"I have something to say," Carol volunteered. "I'd like some help with my conflicted feelings toward El."

"What's going on?" Dana asked.

"We've known one another for three months. Just recently, his emails turned in a direction I'm not sure I want. He told me that he is there for me and invited me out to play."

"Play what? Play where?" Dana was her usual practical self. "You're in no danger, Honey. He may be there for you, but he certainly isn't here!"

Carol smiled. "True, but when we are on the Internet, it all seems so real. I like El. I like him a lot. Believe it or not, there is chemistry between us; I'm drawn to him as I've never been drawn to anyone before, so powerfully drawn. . ." She was going to say more, to tell them she felt crazily happy at the delicious prospect of being loved, being fully known, being appreciated again, but she caught the look on Sophie's face and stopped talking.

Sophie shifted her jaw and bit her lip before saying softly, "He does have a wife."

"Ah, there's the rub," Carol admitted. "I keep telling myself that she isn't there for him. Ironic, isn't it? She lives there, but she's not there. I feel uneasy thinking of her with Alzheimer's, unable to comprehend that her life with El has changed, and there is another woman who interests him—me!"

"Ah, Honey, don't be so hard on yourself," Jennifer advised. "You two are lonely people who have connected in a very special way. He needs you as much or maybe even more than you need him."

"All well and good, "Sophie said, "but it's a serious business interrupting a marriage of over fifty years. Even though ours wasn't a perfect marriage, I would hate to think that Nathan carried on secretly with another woman while I was out with my friends."

Carol frowned. The statement stung, but Carol knew what she had to do: she had to face this uncertainty within her. "You see, Sophie, the problem is, I think, that Ellis's wife is unable to grasp that there is another woman in his life, and maybe if she did understand what was going on, she wouldn't care, particularly; Ellis told me that his marriage died 30 years ago."

"Why did it die?" Sophie countered.

"I don't know," Carol said. "I suppose it happened when she began having memory problems."

"Perhaps, but not likely," Sophie replied. "Can you find out?"

"I guess so." Carol wasn't particularly happy with that solution. "I feel uncomfortable asking in an email, and I'm not ready to talk to him just yet. I want this relationship—this friendship," she corrected, "to grow." Carol realized she had just minimized the reality of her desire. Feeling trapped between admitting her true feelings and the pressure of moral considerations, she retreated to the safety of psychoanalysis: "It fulfills a need I have for an intelligent, caring man to pay attention to me. Can't you see?" She was close to tears. Her face contorted as she pleaded: "Do you know how hard it is to find such a man?"

Carol stopped talking and held her breath, willing the tears to stay put. She was thinking of the intelligent, caring man she once had—Mario. She let a sob escape and then, wiping her eyes, she collected herself. "I'd like for things between El and me to settle out, to know if this friendship has potential for something more, before I pry into his relationship with his wife."

"I hear you," Sophie confessed. "I miss Nathan too. Sometimes I want him back so badly—healthy, of course—that I physically ache for him to be sitting in his chair, carping at me for never being home with him. When I think about it, honestly, I too sometimes fantasize about finding someone else."

"You know," Dana interrupted, "you two aren't getting any younger. I'd say don't wait around for Lady Love to fall into your laps. Look at me. I found a fellow. He's not at all like my David was, and sometimes I find him annoying even." She raised a telling eyebrow. "But he is a companion. It's nice to have someone in your life who cares for you."

Stella looked at Carol and in her soft voice whispered, "Remember that this all started because he told the online bridge group that his wife has Alzheimer's and he is lonely. That's all you need to know for now. Don't let doubts and fears crowd out your happiness. I've seen joy in your face again. So good to see after seeing so much sadness there."

"I agree," Jennifer added. "Give it time. See what happens. Anything that puts a sparkle in your beautiful blue eyes has to have some merit and deserves a chance to ripen."

"I have beautiful eyes?" Carol quipped, breaking the tense concentration of everyone starting at her. Jennifer stuck out her tongue and wrinkled her nose. "*As if* you didn't know, dearie." The women laughed.

It was then Sophie yielded her position. "Okay. Okay. Just trying to help."

"I'm sure if Evelyn were here, she'd vote for a wait-and-see attitude as well," Stella said.

"Undoubtedly." Sophie turned the conversation to a discussion of Evelyn's declining health. The group's oldest member no longer had the energy to attend meetings, but was still clinging to life.

When Carol got home, there was an email from El, reminding her that his health was a real issue. **The smear of the last specimen from my lungs tested negative, but now we must wait five weeks for the culture to mature to see for sure if "negative" is truly "negative." The food restrictions are now lifted, except I can't have any alcoholic beverages.**

There it is again—alcoholic beverages. Was this simply an innocent statement? Carol wanted to believe that it was. She read on. **Now I can eat just about anything I want as long as it agrees with my body. My specialist told me that the shortness of breath will get better over time as I recover, but I will be on medication for ten to twelve months. I will go back to her in January. Meanwhile, I'll see the asthma doctor December the fifth and the internist on the sixth, which will wrap me up for this year. There will be more specimens to run by the lab, and I have been asked to get an eye exam to use as a baseline since some of the drugs I take may affect my vision. Nasty stuff this!**

All in all, I feel good today and took care of some details like filling my truck with gas and going to the grocery store. Today I feel stronger. My legs are steady and stronger. I keep my tummy under control with yogurt, buttermilk, and Pepto-Bismol. Ah, me, this is most likely information overload, but there you have it. Thanks for your concern, dear heart; you are a love.

Carol chuckled. She had wanted reality. *Well, is this enough reality for me?* Like many older people, Ellis came with a carload of ailments, but his mind and spirit were well and attractive to her. Once the lung infection was gone, surely his health would be comparable to hers; she felt well and fully functional. Oh, occasionally when the weather turned really cold, she coughed more often, but that was controllable.

I plan to visit my friend north of Houston on Friday, returning on Monday, if I am feeling up for it. I'm getting a bit stir crazy here in the condo after two months of being incarcerated; the brief trip will do me good. Beth and I have known one another for almost twenty-five years and

are very close. I have nursed her several times: once when she had knee surgery, and again when she broke her arm as a result of a bad fall. I lease the ten acres the trailer is on from her and her son. I am as close to her family as I am to my own, perhaps closer.

The mention of another woman was a shock. *What is the matter with me?* Carol asked herself. I am getting deeply involved with a man who not only has a wife, but also has—*dare she even think it?*—a mistress. *Okay, Carol, slow down. He describes her as a friend of twenty-five years! He is even close to her family. You have a friend—Will—that you've known even longer. She's not necessarily his mistress and, if she is, what business is it of yours?*

She and I will be taking care of tons of paperwork that she's allowed to accumulate over the years and to date has not had the energy to weed through. She promised to let me rest when I feel the need and said she will cook for me— fresh asparagus will be on the menu—but I will take her to dinner one night to say thank you. I plan to take it easy and get plenty of rest so as not to undo the progress I've made.

Well, at least he has someone to care for him. It was good to find an excuse for his being with Beth; Carol could understand craving that kind of attention. She wondered what his wife would be doing while he was away. Could she manage with her Alzheimer's?

Beth has traveled to New England with my wife and me, and she and her daughter have weathered two hurricanes here with us at the condo. Her home north of Houston is located in a flood zone and is not a good place to be in a major storm. I have not seen her in over two months: it will be a good time for both of us.

Hmm. So she is a friend of the family, after all. Carol felt better, but she was a little annoyed at herself for doubting El.

How did your bridge game go the other day? I bet you won!

As always, E xoxoxoxox

What is this "as always," E.? As usual, she answered his email right away: **Hi El, I'm glad to hear that you are doing well today and that you have recovered your ability to eat anything agreeable to you. Sounds as if your infection is beginning to clear.**

Your visit with your friend should do you a world of good. I hope you get to take the trip. I feel less concerned about you now that I know you have a special friend who also cares for you and is within reach. That was the truth. She did feel relief that Ellis had a friend to go to in the Houston area. Beth probably kept him from going crazy from living with a demented wife. Since his wife knows about her, she must be a trusted family friend . . . *maybe.* Carol pursed her lips before making a decision to stop thinking about Beth and Ellis as other than friends. She continued to type: **We need to feel connected to others. I think it is especially true of men who don't bond as easily with other men as women do with other women. Have fun, get some rest, and enjoy Beth's cooking.**

Suddenly, she felt compelled to drown him in detail. She typed rapidly, willing her mind to travel somewhere other than where it had been. *Enough speculation! Enough prattle about connection!*

The bridge game was so-so. We had a new player who is just learning, so that slowed us all down. We made a lot of accommodations for her, but we need to encourage people to learn. I really enjoy playing bridge online because there are some very good players. Even the computers, sometimes, when I play by myself, give me a run for my money.

Ah, and, yes, let's tell him all about the venue.

We played in a restaurant, a sports bar really, which served us lunch for $12.50, tip included. The lunch was su-perb. I had an orange chicken salad with garlic bread.

She was beginning to love the rhythm of the serial depictions of her life. Would doing this cure the unwanted anxiety she felt?

Tonight my son and I are going to the Alkathon. Our AA group is host and will bring food and chair a meeting. I decided I wanted to go this year to support the group. Usually, I go to a church service, which is very nice—a singing service, which we do on Wednesdays in the Advent season. After the service, pie will be served tonight, but I won't be there.

Ta Da! Maybe I could sing this all to him if I knew his phone number! Okay, let's finish this.

I look forward to having Thanksgiving with my son again. Here we are last year in my kitchen. (Carol inserted in the email a picture of herself and Paul hovering over a golden brown turkey. *It's time I became a little more visible, I think. He doesn't know the picture on the back cover of the book is also one taken a year ago.*) She chuckled as she furnished more details.

He helped me cook the bird. See the red curtains in the background? Right under them is my computer where I play bridge and write to you.

Have a good holiday, my friend. She smiled and impulsively added, Hugs, Carol

She had written herself into a happy mood.

Chapter Twelve

*H*olidays weren't happy days for Ellis, especially this year. He had come so close to death a little over a month ago, and was now progressing ever so slowly towards health. Neither of his sons, nor their wives, showed any inclination to cook turkey for the family. El was in no shape physically to plan and execute a family dinner. *Best to go out*, he thought; so, as usual, sick or no, he made plans, called the families, and arranged for all to meet at a pricey downtown restaurant.

He was at his computer, dressed in his sports coat and string tie, ready to leave, when he decided to write to Carol. **Thank you for the picture. I was thrilled to get it. I know you will be busy today cooking for your son, but I just wanted to come by to wish the two of you a very happy Thanksgiving. We do have much to be thankful for despite all the uproar going on in our country.** America was in a serious financial crisis as were most of the other free countries of the world except, perhaps, Germany and Switzerland. There were massive layoffs with a spike in unemployment figures and much bickering among governments on how to address the problems.

Ellis sighed: **I take comfort in knowing that God is in control.** *It sure seems that no one else is!* **I am in my study right now with the TV playing behind me. I feel as if I have been dumped on by all the desperate harangue of advertising** merchants pushing their products in advance of the holidays. It would be nice if our country could be saved by rampant consumerism, but we both know that this alone will never solve the problem. A whole new mindset must take place before we again measure up to what we might be. I am thankful for living in a country where I can believe in the system, even though it has become corrupted by greedy substandard people. There is hope; I hold tightly to that thought. Have a good day, Love. E xoxoxooxxox

Ellis looked at the endearment he added. It had come naturally, almost a blessing, an antidote to the gloom he felt for himself and his nation. Carol was something—someone to call *Love*; she was part of the hope he felt, maybe a miracle of renewal for him.

Joanne came into the study just as he turned off his computer.

"Did you say we were going Christmas shopping today?" she asked, looking at the cascade of Black Friday ads appearing on the television set.

"No, Mam. It's Thanksgiving. We're eating with the family at Lulu's."

"We are?" Joanne's face darkened. "But the television says there are sales."

"Tomorrow. There are sales tomorrow." He didn't dare tell her some stores stay open on Thanksgiving.

"But we are going shopping, aren't we?" Joanne persisted.

Ellis sighed. He could barely stand to try to reason with her. "Later," he said, knowing that she would not remember. "We need to eat first." They had given up Christmas shopping for the most part since the children and even the grandson were grown. *I'll be happy to get out of here tomorrow*, he thought.

Ellis had no idea how to help Joanne. The doctors weren't much help. They were good at prescribing medications, but scant on ideas on how to cope, especially with a wife he resented. While his life with Joanne was not ideal, at least the diseases that plagued his wife before Alzheimer's had some historical understanding attached. She had managed those afflictions on her own, but lately she'd come back from her doctor's visits with nothing to tell him. He wondered whether she even remembered going to the doctor.

The restaurant turkey was unappetizing to him, but the family seemed to enjoy it. James was absent. El's grandson and his new wife were having dinner with her folks. Joanne seemed better around her sons. She smiled as she told them she was going shopping after dinner. George and Henry, used to their mother's confusion, nodded numbly. She asked them what they wanted for Christmas. Both men, reaching for a way of communicating with her, indicated that they wanted to be surprised, knowing full well there was no longer any exchange of gifts. Their mother used to love surprising them with goofy gifts—dental floss or lottery tickets—before presenting them with cashmere sweaters or some other wanted extravagance. Now her woefully wanting memory clashed with the wistfulness of her sons for those vanished happy times. After dinner the family went separate ways: El drove Joanne home. By the time they got there, she had forgotten about shopping and went quietly to the bedroom to read.

Ellis switched on his computer. There was a message from Carol. **Hi El, Happy Thanksgiving to you as well. The turkey's in the oven. Paul and I did our turkey-fixing together again and enjoyed it. He's outside now fixing his burned-out headlight on his car. I may play a little online bridge.**

Yes, I agree with you. We do need a new mindset, but changing minds is hard enough for individuals. Imagine a whole nation shifting! However, we are God's creatures— precious to Him—so I think that we will be given the

wisdom and the power to figure something out. We might have to go through more hard times, though. Enough of that on Thanksgiving! I'm thankful to be alive and full of energy today with friends to talk to and email. I'm thankful you are feeling better. Keep going in that direction. Hugs, Carol

Ellis noticed that the email was friendly, but not especially close, considering what her emails were in the past. He shook his head. Some past. *We hardly know one another yet.* He supposed her switch to a more dispassionate correspondence was a message to slow down. He wondered whether his mention of Beth had anything to do with the distancing he was sensing from Carol. Suddenly weary, he decided to go to bed. He had a long drive to Beth's Forest Cove house in the morning.

The next day he reminded Joanne that he was going to visit Beth and asked her if she needed anything. She signaled she was fine and waved her arm as if saying, "Go, already." On his way out, he checked in at the lobby desk and alerted the staff that he would be gone until Tuesday and that his wife would be alone. He had already told George and Henry to keep an eye on their mother while he was gone. For now, he was reluctant to disturb her independence. He knew Joanne would find her way to their usual restaurant for her evening meals. She would also call him two or three times a day. His stomach churned. He was still resentful that late in life he was forced to be responsible for her care.

Beth met him at the door. She smelled of beer, her favorite drink. The odor was strong when he hugged her, but dissipated as they sat in her living room, talking of his hour's drive to her house and their plans to go to lunch before tackling the work she had for him. Since Charlie's death, Ellis had periodically reviewed Beth's investments for her before she met with her financial advisor. She liked his input, for she was heavily invested in energy stocks, particularly oil. Since Ellis had worked in the field with Charlie, she felt he had a specialized knowledge of the oil companies, more so than the advisor, whom she kept on because Ellis hadn't wanted to be solely responsible for her decisions. Her portfolio statements were already laid out on the dining room table.

"How's Joanne?" Beth wanted to know.

"The same," Ellis said.

"No formal diagnosis?"

"Just dementia. Her neurologist hasn't given her any more memory tests since last year when she did well enough on them to convince him not to put her through the arduous testing to diagnose Alzheimer's. I get the feeling the doctor doesn't want to go there with her." El was sick of the doctor's cautious foot dragging. He was getting no help whatsoever from the medical establishment in understanding or managing Joanne's mental symptoms.

"Have you talked to the doctor yourself?"

"I tried to, but he gets defensive. It's as if I'm threatening him somehow."

"Perhaps he thinks *you think* you know better than he what is wrong with Joanne."

"I *do* think that," Ellis declared. "I live with her. I see her confusion daily. It's getting worse." He imagined himself drowning in Joanne's needs, not being able to either help or to find a place where she could get help and he could get some peace from it all. His face flushed with anger.

"Well, hang in there," Beth stammered, unable to think of anything hopeful to say. "Shall we eat lunch now? I've made a chicken salad."

They ate at the kitchen table. Beth had a beer with lunch. Ellis had his Ensure, the magical potion prescribed to help him gain weight back. Even his food was medicine now, he grumbled. He wasn't hungry.

After lunch they reviewed her investments. The drop in the economy took a big bite out of Beth's stocks, yet Ellis advised her not to sell. She was invested in companies that had a good cash reserve, and he was convinced that the energy stocks would be the first to recover, especially with the President giving stimulus money to save the automobile industry.

That night they went out to supper before coming home to watch an old movie before bed. Ellis slept on the well-worn mattress of the guest room. The next day Beth wanted help with going through her files and deciding what to discard. This ended up being a massive undertaking since Beth was indecisive on so many items. Seeing they were getting nowhere, Ellis made a suggestion: "Let's wrap this up for today, and try again tomorrow."

He got up, stretched, and moved into the living room. The work had tired him. It surprised him to discover his jaw hurt, but then he realized it had been tight all day. Puffing air into his cheeks, he blew out a long cleansing breath and dropped his shoulders, hoping to force himself to relax. When he plopped on the couch, feet up and eyes closed, he gratefully shut out the muddled issues the day had brought and fell fast asleep.

Later in the afternoon, Beth woke him, offering him a cold Pepsi, which felt wonderful going down. She was drinking from a can of beer. She wanted to talk about her son, Larry.

"He wants to come home," she said. "He's been laid off from his job. You know his wife left him last year, and now he is having a hard time making rent on his apartment. He still has to support his two girls, you know."

"How would coming to you solve his problems?" Ellis asked, sipping the Pepsi.

"I don't know," Beth snapped, clearly irritated. She didn't want to tell him that she had been giving Larry money since he lost his job. Ellis might know the state of her investments, but she never volunteered to show him her checkbook.

Beth's daughter was leaning on her too. She and Charlie put Lauren through college and saw her through the impulsive first marriage, which turned into the failure they had predicted. For a number of years after that, Lauren was a lecturer at a private college in Dallas, a well-paying job she gave up when she married Craig, her second husband. The marriage was shaky; Craig was a womanizer. Although unhappy and deeply lonely, Lauren stayed in the relationship. She wanted the security of another job before daring to leave him, but no one was hiring an overqualified woman in her late fifties. She, too, had asked if she could come home.

"Maybe if Larry were here, he could help around the house," Beth said. "God knows, there is plenty to fix around here." Beth had done virtually nothing to improve the property since Charlie's death.

"True enough," Ellis agreed. "However, it is very difficult to have adult children return to the family nest, especially ones who are out of work."

"I know. But what am I going to do? Let him live on the streets?"

"Perhaps if you let him figure it out, he'll find a way. Maybe even go on welfare for a bit."

"Oh, God, no." Beth set her beer down on a small, wobbly end table and got up to pace. "Charlie would turn over in his grave he thought a child of his was on welfare! You know what he thought of people on welfare, sucking the livelihood from honest working people." She stopped pacing and gave El a hard stare. "As long as I have a roof over my head, my children will be welcome in my home," she announced vehemently.

El backed off. "Well, you know what you want to do." He was certain Beth's stubborn resistance to his suggestions was her way of convincing herself that making sacrifices for her children was the right thing to do. Thinking to distract her, he asked, "How's Lauren?"

"What do you mean?" Beth was defensive, forgetting El didn't know that Lauren wanted to come home too.

"Nothing. Just asking." El's nonchalance disarmed Beth. She took a deep breath.

"She's fine," Beth said, finally relaxed. "Still looking for another teaching job. Not much open in Dallas right now."

"Hmm. That's too bad," Ellis murmured. He didn't know what more to say. Beth was sensitive about something, and he wasn't fool enough to provoke her into telling him what that was. He knew she was irritable lately, but didn't know why. When she was upset, she was unpredictable. Once before, when she confided in him that her son-in-law was having an affair, he had asked if Lauren's husband was a drinker or a drug user. Bad move. Beth told him in no uncertain terms that she didn't delve into her children's business and would appreciate it if he didn't either. After that, he watched what he said around her. He disliked confrontation, so he asked, "Shall we get back to work?"

"I thought you wanted to do that tomorrow," Beth said, finishing her beer.

"Well, I'm reenergized after that nap. Let's see what we can do."

They worked on the files then. Beth seemed more willing to throw out old material that had cluttered her files for years. They separated the paper into bags that could go to recycling and others that would need to be destroyed. Beth made an appointment for Monday with a company that shreds paper. They finished the job in an hour. By that time, both were hungry enough to clean up and go out to supper, where Ellis had a steak and coffee and Beth had fried chicken and beer.

Chapter Thirteen

*C*arol was restless. She tried playing bridge with her online friends, but missed El playing with them. Thanksgiving over, he was where he'd told her he would be—at Beth's house somewhere north of Houston. She wondered where precisely, but couldn't guess. There weren't any tangible clues on the Houston map she pulled up on her computer. *No matter,* she told herself, *I don't really want to know too much about her.* Keeping Beth at arm's length mentally was akin to believing she didn't exist. *Oh God, was she jealous of his friends already?* She clung to the belief her interest in Ellis was platonic, though the word *liar* clearly sounded in her thoughts. *Yes, yes,* she admitted, flustered at her lack of control, *I miss him.*

The days crawled, and then suddenly he was back, full of sunshine and cheer. **Four days of rest and good food do wonders for the body and soul. I slept like a baby and enjoyed my brief respite.** *I bet you did!* Carol glared at the email. **A change of scene is always welcomed. It helps maintain emotional balance. I suppose the most difficult part is saying "goodbye."**

I knew it! Carol fumed. *Difficult to say goodbye to Beth, was it? How would you feel saying goodbye to me?* Instantly, she regretted the thought and took a deep breath. *Out with such self-centered feelings!* Although she knew he couldn't possibly know what she was thinking while she read his emails, Carol worried she'd trigger second thoughts in El by subconsciously suggesting a lack of faith in him. *Why do I worry about what he's thinking when I barely know my own mind these days?* It must be the holidays and the approaching anniversary of Mario's death, she decided. *Four years should be enough time to grieve, shouldn't it?* She had grown accustomed to El's engaging attention. *Was longing for more so bad? Not if you can keep your emotions in check, old gal,* she told herself. She was again reminded of Mario. He'd call her "old gal" now and then when he was feeling especially affectionate and protective. She sighed and read on.

Today I make up my bank deposit and go to the bank. Afterwards, I'll need to go to the drug store to pick up some Rx's and drop by the grocery store.

Looks like it's my turn to be drowned in details. Oddly, telling her the ordinary details of his life made her feel forgiving and close to him. His next sentences, however, doused her pleasant reverie. He was going to leave her again! Bitter disappointment flooded her face. *Why so soon? Why when I can't bear missing you another minute?*

Fayette County is on my agenda for December the 8th, since there is work to be done on the trailer. One of the air conditioners has failed; I need to deal with this while it is still under warranty. The heater needs to be checked, and there are other issues that need a bit of loving care. I can tend to myself as well there as here. I will be careful not to challenge my breathing. Beth showed me pictures of the new fence, but there is nothing like seeing it in person. I will be there at least a week, possibly longer. We'll just have to wait and see how things progress.

Details, more details! I'm sick of details. Carol forgot all about the warm fuzziness of details just a moment ago. She was breathing heavily, irrationally angry now. *God, I am crazy—driven stark-raving mad over a guy I have yet to meet. He's taking her with him, I bet. I just know it.* She sighed. *Calm down, gal,* she told herself. *You never were jealous before. Remember this: he promised you nothing; he owes you nothing. He obviously has more of a life than you imagined.*

The Thanksgiving dinner in the restaurant was such a disaster that I have decided to have Christmas dining here in the condo. I don't plan to do it all by myself. I'll use Jake's Deli for Christmas Eve with the customarily served potato soup. Christmas Day, I'll serve honey-baked ham, rolls, and dessert while other family members bring side dishes and help with the cleanup, which I think is only fair.

The litany of Christmas details calmed her. Carol, now able now to focus on El, imagined how lonely it must be for him to be charged with holiday meals. With the mother of the house conspicuously absent, El did all the planning, shopping, cooking, and serving. *There'll be loneliness for me too*, Carol admitted. Even though Paul was coming for Christmas, the holiday wasn't the same as in years past. When the children were little, there was travel and a large family gathering. There'd be no big meal this year.

I have decided to opt out of the usual ho-hum gift exchange on Christmas Eve and contribute money to the Houston Food Bank. For every dollar contributed, the food bank can buy ten dollars' worth of food for those in need. I want Christmas to matter to everyone; I want to feed people who cannot provide for themselves.

Now that's a really nice thing to do. Carol felt centered once more. She thought of contributing to a food bank herself.

Okay. Now, I want to know how you are doing, busy lady. I will be here until December 8th so, until then, you will find me standing under my usual lamppost here on the corner.

He signed off with "take care," but did send the usual "O" and "X" hugs and kisses. She wondered what that omission meant, but stayed subdued. She had been through enough emotion for one day. She wrote to El: **Well, hi, my friend. Lonely at the bridge tables without you. Glad to hear that you got great attention and rest while you were gone. You are one lucky fella! And off again on December 8! I can assume that you are feeling much better; I'm glad of that.**

It took effort to type those words and mean them. Carol sighed again. She knew now that El would go to the trailer often and, almost certainly, with Beth. Could she accept that reality and still hang in there with El? She feared being a second paramour in line. Bah! There was a bad taste in her mouth, but loneliness was worse, she decided.

Christmas is quiet around here. My son will spend time with me as he did on Thanksgiving. We do not exchange gifts anymore. What's the point? After a while, you realize you have more than what you need.

Yes, and then you have to think of getting rid of things, downsizing, giving up your car and going into assisted living. Nice thought, Carol! What has gotten into you?

I think your idea of feeding others is superb. I make contributions in my church. In fact, we have a Christmas in July, complete with a tree and items for the homeless underneath it. Bless you acting on behalf of the hungry. You have a good heart.

She told Ellis about her Thanksgiving with Paul. When she brought out the camera, Paul ran to the bedroom to change into his old faded tee with tiny, tired stripes. "Same shirt I wore last year, Mom!" They both laughed. The shirt was a holiday ritual. Carol gave him $50 on his last birthday to buy a new one, but he never did. They took a picture of both of them then. Focusing and using the timer, Paul raced to circle his arm around his mother and lean on her shoulder. Both grinned over the browned turkey as the flash fired.

"Should I send Ellis another shot of Thanksgiving turkey?" she asked, smiling.

"Why not? Sounds like he's interested in seeing you anyway he can."

Carol blushed with pleasure. "Oh, I think not . . . sending the picture, that is. Too much like the other shot I sent. I don't want to leave an impression that I'm boring."

"No one ever thinks you're boring, Mom." Paul surprised her with his comment.

"Really?"

"No, of course not." The imp in Paul returned. "*Everyone* thinks you are boring."

"Stop it!" she scolded. Mother and son had a history of inane humor, the cushion they used to soften some of the horrendous experiences they had been through.

"Well, that's what you get for not believing you aren't boring in the first place." Paul smiled at his mother.

Carol *had* believed—believed in him. When he told her he was gay, she cherished him. She was there by his side when he needed her most—when Len died and Paul feared for his own health. *Now, it must feel good for him to be of some support to me,* she thought. He knew she was far from recovered from Mario's death. Remembering his own grief over Len's death from AIDS a decade ago, he knew as well as she did, Carol realized, that life was never quite the same after losing a loved one.

"Let's eat," Carol suggested. "Bring that turkey to the table."

The evening before Thanksgiving, they had attended an Alkathon, a holiday round-the-clock support feast for recovering alcoholics.

"I haven't been to an AA meeting since I was a teenager," Paul told Carol as they found seats among the 200 people who crowded the large downtown church hall where the event was held. Most people came early to savor the turkey dinner being served in an adjacent room. Carol's home group hosted the first wave of eaters. The food they brought filled gaping holes of regret for alcohol-drenched holidays in the past that tore families apart. Now there was gratitude for reconciliation and forgiveness found through working the twelve steps of the program. Here in the safety of strong coffee and lukewarm soda pop, newcomers felt acceptance and understanding, some for the first time in their lives. All who participated felt the camaraderie of kindred souls seeking hope and community at a difficult and dark time of the year.

Since her group was a Big Book study group, the chairperson had selected "Bill's Story" for audience members to read aloud, a paragraph at a time, at the microphone up front. Paul listened attentively, later telling Carol he had never heard the story of how Bill found his own sobriety and then, with Dr. Bob, began to help others and together founded AA. After Carol finished her paragraph, she urged Paul to read. He took the book from her, read, and then looked up to encourage another volunteer.

From the back of the hall came a voice: "I want to read."

A young man, dressed in clothes that had seen much better and cleaner days, came forward, stumbling a little, but raising his hands in greeting. "Ho! Ho! Ho. Happy Thanksgiving," he bellowed. It wasn't that he didn't understand the concept of an AA meeting; he was just drunk.

The chairperson pointed to the microphone, and Paul passed the book to the jolly interloper.

The man grinned, ran his finger down the text in the book and, miraculously, found the spot where Paul had left off. Carol could feel the amused, but supportive, identification in the sober audience. All had been there too. The tattered man read then, slurring words occasionally, but with strength and conviction. The gathering knew what a difficult time the journey toward sobriety was for him. All that mattered to those in the audience was that he was there, and he was reading—reading in his drunken, but elegant way—reading of Bill's spiritual experience that gave AA's founder relief from his own alcoholism when nothing else had worked. Carol silently said a prayer for the young man. Then she noticed the tears in Paul's eyes. "There, but for the Grace of God. . . "she thought, knowing that alcoholism runs in families.

On the Saturday after Thanksgiving, Carol and Paul attended an author's reading at Myers' Coffee Shop. She wrote about it to Ellis: **I read a piece I did after participating in the 1995 Mother's March Against AIDS in Washington, D.C. After I read, there was quite a stir as people vied with one another to tell poignant stories about AIDS. As you know, Californians, living with a large population of gay people, were especially affected by the disease.**

Carol read that particular piece reach year and remembered Len as World AIDS Day approached. He mattered to her; her first book, written with the hope of eradicating homophobia, was dedicated to him. She knew the courage it took for Len to move from England to Hawaii—to travel thousands of miles from his homeland just so he could be openly gay—and then, ironically, to have to find the courage to move back home when he got sick and needed expensive medical treatment. Equally, she respected Paul's loyalty and love in going to England with him. It was a terrifying time, a time early in the AIDS epidemic, a time when AIDS was callously called GRID and dismissed as a gay man's disease. Overwhelming shame layered the terror. With every living breath, Len resolutely denied his sickness;

he dared not admit the possibility of AIDS, even in discussions with Paul. But it *was* AIDS. The death certificate said so. Only by the grace of God did Paul escape infection. No one, including Carol, escaped the terror.

Carol felt drowned in sad memories. She didn't want to revisit Paul's grief, let alone hers. She finished the email to El: **Our women's group went to see our friend Evelyn today. She's in rehab with a hip injury. Afterwards, we ate lunch at a Thai restaurant whose owner, I discovered, donates twenty-five percent of her sales on World's Aid Day to the local AIDS Foundation. We've come a long way since the days when President Reagan wouldn't even *say* the word.**

Chapter Fourteen

Beth's son Larry bounded down the hall to answer Ellis's persistent tattoo on Beth's doorbell. "I'm coming, I'm coming," he sang in response, and then, seeing Ellis, pulled him into the house with a buoyant hug.

"Well, hi yourself, Sport!" El boomed his greeting as he wrapped his long arms around Larry's shoulders and gave the younger man three hearty slaps on his back. He liked Larry and sympathized with the problems the recent job loss was causing him. "Here to visit with Mom?"

"Yes, visit, of course . . . of course." Enthusiasm waning, Larry gave Ellis a quick smile and then cleared his throat. "Ahem. And bunk down with her for a while." He grimaced, looked down at his feet, and taking a deep breath added, "Just to give me a little breather." *He's embarrassed*, El realized and then thought, *good*!

Larry raised his head and lifted his eyebrows slightly, risking a look at El. "You know what I mean, I'm sure. I just need to buy a little time to get back on my feet." He nervously shifted his gaze away from El and bit his lip. "It's tough for a man of my age to get a job in this economy."

"Oh?" Ellis was noncommittal. His view of grown children returning to the family nest was quite different than Beth's. He doubted her income was enough to support herself, let alone her children.

But Larry was here now; could Lauren and all her troubles be far behind?

"On the other hand, I'm footloose and fancy free." Larry gave El a big smile to waylay any unwanted criticism. "See, no belongings, except what's in that suitcase there." He gave a quick kick to a large suitcase lying forlornly in the foyer. "After Nora and I split, I rented furnished, you know. I can pick up and go anywhere the jobs are—any day."

"Well, that has to be good," El said, mildly. "Were you still doing welding at the oil patch?"

"No, sir. The work got too strenuous for me when I hurt my back helping the wife move. Believe me; you don't want to lift a sleeper couch all by yourself. I found *that* out the hard way." Larry grinned and absent-mindedly rubbed his right side. "I'm afraid my days working on an active rig are over now that I've turned fifty. I plan to get some computer training and see if I can land an office job. Meanwhile, I'll do a little light industrial welding through a temporary job agency, I hope. I have to do something. Nora's after me for child support."

"Well, good luck with that," Ellis said, thinking he really should be wishing Nora luck, but dared not open that can of worms. He had enough problems of his own to solve. He didn't need Larry's. Turning to Beth, who had joined them with her travel bag, he asked, "You ready to go?"

She was. Ellis hoped for a quiet drive to Fayette County, but that hope soon vanished. They had barely cleared the driveway when Beth started her usual carping. "Larry's landlord threatened to evict him. I swear that man doesn't have a compassionate bone in his body! Throwing a jobless person out on the street! How cruel can you get?"

El was weary of Beth's complaining. For all her grousing, Beth never denied her children anything, and wound up taking care of them at a time when, in El's opinion, they should be taking care of her! She was eighty, after all. Maybe not frail yet, but certainly, as their mother, she was entitled to more than a little respect from them.

He sighed, willing himself to be patient. "I'm sure it wasn't personal. A landlord has to collect rent, after all. He's in business." Ellis kept his eyes on the road. He longed to turn on his music, but knew Beth didn't like classical.

"Well, of course," Beth huffed. "I'm just saying that it was all so abrupt."

"How far behind was Larry?"

"Oh, Lord, I don't know. He never tells me about those things." Beth sighed and calmed a little. "I suppose both of us should be grateful that he was able to leave on his own. He wasn't bodily thrown out, but he couldn't stay any longer." What Beth didn't say was she told Larry that she couldn't pay his rent anymore. She changed the subject.

"Are we stopping at that deli-grocery for lunch?"

"If you wish."

"I thought I'd buy a six-pack there to hold me over until we go shopping at La Grange."

"Didn't you bring any beer with you?" he asked.

"No. Larry drank my last one last night."

"Okay. Maybe we should buy something at the deli for supper too."

They traveled on in silence. Finally, Ellis put on some Beegie Adair piano jazz. His thoughts drifted with the soft music. He found himself wondering what Carol might be doing. Was she thinking of him thinking of her? His face softened as visions of Carol danced a different sort of tune in his head.

When they reached the deli, Beth grabbed two six-packs of beer, saying to El, "They're on sale. Might as well take advantage of it."

Ellis said nothing in reply, but ordered a ham and cheese sandwich and a side of potato salad. Food didn't really interest him anymore, hadn't interested him since he got sick. In the three months since his hospitalization, he had lost an additional ten pounds. His naturally tall and lanky frame did a good job of diverting attention from his skinniness. As long as he was on antibiotics, he would not gain weight, his doctor told him; he believed her. Though worried that he'd lose too much and begin to seriously weaken, he was reassured by the fact that he was still up and about and doing whatever he wanted. The only persuasive reason to gain weight was the possibility of someday meeting Carol; that goal was so far off, it didn't motivate eating.

Beth ate the other half of El's ham and cheese. They decided on a roasted chicken for dinner.

Finally back in the truck, they drove the last twenty miles to the trailer, where Ellis unlocked the gate to the carport, turned on the water in the outdoor well house, and after turning on the heat in the trailer, unloaded the truck. He missed Carol and wished he'd had a computer with him, but Internet service here was unreliable and expensive.

Beth put clean sheets on his bed and stowed some in the living room couch where she slept. Though they weren't averse to sleeping together, she gave up that arrangement when his persistent coughing kept her awake at night. Besides, she had been alone so long now that she just didn't want to be that close to any man anymore. She didn't admit it to him, but she was grateful when Ellis went to bed by ten, leaving her time to finish one last beer on her own.

Satisfied that the trailer was in good shape for their stay, Ellis told Beth he was going to lie down a bit before supper and retired to the bedroom. Beth turned on the television and lay on the couch herself.

The phone rang just as he was drifting off to sleep. He patted his shirt pocket and found it lit up, vibrating tantalizingly against his bony chest. Annoyed at being abruptly pulled from sleep, but momentarily amused by the vibration, he was aware that as skinny as he was, if he'd rolled over in his sleep, the phone would have hurt. He knew who it was before he glanced at the Caller I.D. He had forgotten to call Joanne when they arrived.

"Yes?" His impersonal tone was habit now.

"I can't work the TV," Joanne whined.

"Tell me what you have done so far."

"I can't. I don't know. I just know there is no picture, no sound." He could imagine the deer-in-headlights look that so often now was her only facial expression.

"Which remote are you using?"

"The gray one."

Ellis groaned. She had used the original television remote when she needed the one that operated the cable. Now he'd have to go through laborious steps to switch her from one remote to the other until her snafu was undone. He exhaled deeply. *No rest for the weary.* His cherished peace was fast evaporating.

"Okay. Take the gray one and press Channel 3."

"Nothing happens."

"I know. I just want you to be on that station. *Don't lose it, fella,* he told himself. *She can't help herself, but you sure can.* "Are you on that station?"

"I think so."

"Now turn off the television set by pressing the power switch on the gray one." He fervently prayed she could identify the power switch on the old remote.

"Okay."

"Now put down the gray remote."

"Okay."

"Did you put it down?"

"Yes."

"Now pick up the black remote with the red buttons on it." His patience was stretching thin at this point, but his pride in being a well-mannered gentleman kept him calm. Still, he couldn't help moaning, *Why, dear God, didn't you send Carol to me instead?*

"Okay."

"Do you have it in your hand?"

"Yes."

"Do you see the red button that says 'all on'?"

"Yes."

"Press that button." *It would be handy if there were an "on" button in your head*, he thought. His kindness didn't extend to his thoughts.

"Okay."

"Did the television come on?"

"No." His tongue clicked the roof of his mouth, hiding his frustration behind his teeth.

"Is there anything on the screen?"

"Yes, it says 'cable box.'" He almost lost patience, but, instead, he deliberately lowered his voice.

"Good. Now look at that row of little buttons on the top of the remote. Do you see them?"

"Yes."

"There are two dark gray buttons and three light gray ones. Do you see that?"

"Yes, but what do I do? The picture's not on. This is too hard," Joanne wailed.

"Listen. Just listen, please." *If only she could listen. Damned disease.* He spoke even more deliberately than before. "Count the buttons."

"One, two, three, four, five."

"Okay. Now count up to three and press that button."

"One, two, three." She seemed to need to hear herself say the numbers. There was a pause, and then Joanne said with obvious delight, "Oh, good. I can see the program menu on the bottom."

"Great."

"Now the fourth button is the power button. Put your finger on that and press it."

"Okay. But the television went off!" Her voice was near panic.

"Press it again." He heard her suck in her breath.

"Oh, good," an elated Joanne shouted. "There's my program." There was an abrupt click. Joanne hung up without saying goodbye. Ellis stared at his phone, sighed, put it on the shelf, and lay down again. He was too agitated to sleep. *I guess the woman has forgotten how to say thank you.* He wished he had Carol's number at times like these, but she hadn't offered it. Not that he'd ever burden her with his problems. He just wanted to talk to a sane woman with interests beyond television or suck-the-life-out-of-you adult children.

Now that he was older, it was wearying to be called upon to solve other people's problems, especially Joanne's. He kicked himself for not going through with the divorce when he had the chance. He was stuck with a woman he didn't love, yet felt obligated to care for as she lost the capacity to care for herself. *What a maddening disease Alzheimer's is!* El could hardly stand to give Joanne the detailed instructions she frequently required, yet he couldn't simply give up on her. Not yet. Not while she still had a modicum of awareness, even if it was just to watch repeats or old movies on TV, or to eat their evening meal together at Jake's.

Bless this trailer, he thought. *If I couldn't get away now and then, I would go mad, locked up in that condo with that woman.* He rarely referred to Joanne as his wife—only when necessary—never in his own thoughts. He deliberately worked at emptying his mind of *any* thought of Joanne. El looked with satisfaction at the walls of his trailer cradling the bedroom. *Like a little cocoon,* he thought. *My cocoon.* He smiled. The chicken would be good tonight. Maybe in a night or two, if his appetite cooperated, Beth and he could take a trip to Moulton and eat one of those luscious Kloesel's steaks. How a world-class steakhouse ended up in tiny Moulton, Texas, was beyond him. Such food would be worth spending an hour on the road to get to.

Beth's phone rang. He could hear her say "hello" to Larry. Beyond that, he wasn't interested in the conversation. Soon enough, Beth would tell him whatever she wanted him to know, no more than that. He was grateful he wasn't sitting out there with her. He got up, locked the bedroom door as a signal to Beth that he didn't want to be disturbed and, taking off his clothes, slid into bed, slipping easily into his favorite fantasy: Carol, crab cakes, and a massage table.

Chapter Fifteen

And just where are we going with all this? Carol wondered when she read the email. El sent this one just before he left for his trailer retreat with Beth. The words were wonderfully provocative—**I like to see the reluctance in nature as she disrobes.** Carol blushed, envisaging another disrobing—she and he flirting, baring their bodies ever so slowly, holding back, tantalizing, teasing . . . She pursed her lips, closed her eyes, breathed deeply, and slowly let her head clear.

When she looked again, she found more in the email than delicious sensuality. El's philosophical and spiritual side emerged, surprising her with his wisdom. *Good. I didn't much like those dry travelogues you've been sending recently, Mr. Thompson.* She suspected El was abiding strictly with boundaries she herself set after his invitation to "come out and play." Too quickly distancing herself from sexual word play—*what was I so afraid of?*—she had turned his *play* into a simple exchange of wit by intellectualizing *play* itself. *Groan.* Sometimes she was too smart for her own good.

Come out and play. The truth was her heart danced when she read those words! The compelling invitation came after a carefully crafted description of intimacy, designed, no doubt, to disarm and persuade her that they were *just* discussing ideas. Then, oh so cleverly—*as if I'd know there is no ulterior motive*—he stated his belief that life should be shared with a significant person, **"one who satisfies**

physical needs and brings out thoughts and feelings privy only to one's very soul." *I see your "privy," Mr. Thompson. You're thinking you're distracting this intellectual, aren't you?* She grinned then. She knew herself well; *privy* could go into the recycling bin; she was firmly fixated on *significant person.* Was *she* his significant person? The audacious idea made her dizzy.

On the other hand, that email frightened her as well. *Who was she to feel that they were significant persons to one another?* Perhaps the scary notion had spurred her to deliberately set boundaries in response to him. She remembered being troubled by the feeling that they were perilously close to falling in love, and there were compelling reasons not to. The physical distance—1600 miles—and the reality of a wife, albeit one not available to him, made her anxious. For her own peace of mind, she had needed to assure him and herself that the "play" they were savoring was just that, even though she was wasn't sure she was telling the truth.

So she told him: *The reason our literary exchange is so magical and fun is that we are experiencing all the joys without the physical presence and hard work of actually being in a relationship.* Yet, even having said that, she couldn't help adding: A*ll I know is that I smile a lot when I think of you.* Then, in an approach, inscrutable even to herself, she wrote, *so, I send you a measure of love equal to the one you have sent me,* and signed off with *"Hugs, Carol,"* no less.

That email surely reflected the intense ambiguity she felt. No wonder they both escaped into mundane territory after those exchanges. For all the talk of intimacy, they had yet to share more than hints of deeper feelings.

Now, in the middle of December, came this captivating email that offered more than hints. It was definitely a new approach: a poetic reflection of the great outdoors in his area of Texas. He began by casually observing that the trees had yet to shed their leaves;

some of the leaves were brown and ready, others were still colorful. Then the words turned cryptic as well as suggestive. **I like to see the reluctance in nature as she disrobes. The leaves and branches clinging to one other remind me of lovers holding desperately to that which is no more. It's as if they hold on, even when knowing they must let go, for letting go is yielding to an uncertainty they cannot comprehend. You can see that this season brings out the melancholy in me. Beginnings and endings are so confusing.**

Carol's heart sank as she read the words "letting go." *Was this a call for them to stop?* Reading on, she decided, with relief, that he was not writing about their own budding relationship, but exploring life issues.

Never mind me, he wrote. **Comfort comes when I remember how good life is, how God provides for us even in the midst of our paradoxical muddles. In order to live, we must die, the trees tell us. Their bright leaves make a royal carpet to shield the earth from the coming cold. I'm no theologian, but I think that the secret to all this is love. It seems to me there is a loving forgiveness in the way leaves spend themselves in nourishing the earth. Then, again, maybe all this is just nature's "thank you" for a lovely summer. E.**

Carol sat at her computer monitor, absorbed in reading the words, over and over, fixing images in her mind until she convinced herself that she had gotten ahead of herself, making mountains out of molehills. What was important, she decided, was the discovery of his deep creative thinking. Pleased and feeling on common ground with El, she released her fear and let her words flow freely.

Dear El,

What beautiful thoughts! I love the way leaves cling like lovers reluctant to part. Fall is a time when beginnings and endings are confusing, a time for melancholy, indeed.

Your words are full of the unfathomable promise of life beyond, yet suggest that promise is always there before us, incomprehensible and uncertain, but real, a kind of now-you-see-it-now-you-don't wonder. I think it paradoxical that we live life as if we have forever, and yet never realize that we are truly living in eternal life; the seasons teach us that lesson.

My dear El, you impress me so much. You stir in me longings, remembrances of good times in nature with Mario and the complexities of *his* mind, and also thankfulness that God has given me the gift of you.

Thank you for sharing your insights in such an appealing way. Stay well, my extraordinary friend. With warm and loving thoughts, Carol. She sent the email impulsively without even running a spell check.

He's a poet, a thinker, and a sensitive soul! Carol was intoxicated with the thought of him. She adored his passion, a passion that matched hers. She was happy.

When El did not respond to her email, Carol second-guessed herself, thinking *maybe I was a bit too eager in my spontaneous reaction* to his poetic musings. She feared she had scared him off. He was leaving for La Grange in a few days and, uncharacteristically, there wasn't even a "goodbye-stay-well" email from him. Could it be he didn't get her email? Or, maybe he wasn't as interested in her as she thought. *No. That just can't be*, she soothed herself. Still, no word. When he finally left for La Grange without an email to her, her happiness withered.

Carol was lost without El. To top off her despondent mood, she lost a crown off a back tooth while biting into an apple. The jolt of looking at a $1200 repair brought back reality. Although fixing the tooth was a financial burden, she was actually glad to be distracted by something she understood. The women in her group were busy with Christmas plans, shopping for their grandchildren, and gathering family input on what to cook for the holiday dinner, so she withdrew—sullen, sulky, and reflecting endlessly on what she might have done differently. She was reluctant to burden celebrating friends with her gloom. Besides, it was embarrassing to obsess over a man with whom she could see no real future.

Playing bridge online without El wasn't much fun either. She showed little interest in her online bridge buddies. Internet friends are superficially close, she decided. Even though they seem open and friendly, they tend to be here-today-and-gone-tomorrow friends. She never knew whether such friends moved on to other sites, died, or just didn't give a damn about relationships. Developing the kind of intimacy she had begun to feel with El required a willingness to share daily life. Such conversations simply don't fit the narrow confines of chat rooms; she understood that, at least intellectually. How strange to be in a world where instant communication made people feel lonelier than before.

Carol moped through the two weeks El was gone, chastising herself for her apathetic mood. All she wanted was to have him back online with her, yet she had no valid claim on him. He had a life of his own in Texas. She was an Internet friend to him. The constraint in keeping the relationship platonic conflicted with all they had said in their emails. Those emails undeniably implied more than friendship, yet here she was, alone again.

A few days before Christmas, a welcome email popped into her inbox. **Dear Carol,**

I have returned and seem no worse for wear after two weeks in the "outback." I got eight to nine hours of sleep each night with a few afternoons devoted to two-hour naps. Sleeping during the day is rare for me and speaks

to the point that I am not back to my usual self yet. My cooking left much to be desired; most of it was microwave "cuisine." After a while, that wears pretty thin. Next time, I will be using my slow cooker and whipping up more inviting dinners.

So, he *was* still interested in her! Carol sighed. *Back to writing mundane details of his life though,* she thought, *but back, thank God, back.* She was a little annoyed that she needed to hear from him, needed to know that he still wanted her. Would she ever outgrow the need for a man, especially a man as elusive as El?

Most of the work that I needed to get done was accomplished. I just got under the wire with all these repairs, but I did get the urgent ones done so I can now move on to other matters.

Despite her annoyance, Carol chuckled. Ellis seemed so happy to be busy with the tasks he had set up. Replacing the air conditioner and checking on a heater were on the list, she remembered. The fact that he was engaged with life's activities, though still obviously recovering from his illness, made *her* happy. *How quickly I seem to get over my insecurities about him!* she marveled.

I will be out and about today with grocery shopping. Thirteen family and friends are coming for the holiday. On Christmas Eve, I serve the traditional potato soup, cookies, and crackers for supper—followed on Christmas Day by honey baked ham, spiced peaches, rolls, and dessert. I ask others to bring side dishes. If I can find an already prepared sweet potato casserole, I will get it, but otherwise it may well be mac and cheese. I have also made it plain that I expect help with the cleanup, since this isn't going to be a free ride.

Yeah, yeah, yeah. Her mind grew numb with detail. *More mundane stuff!* Then she read the last sentence and the closing; her heart stopped.

I hope the last two weeks have been kind to you and that you are well. More later as time permits. Love, E

Love! The word leaped at her. *He had written "Love, E."* Carol was suddenly transformed. No ambivalence now. Only wholehearted delight. There in Times New Roman font was the word she had longed to see: *Love.* Her heart beat a joyous refrain: *Love, Love.* She sang along, whispering the words: *I am loved! I am loved!* For the first time, El had replaced the "x" kisses and "o" hugs with a solid affirmation: *love.*

Thank you, God, she prayed. For once she didn't feel like a widow. She was loved, loved, loved! *I am alive once more*, she exulted. *Mario, my love, be happy for me, please. I am moving away from my grief for you. Not, you, my love. I am not moving away from you. I will always love you, but now I have room to love another and be loved by him.*

She reached for her computer keyboard. She wanted to take it slowly, to match some of the ordinary thoughts in his email with ordinary words of her own—*funny how "mundane" quietly becomes "ordinary," after a declaration of love.* Most of all, she wanted him to feel her need for him as well. The two weeks without a word from him, however, advised caution: *Easy, Carol. Easy.*

Dear El,
Welcome back. I missed you.
That's a good beginning. I can admit to missing him.

I can't believe you are doing all that work for Christmas! Take care that you don't consume the vacation energy you just collected. I know you will have a rousing good time with your family and friends.

Our Christmas will be a quiet one. Paul is here with me, now, and will stay through Christmas Day. Then he will

drive to Seattle to visit his father for the New Year. There are no other relatives here. On Christmas Eve, Paul and I are part of the church program; we talk for three minutes about Christmas blessings. I will mention our bridge games because they are a real source of blessing to me.

Carol really wanted to mention El as a blessing, but it was much too soon. She wondered whether people in the congregation would frown on her corresponding with a married man, even though his wife has Alzheimer's. Still, it was Carol's task, not the responsibility of any of her churched or unchurched friends, to reconcile her need and affection for him with the fact that he had a wife. Someday she would talk to him about it, but not now.

Not having you here made such a difference at the bridge tables! Partners were sparse, and not as friendly, except for the day I was able to play with Bonnie and Peggy and a friendly stranger. I look forward to more bridge with you.

I've grown wise about our Christmas dinners. This year there will be a fancy beef pot roast, bought ready-made and served with lots of vegetables. For dessert? Perhaps some cookies we'll make tomorrow.

I've been plagued with coughing recently. When it turns cold, I have more coughing fits, which I hate. My doctor says my lungs are clear, but knowing that my lungs are clear is really no help. The coughing exhausts me, so I've been trying to rest more.

Between activities in church, my writers' club, and selling the book, I've been unusually busy. Last Sunday, I was a guest on a local radio show, a gig I thoroughly enjoyed. When it is posted on their website, I'll send you the address so you can listen.

Is that enough interesting minutia? Can I get to the heart of this exercise now?

I'm glad you are back. Take good care of yourself. Love, Carol

There! I get to say it, too! Carol reveled in the joy of finally saying what she wanted to say and making the connection with El. Still, she wasn't ready to share her feelings directly, not even with Paul. When he got up, she fixed him a late breakfast. Since Paul had a cold, his condition allowed her to funnel what she felt for El into loving attention on her son.

"Go back to bed, Sweetie," she said to him when he complained he felt stuffed-up. "You can rest today, so you'll be able to do Christmas Eve at church tomorrow."

"Maybe," Paul said. "I hope I make it to church. I'm not feeling that well, Mom."

Carol reached in the kitchen drawer for some Vitamin C. "Will you take this? It really works for me." Paul took the vitamins back to his bedroom where he could prop himself up and watch TV.

Carol was proud of her son. After his partner Len died, he closed out his affairs in England and moved in with Mario and her, alternating time with them and his father and step-mother. For a while, she worried that Paul would never get his life together—his grief was so overwhelming. When he finally decided he could build a life without Len, he began to take menial jobs, and then, when employers noticed how capable he was, he found a permanent job with a Silicon Valley corporation as a project manager. In time, he found a new partner, Joseph. Paul bought a house in Sunnyvale, and they settled down. It was worrisome to Carol that he was now having problems in his relationship, but she knew better than to interfere.

She sighed. Introspecting about Paul nearly always resulted in thinking about her older son, Patrick, her two grandchildren and, now, a great-grandchild. Eighteen years without a word from them! Was the estrangement her fault? She was never entirely sure. She knew her daughter-in-law didn't like her from the beginning. Was it simply a wife's natural instinct to draw her husband away from his mother, or was it something Carol had done? *No sense going there.* Carol willed those thoughts to stop. Nothing she had ever said or done, including giving expensive gifts to her, seemed to make a difference to Patrick's wife. The younger woman never would engage her mother-in-law in any meaningful conversation; indeed, she even told Carol once that she wasn't interested in hearing about her life.

For years, Carol was heartsick about her loss, particularly the loss of her grandchildren. Then, something happened. She began to talk about it with other women and found, to her amazement, that estrangement among family members was all too common. Even those not estranged from sons and daughters often felt left out. *Someone ought to do a study*, she thought. Knowing she wasn't alone comforted her. She began to bury her hurt—she imagined the pain contained in a sealed pocket in her solar plexus, tender when triggered, but mostly, blessedly, quiet. She also prayed nightly that Patrick and his family be happy. The habit helped divert her from thinking them cruel. *I wonder what Patrick does to disremember his mother?*

Enough melancholy! She scolded herself. *Get on with Christmas. Yes, and get the whole holiday business over with.* It wasn't like her to be so agitated and dismissive. She wondered where her earlier joy had gone.

Chapter Sixteen

ove, Carol—there it was at last. El, goose bumps rising on his arms and legs, leaned back in his computer chair, his gaze fixed on the magical words. *You're one lucky fellow, Thompson,* he told himself, shaking his head in wonder. *Your charming lady sends her love!* Instinctively, El knew Carol wouldn't carelessly toss around the *love* word. Using it in her latest email almost certainly was permission to move in closer.

He longed to abandon all common sense and shout, *I love you, I love you.* Instead, he reluctantly let passion drain. Revealing too much too soon might scare her off. He knew Carol was unsettled about Joanne, but he couldn't reassure her until she raised the subject. Would she reject him then? *Good God, please, no!* He couldn't stand the thought of losing her. *Not now!* He scratched his head, puzzling over the next move. *It's too early,* he thought. *Only three months of emailing one another. Best to stick to everyday news and let things develop.* He sighed. There, too, was Beth's invitation for New Year's and their annual income tax paperwork project. He had to let Carol know he was leaving again.

Carefully, he composed his email. **Is it the Christmas blues or am I just bushed after two days of feeding those thirteen hungry descendants of mine? After all that fuss, I'm a mere shadow of my former self. No more, I say! From now** on Christmas is up to others! I'll stick to living my life one day at a time.

I hope you are no longer coughing and you are feeling better now. Have you been to the doctor lately? If not, then may I gently suggest that you go for a checkup?

I'm off to my ophthalmologist today for a vision baseline because of my lung infection. The only thing I can think of as a reason for all this testing is the high-powered antibiotics I am taking.

If I feel well enough this weekend, I will visit my friend who lives north of Houston and is not having an easy time of it these days. I can't figure out if she's depressed or if there is a physical health issue. Her children's marital problems are taking a toll on her.

We have known each other for 25 years and are very close. I'll stay a few days to help her with some household matters. She never goes out to eat, but I will remedy that, except on New Year's Eve when sane people leave the highways to the revelers; I'll either cook dinner for her or bring some of that leftover ham from Christmas. For New Year's toasts, I'll buy some eggnog and bubbly, libations she loves.

I'm just dropping by to say "Hi" and let you know that someone in Texas is thinking about you. Love, E

When she read El's email, Carol seethed. The "friend" north of Houston was undoubtedly Beth. *Why is he going to see her again? Wasn't he **just there** helping her out?* Carol was breathing heavily, blowing out puffs of air while thinking. *This pattern is all too familiar.* The phrase "we are very close" rang a warning bell in her. Would there be room for her with such closeness between Beth and him? Should she back off? *No, no, no, no. I can't do that! I need this love; I want this love.*

A cold draft shivered her spine. *Okay, okay. I can handle competition with Beth.* Carol knew she was sufficiently attractive to hold El's interest, *but what's this talk of bubbly libations?* This was the third time he had casually mentioned alcohol, as if getting ready to tell her something more. *Was he drinking again?*

A wife, girlfriends in two states, and romance fueled by alcohol were matters toxic to her hopes. How cruel to find love with Ellis and then have to break with him. Not over his women, she mused, but *if* he was an alcoholic and drank, she would have no choice. She looked in her file of El's emails and reread all the ones addressing alcohol. Ferreting out information and following clues, she studied them as closely as a detective would. In one email, El said he occasionally thought about drinking; in another he told her food restrictions around his lung infection had been lifted, but alcoholic beverages were prohibited. In the most recent email, he was buying alcoholic beverages, supposedly for Beth. She found nothing conclusive. Was she too sensitive? Too critical? Or was she simply reacting to her own fear of the power of alcohol to ruin everything? She sighed. *If he is drinking, there is nothing I can do about it, so until there is reliable evidence he's drinking, I'll just let go and wait and see what happens.* She was relieved by her decision. She didn't want to break with El.

She wrote: **I am touched by your letter. Thinking of you in Texas thinking of me in California leaves a very sweet feeling within me. It's nice to know that someone cares. I am grateful for your friendship.** *He doesn't know how true that statement is.*

It's good you are so supportive of your longtime friend. God should bless you as you bless others. *Okay, that was a little dig clothed in supposed gracefulness. That's what you get, mister, for telling me about the special attention you pay to Beth.* Being pleasant, but thinking nasty, brought a satisfied smirk to Carol's face. *So, I'm not perfect,* she chuckled.

My cough has quieted since I have been resting, but, as instructed, I'm off to the doctor's on Wednesday. Paul caught a cold while here; I was able to mother him. He, in turn, was very helpful to me, giving me the freedom, permission, and constant reminders to relax a little. The tension in living alone is thankfully relieved with others present.

I'm glad you are retiring from being the chief cook for Christmas. Big parties like that take the stuffing out of you. If we are both around next holiday season, I'll remind you of your vow not to take on so much.

I'm sorry that your lung infection has not yet cleared. Were you a smoker? I was diagnosed with emphysema 28 years *after* I quit smoking. I'm lucky. If I had kept it up, I wouldn't be writing you today unless you receive mail from heaven—assuming that place is where I'd be. Carol was feeling much better about El. *Life is short, after all*, she reasoned. *I'm not there to give him pleasure, so why not Beth?* **I'm going to step up my praying on your behalf and see if that infection will leave you.**

I'm looking forward to the New Year. It's always nice to feel that there is a new start to life even if only an illusion. Love, Carol.

Ellis, filled with the idea that Carol loved him, had no idea of the mental anguish his words had caused her. He was so thankful for Carol. What a blessing to have a woman of her quality express affection for him. Feeling the urge to spread the joy, and judging himself well enough to make the drive, he made definite plans to see Beth and lift her spirits.

Ellis was genuinely fond of Beth; however, he had decided long ago he didn't want to have a day-to-day relationship with her. Keeping up with her problems, let alone those of her grown children, was just too stressful. He hoped in the New Year his relationship with Carol would flourish, a welcome relief from the constant calamities of Beth's life. Thinking of Carol, he opened her email. As he read, the light in his face faded. He frowned. He couldn't put his finger on why her message seemed incomplete. She answered his comments, but seemed subdued. He had expected more. What did she mean by "a new start may be only an illusion?" That remark was troubling.

We seem to relate to one another in fits and starts, he thought. His mind flashed back to tortured love affairs in his youth. Could it be that even in advanced maturity, love is also tortured? *Oh God, do I need to go through all this again?*

It annoyed him they couldn't talk face to face. He needed to see her body language to better know what she was telling him. Come to think of it, he hadn't yet heard her voice, only the one imagined in his head, and that was inadequate.

In the morning he told his wife that he was leaving the next day to visit Beth. Joanne looked at him blankly; for a moment he wondered if she remembered who Beth was. *It doesn't make any difference*, he thought. *She doesn't care anyway. I wonder if she ever did.*

Joanne peered up from her coffee cup. "Are we going to Jake's for dinner?" she asked, confirming his suspicion that she had no interest in where he was going.

"Sure, if that's what you want," he said.

She left him then, taking her coffee into the bedroom. El picked up the phone to talk to the building manager and remind him that Joanne would be alone for a few days. He also wrote an email to his sons, telling them to check on their mother while he was gone.

Then he wrote a short email to Carol. **I will be heading north about this time tomorrow and plan to return next Monday or Tuesday. I can use Beth's computer while there, so I will keep up with my email. I hope you are feeling better and** that the New Year will be full of good health, love, contentment, and prosperity.

I have no big plans for New Year's Eve, but plan to assist Beth with cooking dinner that night. She has lots of leftover turkey, so we are going to whip up some tetrazzini. Overly excited with the thought of being away from Joanne and celebrating New Year's with someone who could actually converse with him, he impulsively joked with Carol, thinking: *Maybe she needs a little humor from me.* If the two of us are still awake at midnight, we may have a Nutty Irishman or some Bailey's. Since I really don't drink anymore, one or two drinks will probably put me down for the count. She promises not to take advantage of me. (Hee! Hee!)

Take care, dear heart. See you later.

Love, E

Well, that does it! Carol resolved. *I am going to disentangle myself before I'm completely bamboozled.* Suddenly, the absurdity of it all hit her. She laughed. *Bam-boozled! What an adjective!* Was she really being tricked by misleading statements or just plain set up to be perplexed? And who was doing this to her? El? Or her own strict standards of not getting involved with active alcoholism? Besides, there's been no telltale evidence of alcohol abuse in El's writings. In fact, *if* he were drinking, he probably wouldn't jest about it.

She sighed. You'd think a trained psychologist and a writer could figure out inferences in written words. *Yeah, maybe— if it's not happening to you, girl,* she reminded herself. She felt diminished and helpless, embarrassed by misreading simple logic. She hated that feeling.

Okay, then, let's get honest. You are jealous of his relationship with Beth, she said slowly to herself, emphasizing each word in pointing out the obvious. *You don't feel secure enough with El's affection for you.* Another thought struck her. *Or, maybe your grief is catching up with you again—that anger you feel every time you think everyone else but you is in a close relationship.*

Be gracious, she told herself. But she couldn't be. She wrote: **Sounds like a good start to the New Year. I wish the same wishes for your New Year. I won't be doing anything for New Year's except sleeping. This is short and sweet because I have household things to do. Take care of yourself and Beth. Love, C.**

And so New Year's passed for both of them. True to her word, Carol went to bed at nine and slept through until morning. She didn't know that El and Beth also retired early in separate bedrooms. Beth had drunk a little more eggnog and Bailey's Irish Cream than she planned, while Ellis drank his diet colas.

Beth's anxiety over filing her income tax this year drove Ellis wild. He wished she'd stop investing in exotic real estate trusts that required him to pour over endless IRS instructions just to get a single figure right on the 1040. The endless task was eye straining and exhausting; he felt resentful—*why couldn't she stick to mutual funds?* He had no time or energy left to write Carol.

When they weren't deep in tax law, Beth's voice filling his head with the latest in her children's chaotic lives exasperated him. Larry was seeing another woman now that his wife had left him. *So is he living with her or you?* He didn't dare ask and Beth didn't tell him that, though she had tons to say about Larry's wife keeping the children from him.

El listened without much comment. Despite his annoyance, he was sorry for Beth, sorry that she couldn't let go and let her grown children be responsible for their own lives. Convinced that most of her depression was grounded in trying to change their impossible situations and, consequently, not doing much for herself, he hadn't yet figured out a way to tell her that.

Beth droned on. Lauren was still looking for work, while living in unbearable stress with her husband. She wanted to escape, but felt she couldn't afford to leave permanently.

Home at last on Monday, Ellis wrote Carol: **I am back now, mustering up as much vigor and optimism as I can for this New Year. How have you been? I've been meaning to ask how the book sales are going.**

He didn't bother to sign the email. *Why no signature?* Carol leaned into her computer as if she could see him there. *Oh, dear El, where have you really been?* She typed: **I'm feeling better today, but I've been plagued with tendonitis. I'm under a doctor's scrutiny right now. They think it might be arthritis. I hope not because it is hard to walk with pain in the ankles. I'll let you know.**

Other than that, I am too busy with the affairs of living with no time for my writing. Emails, letters, closing out household accounting, and making a new budget for this year are tasks taking up all my time.

The book is selling slowly right now, though I keep publicizing it. I have been on radio, and have done several reading events. Sunday, I'm the featured reader at our Santa Bella Writers' meeting, which I hope will generate sales.

Well, back to work. Maybe I'll get to play a little bridge later. Hopefully with you. Hugs, Carol

He answered: **I have not felt at all well today. Sorry can't do bridge. The antibiotics are doing a number on me, making me unsteady. I need more rest.**
More later. xoxoxoxox El

It was a low point for both of them. Neither could quite understand what was happening. Then an email came from Ellis that shifted Carol's focus.

My dear Carol,

My life these days is not terribly exciting. The thing I fear most is the thought of being a bore. The possibility of such an occurrence petrifies me. I am not accustomed to living such a limited life; I resent not being able to give free reign to my passions. *Something is definitely going on with him*, Carol thought. His next sentences thrilled, yet disturbed her. At last, El trusted her with the reality of his life, but such knowledge has a price: their budding relationship moved into complex territory.

The woman I've lived with for 57 years has become a stranger to me. I cannot tell you how sorry I am about this. Everything worthy in marriage went away about 30 years ago. When that happened, I essentially gave up. I figured that my life would be one of simple maintenance—that is, until I met Beth, but that's another story.

My wife's short-term memory is getting worse. Although she seems to get by for the most part, I believe she has Alzheimer's. A neurologist told us she does not think my wife has the disease. I disagree. I will make an appointment this week to ask for a full-scale workup. A discontinued drug that she took some time ago is known to cause short-term memory loss, so we blamed her condition on that, though it seems unlikely the effect would last this long. I feel so sad for her. Her life has spiraled into ever-decreasing capabilities.

I see that I have rattled on for some time now, so I'll give this a rest. So far this year our weather does not seem as cold as last year. But then the winter is not over yet.

Hope your weekend is going well.

E xoxoxoxox

Carol's heart ached. She had seen Alzheimer's in her friends. The disease was terrifying to her. A person's rational mind is replaced with mind-numbing repetition and maddening obsession. She had seen afflicted people turn inward and fearful. Others became silent or rattled off accessible memories like a stuck needle on a phonograph. Her sense was that his wife was not yet there, but the disease was progressive. Ellis had to confront it and do something—she didn't know what.

Carol, who had offered him a sympathetic ear in September, couldn't answer this particular email. She was struck dumb by El's stark admission of helplessness. She felt helpless herself and ashamed.

In a few days he wrote her again. **I read your blog and see that, in addition to your other activities, you are now committed to a weight-loss program. Good for you, Carol! You will be in my thoughts and prayers as you move through this process.**

Life, at least to me, is about struggling to overcome adversity and staying the course. I'm convinced I have an addictive personality, for I have always been self-indulgent and have partaken of about all the sensual pleasures that life had to offer. Alcohol, women, food, work, sex—you name it—I've been there. Well, at least I didn't do drugs. God help me if I had. I tell others that being me is not easy. Managing El is a full-time job.

I tend to let passion rule me. I remember that fateful day when my doctor told me that if I did not stop smoking I would be dead in a year. I stopped smoking and drinking on that same day. Threats on my life have always been effective means for course corrections. At first, I refused to face the reality of it all, but reluctantly I joined AA and, to my surprise, found something to replace all those urges

that were killing me slowly. I now think highly of 12-step programs. I am not telling you that I live a monkish life because I do not. I just stopped smoking and drinking.

Carol was stunned. First the confession about his wife's affliction, and now he confirmed what she had come to believe: he is an alcoholic.

My addictions separated me from others; I had become more and more introverted. Coming out of that hell took help from my newfound friends and the love of God. I could *not* simply pull myself up by my bootstraps. No matter how hard I tried, I could not do it alone. I think what I was really looking for in my drinking was intimacy. I will be here if you want to talk. Just let me know. Her silence had primed his willingness to be open. He prayed she'd answer. Have a good day. E. xoxoxoxox

When Carol finally breathed, she did so with relief. "Thank you, God. Thank you." She was ready now; she knew exactly what to say.

My dear El,

My name is Carol and I am an alcoholic. I joined AA on April 1, 1973.

So, I guess we've recognized one another, eh? No wonder we are intimately connected! We're both been-there-done-that kind of people. (Imagine a big smiley face here.)

She was overjoyed, willing now to share herself completely with him. Fears about active alcoholism in El were groundless. She and El were peas that God placed together in a pod.

I still go to AA once a week, a Big Book study on Tuesdays at noon.

Yes, life *is* about struggle. Paradoxically, it is also about surrender. We are so lucky to have a program that teaches us to surrender. I really get myself in a tangle when I try to control things or become overly responsible. It is such a relief to remember that I am not in charge of this universe; God will not give me more to carry than I can handle.

Thank you so much for sharing this with me. I am really delighted. I look forward to your support in working my weight loss program. Already, I know it is not about losing weight; it is about change in my perspective and attitude.

I am also humbled by your sharing your wife's memory problems. Even though your marriage is "dead," it must be difficult to see someone you've loved all these years go into such a place. We all fear memory loss in our own lives. What we can't imagine is what caregivers go through watching the disease progress. I am sensitive to your feelings, and I hope you continue to feel free to express them to me.

Carol thought for a moment and then decided: *yes, it's time for this*. She typed in her phone number. **Call me at any time.** However, she did not send her cell phone number, but she smiled when she wrote: **Kind of crazy isn't it—that we can develop a virtual friendship that is so real? Love, Carol**

Chapter Seventeen

The phone's sharp ring alternated with caller ID: "Call from Houston, Texas." *Brrng.* "Call from Houston, Texas." *Ellis!* Excited beyond belief, she grabbed the phone. At long last, a voice— his voice.

"Hello." Her own voice was light, restrained by concern she'd unleash the wild gladness surging through her.

"This is the Texas Roadrunner," a deep, pleasant voice greeted her. "Is this the world-famous author of *A Journey in Time?*"

She laughed. "Well, at least 'author' and the book's title are not up for debate. How nice it is to hear your voice at last." Politeness covered the excitement she could hardly contain. His voice was velvet. The Southern drawl he had owned all his life, his merry tone, and his obvious command of the language captivated her. No old-man cadence here; Ellis projected youth, energy, and an intense focus on her.

"I'm not so sure about that," he countered. "I've read your book, and if it is not yet widely known, it should be. You are an accomplished writer." He reveled in the sweetness of her voice. He liked strong women, but he also liked independence combined with a soft, feminine quality promising passion. Though his heart beat wildly, he knew he'd control his words. Strength and gentleness were qualities most women liked, he had learned.

"Thank you," she said. "I'm glad you liked the book. *Please find something else to talk about*, she urged in a silent message to him. She didn't want this conversation to end until she felt sure he'd call again. She knew he would, yet somehow they needed to slog through the amenities before the real sharing began.

"I hope you don't mind my drawl," he said.

"No, I actually like it. I was raised in Virginia, so I'm accustomed to Southern accents, though most Virginians don't have that deep resonating quality that you Texans have."

"Oh, really? Most people I know in other states think the accent reeks of longhorns mounted on Cadillac fenders and ten-gallon Stetsons on bowlegged men. I've been seriously asked if I own an oil well."

"Do you?" Her voice was full of laughter.

"Stop it," he ordered, signaling a willingness to be teased. "No, I'm about as ordinary as they come down here. I come complete with a white pickup truck, which I drive constantly."

"Ah, so that's the roadrunner in you, eh?"

"Yep, it is. I enjoy my truck. Comes in handy when I go out to the country. Tell me," he said, changing the subject, "What is life like in Santa Bella?"

"Well, you have a pretty good idea from my emails."

"Yes, you seem to be one busy lady."

"Too busy, I'm afraid. I'd like to take some time off and go somewhere."

"Why don't you?"

"Oh, I don't know. I'd like to go back to Hawaii. Mario and I used to spend a month there every January. I haven't done that since he died, except for the cruise to Hawaii I took last year with Dana. She wanted a cruise, but I missed staying put on a single island." She was suddenly aware of talking to Ellis as if a telephone call between them were routine—as if he already knew Mario, Dana, and her other friends.

"I'm not much for cruises," Ellis said. "We had a big storm in the Atlantic on the way to the Panama Canal, the only time I cruised. I felt so nauseated, I couldn't stand up straight. Kept sliding and bouncing off walls inside. I didn't dare go out on deck."

"No sense of adventure, eh?" She was laughing again, remembering a time in her youth in a ship bound to Hawaii and the tail end of a typhoon that left Harold and her sliding across the dance floor while their sons slept in their cabin. When she checked on the boys, she glided in narrow passageways from wall to wall like a skater full of wine, a sensation she rather liked. The wildness of the weather with the sense of being tossed about and surviving gave her a feeling of invincibility.

"Well now, I'm not saying I'm not one for adventure," he explained. "Just not shipboard adventure. No sir, not again. That was a trip to last a lifetime."

"Was that a recent cruise?"

"A few years back. We were on our way to Central America. If there had been a choice to helicopter off that boat, I'd have been gone in a heartbeat. I thought we were going to sink. Water flooded the salons and made the floors treacherous."

"Oh, my, it must have been a tremendous storm!"

"It was. By the grace of God, we made it out and sailed quite smoothly into Cozumel after that. We almost flew back to Texas from there. I had lost all interest in the Panama Canal, but my wife insisted we'd be all right since another storm like that one was unlikely."

They were silent for a bit, each lost in their own thoughts. Then both started to talk at once. "Will you be home tomorrow?" he was asking just as she was telling him, "I'll call you tomorrow if that's okay."

They both laughed.

"That would be just fine, very fine, in fact," he said.

She blushed, radiant with success. "Okay then, see you tomorrow. Thanks for calling."

"Thanks for being there," he said, and with a quick "goodbye," the call ended.

Carol cradled the phone to her heart. It wasn't so much what they had said in that first call, but the nuances in his voice that gave her the hope she felt. *I am loved*, she told herself. *He is real, and, oh my God, he sounds so good.* She thought of the young men in her high school class, the ones who were so attractive and yet beyond her reach. "Boys don't make passes at girls who wear glasses." The popular adage of that era was painfully true then. Alpha male classmates copied her homework, but didn't ask her to a movie. Laughingly, she dismissed the notion of her braininess. Her class was so small, it wasn't hard to be the smartest person in it; that position turned out to be a very lonely spot for a budding young woman who had little clue she was more than a scholar.

Hearing Ellis's voice so full of desire—yes, desire, she could *feel* it in the way he spoke to her—hearing that voice, that smooth, silky voice, reminded her of how far she had come since high school. Though it had taken a trip through perilous sexual adventures during the days of her own active alcoholism to discover she was a sexual being worthy of finer attention than she was getting then, she was confident now that she was an attractive woman. *Yes, attractive and*—she groaned—*old!* Laughing at the absurdities of life, she told herself: *Okay, Carol, you can now have that handsome young man that you wanted then, only. . . oh yes, he'll be old too!*

Nevertheless, she clung to the phone like an adolescent maiden. She was delirious with desire for him, exuberant to be the focus of his affection.

She knew what younger people would think about romance among elders. *Yuck*, she thought, even now. Couldn't there be a better word than *elders*? She felt as if seniors lived in a different world, a world that younger people ignored or demeaned. Vivid images of old *Carol Burnett* shows reminded her that she laughed too, when Carol and Harvey Korman and Tim Conway portrayed old men and old women as bent, stumbling, and mumbling, beating on one another with their canes. *Oh, hell, yes*, she thought now, *we're funny and will probably always be funny old people to those much younger than we.* She grinned. *But let them think what they think. We know what we know, don't we, old man?* It comforted her to know that Ellis must be thinking similar thoughts. She hoped he was hugging the phone too.

Ellis did hug the phone momentarily. He was flush with the excitement of hearing Carol for the first time. Her voice had rung in his ear from reading her personal narrative in *A Journey Through Time* and in the tone of all the emails exchanged between them, yet the fantasy of it was pale pickings compared to the ultra-soft sweetness and the sexy promise he sensed in the way she articulated the most innocent of words.

Oh, yes, I have to meet this woman. I just have to meet her, please God.

The phone rang in his hand. He resented the intrusion and answered somewhat abruptly.

"Well, hello to you too!" Beth's sarcastic scold was unmistakable.

"Oh, Beth, I'm sorry," Ellis said, returning to his normal civility. "I was deep in thought when you called."

"Sounds more like you were on the phone, the way you answered on the first ring."

Her accurate perception annoyed him. He decided to distract her.

"Well, yes, what is it I can do for you today?"

"Lauren's left that son-of-a-bitch she's married to."

"Oh?"

"Yes, she came here yesterday. I don't know where I'm going to put her. Larry's in the spare bedroom, so she slept on the foldout couch, but that's not going to work forever."

"Slow down, Beth. Did you invite her to live with you?"

Beth was immediately defensive. "Nobody turns their back on a child who needs help."

"I understand," he said with more patience than he felt. "I was just wondering how you are going to manage with both of them underfoot." He could barely bring himself to focus on her voice, let alone her problems. The magic of the telephone call with Carol was fast becoming memory; he resented its contamination with long-standing Nelson family issues.

"I'm not sure I'm following you," Beth said. "Larry and Lauren are adults, not children underfoot."

Precisely, he wanted to say, but temporized. "Well, your house is rather small for three adults. That's all I meant."

"Oh. I see your point. It's a little inconvenient, but they won't be here forever."

Wanna bet? The thought popped up in his mind, but the words, thankfully, stayed in his mind as well. "Beth, I'm not quite sure what to say, except I'm sorry your kids are in such difficult situations right now."

"God, Ellis, that damn son-in-law of mine is something else again. I swear if I had a gun right now, I'd shoot Craig. He got drunk the other night, called that woman he is seeing, and when my daughter walked in on him talking to her on the phone, he shouted at Lauren to get out of his life."

"And?" Ellis knew there was more to be told. There always was with Lauren stories. That girl had a propensity for making bad situations worse. If he were Lauren, he would have turned on his heel, walked out on the son-of-a-bitch, and said *good riddance*— that's what *he* would have done!

"Well, naturally, she wanted to know who he was talking to, and when he wouldn't tell her, she grabbed the phone from him and confronted the bitch herself."

"Oh, no!" Ellis was shocked. He couldn't picture Lauren being that aggressive. Usually, she argued and screamed at Craig but, to his knowledge, she had never dared to make a move against him.

"Oh, yes!" Beth was adamant. "She had a right to know what was going on between them but, Ellis, she badly misjudged Craig, and so have I for that matter. That miserable monster grabbed the phone back and beat her in the face with it. She has two black eyes and a badly bruised arm she raised to defend herself."

"She should have called the police."

"She didn't. She called me." Beth paused. "When Craig saw what he had done to her—red marks on her face and arm and a cut that was bleeding on her forehead—he grabbed her and held her tightly, practically sobbing, and telling her he didn't mean to hurt her and to please forgive him."

"Good Lord, what is she planning to do?"

"She wants to stay with me until she heals. She figures she can look for work here, maybe teaching in the public schools."

"She's nearly retirement age, isn't she?"

"Well, yes," Beth admitted, "but retired teachers do go back into schools as substitutes. It's probably her best chance of getting a permanent position, though she's never really taught below college level. When and if she gets a job, she says she is going to leave Craig."

"Is she going to bring charges against him for assaulting her?"

"No. I wanted her to, but she says she needs him to support her now. She can't afford to leave him permanently yet."

"Ah, Beth, you sure do have your work cut out for you." Ellis was sorry for his friend. He knew she just wasn't able, somehow, to say no to her grown children, and things kept getting worse.

"I know. I'm not feeling all that well myself," Beth told him. "I was wondering. You think we could slip away to the trailer sometime soon? I could use a little peace and quiet just now."

The thought of leaving with Beth so soon after connecting with Carol made El's head spin. "Hmm," he replied, taking a moment before making a commitment. "I've been thinking of getting away myself. Joanne's been obsessing more lately. She keeps telling me she needs new clothes, but when I offer to take her shopping, she says she doesn't want to go. Then she tells me again she needs to buy some new clothes. I know it's the Alzheimer's, but she's driving me up a wall."

"Then we both need to get away for a while." Beth made the decision. "Let's go next week."

"Okay. Let's do it." Sliding shut the phone, Ellis tried to recapture the magic of the first phone call to Carol.

He had purposely picked a time to make the call when Joanne was out to lunch, wanting to be utterly alone with Carol, wanting to be without ties to a wife that was more millstone than partner. *Maybe Beth, too*, he thought, sighing. *Who has she become to me? Once again he wondered why he hadn't gone through with the divorce so many years ago. Abruptly, a new thought struck him. Because you'd be unavailable now to the promise of a newer, truer love. Knowing you and your luck, old boy, you'd probably have picked another Joanne to settle in with. Maybe that's the real reason you didn't get that divorce.*

Water over the dam, he told himself. It felt really good now to focus his mind on possibilities and not ruminate on what might have been with Joanne or Beth. Curiously, he felt free—free to feel a growing yearning for Carol. Maybe God did have a hand in this, after all.

Ellis didn't tell Carol of his plans to go with Beth to the trailer in the country. Somehow, it was sufficient to hear her soft voice on the phone, telling him of the events of her day. She had been a guest on a local radio show and was interviewed about *A Journey Through Time*. She sent him the Internet link to the show. It was exhilarating to hear her in a professional capacity, competently touting her book, yet sharing so much of herself without fear or embarrassment. He admired her quiet self-confidence. *This woman knows who she is*, he thought, thankfully. *I don't have to solve problems for her.*

"I had such fun, Ellis," she was saying in that second phone call. "My friends liked the show too. By the way, speaking of my friends, at our last meeting I told them we have talked on the telephone."

"You did? What did they say?" Ellis knew of the weekly group meetings she had with Sophie, Dana, Stella, Evelyn, and Jennifer. Her women friends were becoming a reality to him. He was curious to learn what they thought of him, though nothing they, or anyone else, said was going to discourage the growing love he felt for Carol.

Carol laughed. "They wanted to know when you are coming to see me." She hoped he couldn't sense her blushing with the audacity of the suggestion.

"Well, that, my dear, is a very interesting idea." She wondered how interesting? The answer was quick in coming. "Don't be surprised if my white pickup shows up at your door someday."

"If only you could," she said, excitement building. He paused before answering.

"I know," he said quietly." I may have to look into that possibility when my doctors give me clearance."

Carol didn't want to talk about his illness. She looked up bacterial lung infections on the Internet and was not happy with what she found. One type, Mycobacterium, caused serious diseases in humans and other mammals and was life threatening to those whose immune system was compromised. The fact that he was still on powerful antibiotics three months after he was hospitalized made her suspect that this particular bacterium was the cause of his lingering illness. *What if he never got better?* She didn't want to face that outcome. Not yet. How ironic that she would find the possibility of great love and not be able to access it.

"Oh, well," she said aloud, not really conscious of her words. She changed the subject. "It was interesting in group. Seems like whenever I bring up something, it becomes a springboard to the others to discuss similar experiences in their own lives."

"How so?" He was wondering about that stray "oh well," she had uttered, but didn't ask her.

"Dana was moved to tease a little about male virility at advanced ages. We all laughed as she explained exploits with her new boyfriend— we're so pleased for her. You know, she lost her husband less than two years ago, so being with someone else is very new to her. I guess dating at our ages has an uncertain quality to it. Still, we women are always hopeful." She paused and then laughed. "We end up more often talking about using canes and walkers rather than our womanly charms."

I didn't tell them, she wanted to say, *that I think I have fallen in love with you.*

"I am pretty sure," he said in the voice she found so alluring, "that all of you still have the womanly charms you enjoyed as teenagers. Perhaps, though, you know more about *using* them now than you did then." His laugh was deep and hearty, matching her own startled burst of appreciation at his playfulness.

"You're a rascal, aren't you?" she said lightheartedly.

"Caught and recognized," he confessed.

They lingered on the phone a little longer—long enough for him to tell her he was leaving again, only he didn't. *Time enough,* he thought, *when I do go. I'll tell her then.*

Chapter Eighteen

$\mathcal{E}$velyn missed another group meeting.

"What is it this time?" Stella asked.

"Her daughter said it was another bladder infection," Sophie told the women. "She called me to say Evelyn probably won't make many more meetings. It's too hard for her to get around."

Carol was surprised. "She seemed all right when I saw her at the symphony last Sunday. She told me she had mostly recovered from that tumble she took before Christmas."

Sophie shrugged. "These things happen all at once. I suspect her immune system isn't handling all her ills very well anymore." Morning light bounced off the glass top of Sophie's coffee table, giving the room a cheerful quality, not at all a match for what the women were feeling.

Dana broke their somber silence. "Well, what can you expect at 97? That woman is a walking miracle, if you ask me. She's in constant pain, yet she still shows up at the symphony. Look at all she's gone through. Enough osteoarthritis to cripple a horse, let alone a tiny woman like Evelyn. Have you noticed how bent her fingers are? She can hardly hold her coffee cup."

"Yeah," Jennifer agreed, twisting the knobby fingers of her own arthritic hand. "And her legs are truly toothpicks." She shuddered. "I used to think that expression overblown but, in Evelyn's case, I don't see how she manages to stand on them."

"She's got spirit," Sophie said softly. She tilted her ample chin, straightening the wrinkles in her neck. Her thinning silver-white locks met her shoulders momentarily, but settled into tiny curls when she dropped her head. "Would to God I had the iron will that lady has. Maybe my own aches and pains wouldn't get to me as much as they do."

They all grinned, seeing in Evelyn a tiny woman warrior, a walking ghost still wielding a mighty sword and shield. Carol wasn't about to bring up the obvious, the dementia she'd recognized in Evelyn. Dementia in Ellis's wife in Texas was one thing—an abstraction for her, since she didn't know the woman—but here in Santa Bella, in Evelyn's own cozy living room, they watched their old friend struggle, seriously lost for words and barely making sense of subjects she once knew as well as the back of her hand. To face losing Evelyn's intelligence and wit to Alzheimer's invited unbearable anxiety, especially after watching Irene, who once belonged to the group, slowly melt away with that cruel disease. Carol's mind flashed on an image of a smiling Irene sitting up in a nursing home bed speaking gibberish, convinced that she was communicating clearly. Irene had mercifully forgotten she was confused! Carol shivered. She didn't know if she could go through that again.

"I hate to say it, ladies, but I think our friend is circling the drain," Sophie said.

They all nodded.

"Well, maybe it's for the best, after all," Dana said, pulling her sweater closer to her rail- thin body. "She keeps hinting herself that it is time to go."

Carol had had enough. "Let's get on with group," she said abruptly. The women, surprised at her tone, but relieved to be off the subject of Evelyn, stared at her.

"Okay, I'm for that." Jennifer lifted a hand in surrender and leaned back in her chair. "Tell us what's happening between you and your man in Texas. I'm all ears."

"He's hardly *her* man," Sophie interjected.

"Whatever." Jennifer waved away the comment. "We know there's a wife in there somewhere, but she's not really there, is she?" Silence. "I mean. . . "She paused. Sensing she had exceeded the forbearance of her friends, she quietly added "considering the circumstances."

"I'm just saying that a relationship like this can get complicated, that's all." Sophie retorted.

Carol exhaled, calming herself. The last thing she wanted was to be the center of a gathering storm. "I'm well aware of the complications. Right now Ellis's health is more of a problem to me than him having a wife. He can't shake the lung infection; at least, I think that's the situation since he's still taking antibiotics, *and* it's been over three months since he was in the hospital!"

"Maybe you should cut your losses before you get in too deep, Honey," Dana advised. "You know how hard it was in the end for you to take care of Mario."

"I know, Dana. You, of all people, know how demanding caregiving is." Carol hesitated. "There's something about this whole encounter I just don't want to give up." A quick sparkle in her eyes and a momentary soft, shy smile told it all before fading. "Besides," Carol said in a plaintive voice, "it's not likely that we'll meet anytime soon, with me on night oxygen and he still fighting to get better." She cleared her throat and then shifted moods; she could always rely on her intellect. "I looked up lung infections on the Internet and came up with one called Mycobacterium."

"Good grief, what is that?" Stella asked.

"It's a common bacterium found in water and soil. When it caus-
es an infection in mammals, it can be serious." Carol felt an odd
sense of relief. She smoothed her hand on the charcoal sweats she
customarily wore everywhere in the winter.

"How serious?" Sophie wanted to know.

"Tuberculosis. Leprosy." She shrugged. It felt good to face the
truth.

"My God, Carol, run," Jennifer advised.

"Those are the worst outcomes, I think. There are all kinds of
other manifestations too complex for me to comprehend." Carol
slowly shook her head. "I don't know what Ellis has, but I do know
that there is a very long period of treatment with antibiotics for
Mycobacterium infection, so I'm thinking that might be what he
has."

"But TB and leprosy? Aren't you terrified?" Stella asked.

"No." Carol actually laughed over Stella's overreaction. "El told
me that in the hospital they thought it was TB, but tests were negative. If it had been TB or leprosy, they certainly wouldn't let him
walk around with them in public."

"You sure know how to pick them, Carol," Sophie said bluntly.

"Yeah, I do," Carol admitted, gritting her teeth at the ignoble
quip. "I do know how to pick them," she firmly repeated, suddenly
cheered. "He's intelligent, he's attentive, he is a gentleman, and—
most of all—I am attracted to him, as he to me." Satisfied, she
chuckled. "At our age, ladies, that feat is known as a miracle."

They all laughed, even Sophie.

In the week after the first phone calls, Carol and Ellis couldn't
get enough of one another. **How are you?** Carol emailed him.
**Better. I hope. I feel a little restless today. There's a coun-
cil retreat scheduled for tomorrow where we select new
officers. Since, I already told them I would not run for a**

third term as president, I hope someone willing and able to take charge will show up. I need to lighten my load.

I haven't written anything creative in a while. I think that is why I am antsy. I always want something to be going on, something fun. Indeed her creative juices had been used up lately trying to solve ecclesiastical financial matters. Though she loved her church and enjoyed being a leader, keeping everyone focused on the budget drained her time and energy. Thinking about, writing to, playing bridge with, and talking to Ellis was thankfully restorative.

I read a good article in *AARP* today saying that dealing with chronic illness is similar to dealing with aging. I agree in that we need to stay in some form of denial to age or live successfully, but I certainly don't have to tell *you* that.

Ellis responded. **I understand completely. I get edgy when I feel confined and limited. I have, as I've grown older, lived my life more and more aggressively and with purpose. I am unwilling to limit my activities or relationships. To resign myself to the inevitable is not for me. I whole-heartedly agree we need some denial in life. You and I have, or have had, enough reality in our lives. Phooey on reality. Give me passion; I *must* be passionate about something—anything.**

He sat back, sipping a cola and thought of all the years he had spent with Joanne—was *still* spending with Joanne—in a loveless condo cocoon, escaping, too infrequently, to the trailer in the country. *I know I'm not masochistic,* he told himself. *I guess I just didn't have the nerve to leave a sick woman.* Propriety lived in his bones, served to him with his mother's milk. He could still hear her lecturing on duty and civility. He pounded his fist on the computer desk, rattling the cola can, as he recalled the fibromyalgia that first turned Joanne from sexual intimacy and the insidious progression of subsequent illnesses that made her refuse sex with him long before dementia set in. *I'd have left if Joanne had gotten better, but she never did. And, now? Oh God, how impossible it all seemed.* Gratefully, he turned back to center his attention on Carol's email.

I guess keeping busy or looking for something to focus on other than oneself is a really good strategy. Think about it. When we were younger, we had things to concentrate on—our work, our children. That's what kept us going. Things narrow as we grow older; we need to become more creative.

When we were younger, we tended to compare ourselves to others. The older I get, the more I know that others are pretty much like me—having the same kinds of feelings and desires and thinking thoughts similar to mine.

What is it all about, anyway? Who knows? We just keep inventing our lives until we run out of life. Take care, my friend. See you at bridge. Love, Carol.

Pleased with her viewpoint and especially pleased with her casual expression of love for him, he responded:

You and I need to be involved in life or we feel limited and frustrated. I'm not surprised you get restless: you are talented and creative. That gift is life-giving to you. I get restless with the lack of intimacy in my life, that is, when I allow myself to feel that void. My ability to responsibly sublimate emotions is an art form; maybe that's creativity.

Ah, yes, I do know how to shut down after all these years. Ellis pursed his lips and nodded. Only now, with Carol, he was beginning to allow more latitude to his emotions. *For better or worse,* he thought.

I try not to be too hard on myself for all the feelings running inside of me. We live within a paradox and are

better off understanding that we do. Have a good evening, dear heart. E. xoxoxoxox

A couple of days passed without emails, phone calls, or even their bridge game. Carol was busy with her church retreat, which went exactly as she had hoped. She was no longer president. She wrote Ellis: **When I say my prayers, I thank God that you have come into my life. You are such an intelligent, interesting human being. I feel protected by you, which may seem strange since you aren't physically here. You come up with the right words when I need them.**

Ellis read the words with a mixture of pride, hope, and regret. *If only, my dear Carol, I was able to be that knight in shining armor you see in me.* He absent-mindedly rubbed his arm, noting, with sour dissatisfaction, how thin he had become. How had this damned infection got into him anyway? He turned back to her email. **I know we are unlikely to ever meet in person, and that is okay with me. We have a really nice relationship online and don't need to complicate it. If we were younger, I might feel differently. We are blessed just to be able to enjoy corresponding with one another**.

Was she setting boundaries again? He hoped not. Up to now, he hadn't fully admitted it, but he wanted badly to meet her, to see her in the flesh, to touch her.

It is really nice when you pop into the bridge game even if we don't have our usual lively conversation, she wrote. **I feel your presence and your caring, and that makes me happy. After a while, I also know it is time to go, and I feel fine about that too, because I know there will be another day with you.**

Ellis grimaced. *Worrisome tone to this email, he thought. Was it something he'd said or not said?*

Yes, we live in a paradox. We have no idea what life really means, except, I suspect, it means living in the moments that we are given. When I am consciously appreciating what I have, I feel full of life. Being human, I cannot sustain such heights of grateful awareness, yet knowing that there are such heights can carry me through the down times. To be consciously grateful for those down times is harder. Perhaps, these times are periods of growth.

Our creator has obviously made life so infinitely varying that we can never in a human lifetime work out all its mysteries. Still, I sometimes feel we know the answers; they are built within us. The greatest mystery is why we can't intelligently expose them.

Be well. I'll see you in bridge. Love, Carol.

Ellis pulled the keyboard toward him and wrote: **I have a friend who told me that her great grandmother once said that circumstances change outcomes. One small event can radically change an individual's life as well as those around them. How events will play themselves out is a total unknown.**

He stopped writing. *One small event*, he thought. *Being in an online bridge room at the right time with the right person has miraculously changed my life. I do not know where we are going, my beloved Carol, but my hope is that we are going there together.* Bobbing his head as if to affirm his own notion, he continued to write.

Life is truly a mystery. Being able to live within the framework of mystery makes us free. The only thing I know for certain is that I don't know.

For some reason, he felt compelled to add a stray thought. **One cannot love with the idea of controlling another. If love is not freely given and received, there is little hope of having** anything meaningful and lasting. *How well I know that*, he thought. **We live in the here and now and need to play the cards we hold. What went before has shaped us—we are what we are today and must proceed from this place, this circumstance.**

Will she understand what I'm trying to say? Do I understand what I am trying to say? I'll just say it. He wrote the last lines to her. **Knowing you has become a joy to me. We may never have the happiness of meeting one another in person, but life is very, very strange, so let's not be limited by the naysayers. We can't replay the past; the future is our hope and promise. Love, E.**

Soon, very soon, he was going to the country again, with Beth. He didn't tell Carol this.

Chapter Nineteen

*C*arol couldn't believe it. **Tomorrow I'm off for Fayette County once again—much to my delight,** Ellis wrote. She nearly choked on the hot coffee she was drinking. *But he was just there!* Bewildered, she ticked off the times he's left her without any means of communicating with him: two weeks *before* Christmas, two weeks *after* Christmas, and now barely two weeks *after* New Year's! All that time was spent with Beth. Now, he's off again. *How irritating!* Is he going with Beth? *Of course, he is going with Beth.* Her resigned acceptance was no help.

Carol felt faint and a little nauseated. It wasn't the trailer retreat that bothered her. It was the idea that she was in competition with Beth. *That idea again!* Why did it trouble her so? Because she felt diminished—diminished over a man she had no real claim on. *Who's crazy here,* she wondered? An exasperated breath escaped. She had not realized, until then, the extent of her bottled-up anger. *We've just begun to talk on the phone, for God's sake. Don't you know we are building a relationship here? Why do you need to run off now? Can't you just stay put and play with me like you said you wanted to?*

Carol was appalled at her own tumultuous feelings. Apparently, love in later years comes with all the same maddening problems of young love. She never was jealous before. Why now in her 78th year? She left that thought hanging and read the rest of his email.

I'm leaving a little later in the morning to avoid the congestion that characterizes Houston's commuter traffic. Continued growth of this city will ultimately gridlock all the freeways and bring on Armageddon. Why do I live here? I live here because I must. This is where I made my living. Otherwise, I would move to my place in the country and bid the city life a wholehearted goodbye. I am sure my little family of resident deer has missed me.

Ellis's mention of the deer at that point seemed out of place. He was pussyfooting around with all this overkill of information, avoiding an explanation for his conduct. *Ha! You do sense how I must be feeling, don't you, you cad?* Instantly, Carol was sorry for the mean-spirited label. Ellis may be habitually attached to many women but, as far as she could tell, he was not unscrupulous or dishonest with them. He had told her about his wife from the beginning and about Beth soon after.

Carol felt better when she read: **I have been thinking about buying a laptop for the place. I would need to get a wireless server card to connect to the Internet.** *Ahh, you are thinking of us after all!* Her mood brightened. **I'm not sure I want to pay so much for the convenience right now, but I will mull this over and see if spending the extra money feels right. There is no landline on the place, but my cell works very nicely.** *Yes, and I guess we can use that if Beth isn't listening.* She grinned.

I will miss *seeing* you and playing bridge, but I will be back at the card tables as soon as I return. Take good care of yourself. E. xoxoxoxox

"*Aww,* that's sweet," Carol murmured. *He's missing me already.* She noticed hugs and kisses were back, but not the *love* word. Biting her lower lip, she made a decision, once more, to stay involved and think positively about the relationship. Telling El about her doubts and fears could only muddy the waters at this time and might even prove embarrassing if his prior use of the *love* word was casually meant. *Oh, God, there I go analyzing every little thing again.* She scolded herself. *Just do it, or don't do it, Carol!*

She wrote to him: **Dear El, I shall miss you too. I'm glad that you get to follow your heart and have time for relaxation and enjoyment. It is good that you are taking care of yourself. This is a quick note. Perhaps I'll have time for more later. Love, Carol**

Her *love* word wasn't casual. It was defiant.

Ellis noticed the defiance, not in the word *love*, but in the short business-like politeness of her email. He knew he had upset her, leaving her so soon after their exhilarating phone conversations. It wasn't as if they couldn't phone one another while he was in the country. He had suggested that option in his email. Maybe he should have said outright that he'd call, but—he felt a surge of irritation—she had drawn a line recently when she wrote they were not to complicate their relationship. What was he supposed to think—or do?

He wasn't in the best mood, anyway. Going to the trailer with Beth and her problems was a complication in itself. He decided not to answer Carol's email. He'd call her once he got settled.

Carol went to her group meeting on the day Ellis and Beth drove to the country in his white pickup truck. By now, the women were poised to question Carol about the latest developments in her love life.

"I don't know what's wrong with me," she said. "I was so excited about him calling, and now I'm not so sure."

"What is it, Honey?" Jennifer asked.

"I had such hopes for this relationship." Carol noticed the slight frown on Sophie's face and turned to her. "I know, I know—he has a wife! But that fact doesn't seem so important, given there's been no intimacy between them for thirty years and the further complication of dealing with her Alzheimer's. But, now, I have this nagging feeling that there's more to his going to the country than retreating from his home situation."

"Oh?" Jennifer's uplifted eyebrows signaled Carol to explain.

"He goes there with Beth."

"His girlfriend, obviously," Dana offered.

"No, not exactly. She's been a friend of the family's for many years, had traveled with Ellis and his wife. They have been very close; he nursed her when she had knee surgery and again when she broke her arm."

"No husband to do that?" Stella asked.

"Her husband died some time ago. I don't know much about her, except that El goes to the country with her."

"Then why aren't you asking questions?" Sophie cut right to the heart of the matter.

"Because I'm not sure where I stand with him," Carol blurted out. "I know how I feel, but I'm not exactly sure how he feels."

"And how do you feel?" Sophie's tone softened, though her eyes remained intently focused on Carol.

"I love this man," Carol said quietly. "I didn't expect to love him, but I am so strongly attracted to him that I care whether there is a chance for me to be fully loved by him." She closed her eyes and moved her head slowly back and forth. Noisily sucking in and blowing out air, she opened her eyes and told them, "I feel loved by him, so intensely sometimes, that I wonder why I have any doubts—why the presence of Beth in his life bothers me."

"That's what happens in long-distance relationships," Dana said. "You won't know for sure until you meet him in person."

"*I* know. I really do *know*," Carol said, surprising herself. "I have this very secure feeing in me that we love one another. Yet—and this is what bedevils me—our lives have been largely lived with-out each other. I wonder if we can ever build a life together. I don't want to disturb his family life—his relationship with his sons and grandchildren. He has a life in Texas with friends, doctors, and routines."

"And you have a life here, my dear," Dana said. "You're trying to get over your grief for Mario. Maybe your loneliness has fanned the flames of this love."

"Maybe so," Carol admitted. "I do feel less lonely with El in my life."

"Well, I say," Stella leaned precariously forward, excited to make her contribution, "you need to relax. You don't have to make any de-cisions now. Take your love for one another one day at a time and see where it goes. Forget Beth. If there was anything binding between them, other than friendship, he wouldn't be playing bridge and trad-ing emails with you."

"Maybe." Carol paused. She raised both hands and ran her fin-gers back through her short, curly, silvery hair. "Okay, you've heard enough from me for now. Thank you, my friends. I'm feeling better. Someone else talk."

When they arrived at the trailer, Beth was feeling the effects of the two beers she had had at lunch. Ellis noticed the drinking, but dismissed it, thinking that the stress of having two adult children descend on her household was too much. He unpacked the truck without her help.

It was getting late. The barbequed chicken they bought as takeout from the deli and the peas from the freezer would be their evening meal. He'd have liked a little starch with the meal, but that would have to wait until tomorrow when they made a grocery run into La Grange. *Should have bought the potato salad,* he thought. *It would have kept in the cooler. Maybe there still is some boxed stuffing in the pantry.*

Beth had already set the table, retrieved peas from the freezer, and the box of stuffing from the pantry. He was surprised since he usually cooked.

"You've got the chicken?" she asked. "I'll stick it in the microwave."

"Well, thanks," he said, giving her the food package he had just brought in. "That's all the stuff we need to bring in from the truck. If you don't mind, I'll go change into my robe and slippers. I need to make a phone call, anyway."

"To Joanne?"

"Yes."

"Well, don't take too long. We'll be eating very soon."

Ellis really wanted to call Carol, but knew he'd better check in with Joanne first. Carol's call would have to wait until after supper.

Joanne answered on the first ring.

"Everything okay with you?" he asked.

"Fine," she said. "Where are you?"

"In the trailer in Fayette County. I told you I was going, remember?"

"You did?" Joanne seemed more confused than usual. "Oh, I guess you did tell me. I forgot."

"Are you going to Jake's for dinner?"

"I can do that," she said. "Sounds good."

"You have my number if you need to call," he told her. "I'll call you tomorrow or you can call me."

"I will," she said and hung up.

He knew she was intent now on getting herself to Jake's for dinner. He stripped to his undershirt and boxer shorts and reached for the new robe they had bought on an earlier trip to the trailer. He felt better now—ready to eat.

Beth had supper on the table when he emerged from the bedroom. He got a diet cola out of the refrigerator and sat down at the table. Beth was pouring a glass of beer for herself. They hadn't talked much on the way to the trailer. They were used to riding in relative silence, since he liked to listen to his music; she seemed content to sit and stare out the window. The traffic was light—the scenery fairly soothing. Once there had been Burma Shave jingles in a jaunty line on the side of the road to break up the monotony of travel. Kids of his generation glued their eyes to miles of roadside to be the first to successfully read the fast-moving signs and shout "Burma Shave!" before their dads sped by them. He remembered a favorite: *Clancy's whiskers tickled Nancy. Nancy lowered the boom on Clancy!* Now, there was nothing to pop out at anybody in miles of rolling winter-brown fields except scarce patches of unexpected greenery.

He was glad they hadn't talked much. He still didn't know what to do about Beth's fixation on her children's lives. It was maddening to have her go on and on about them without resolution. With no solution in sight for Joanne and her failing memory, he had enough to bother him. The ever-increasing and certainly *unwanted* necessity to take care of his wife was hard to ignore. The last thing he needed was *another* woman to take care of. He sighed. He longed to call Carol.

"Such a big sigh," Beth said. "What's troubling you?" She took a sip of her beer and put a slice of chicken breast on her plate.

If only I could tell her without her going ballistic on me, he thought.

"Hmm. I just talked to Joanne," he said, hoping Beth might assume his obvious irritation was focused elsewhere.

"Is everything all right?" He suspected Beth's concern for Joanne was feigned; he knew she felt threatened by the possibility that they might have to return for some emergency, which had happened once before when Joanne had become seriously dehydrated.

"Oh, it's the usual thing," he said. "She can't remember where I am most of the time. I'm not even sure she cares, except when she wants to go out to eat." El reached for a chicken leg and thigh.

"I know it's hard on you, El. Be thankful you have this retreat from the constant demand that disease makes on you. Others in your situation don't always have a choice."

"I am thankful, Beth. Believe me, I am."

They ate a little then. He felt better. It seemed as if Beth really was concerned for him and his predicament. She poured more beer into her glass. "I am thankful too," she said, her eyes softening. "Wading through the problems Larry and Lauren have brought into my house is crazy making. If only they would listen to me."

"Hmm," Ellis murmured, hoping she'd stop there.

"You know, if I were Lauren, I would put that husband of hers in jail! Look what he did to my baby!" Beth swallowed some beer.

El put down his fork and leaned toward her. "Getting angry isn't helping, is it, Beth?"

"What?" She was surprised by Ellis's intrusion. Usually he listened and agreed or changed the subject.

"I said 'getting angry . . .'"

Offended, Beth didn't wait for him to finish. "You're darn tooting I'm angry. Wouldn't you be?"

"That's not the point," Ellis insisted, deciding for once to give her a straightforward answer. "Did you ever think that, by giving her advice and shelter, you are enabling Lauren?"

"Enabling her?" Beth eyes smoldered now. Raising her arms in protest, she stabbed the air with words. "I've done nothing but help her ever since she married that bum."

El was not cowed. "My point exactly," he said, triumphantly.

Beth rolled her eyes in disbelief. "How in the world is that enabling? I'm doing what any mother . . ."

Ellis interrupted this time. "Whoa. Wait a minute. Just listen, will you?" Beth stopped talking. "Of course you are concerned for your children, but if you step into every crisis they have, you are, in effect, living their lives." Beth gave him a blank look. "Can't you see? When you make their decisions, you rob them of any chance to think their own way out of dilemmas."

"I don't see . . ." Beth began, but he raised his hand as a signal for her to let him finish.

"You obviously don't. Let me put it this way. What your children, or my children, or anybody else's adult children, do with their lives is none of our business. We made our own mistakes, God knows, and we worked them out, thank you, without help from our parents. Dealing with our own problems gave us strength and endurance."

"Yeah, I can see that." Beth's tone softened. "But, El, it's so hard to see your children going through tough times." She was near tears, a state El seldom saw in Beth. He put a hand out to touch hers and comfort her.

"I know," he said. "However, if you encourage them to find their own way, you are not abandoning them. On the contrary, you are giving them a sense of your confidence in them. They know, then, that you can be counted on to back them up, but not carry their load."

His phone rang. It was Carol. Without thinking, he answered it.

"Hi." Her voice was cheerful. "I was just thinking about you, wondering how the trip went. You are in the trailer, aren't you?"

"Well, hello," he said, thrilled she was calling. "I was just finishing my supper."

"Oh, go ahead and eat. I don't mean to interrupt." He could hear a note of hesitancy in her voice.

"No, no, it's fine. Really. I've had enough."

Beth gave him a quizzical look. He had barely touched the food on his plate. "Joanne?" she mouthed.

Ellis shook his head, held up a hand seeking excuse from Beth, and murmured to Carol, "Just a minute. I need to get into a better position to hear you."

Beth frowned. She reached for her beer as El took the phone into the bedroom.

"So, how are you today?" He lay on his bed, enjoying the chance to talk to her.

Carol's quiet mood was welcoming balm to him. "Oh, pretty good. Still not writing much and feeling guilty about it."

"Oh, and what is taking up your time, pray tell?" Ellis just wanted her to talk, to relish in her company. She filled him in on the details of her life since their last emails. He chatted with her about his drive to the country. Both cloaked their true feelings, saying instead, "It's so good to hear from you" or "It seems so long since we talked." Carol ventured a "miss you at the bridge tables," which he already knew, while he repeated his idea of buying a computer for the trailer so they could play bridge while he was away.

"Oh, don't spend the money," she advised. "We have your cell phone."

"As long as the reception holds up," he said, thinking that now Beth would know about Carol, but he didn't care at this point. An hour passed before they finally said goodbye. He promised to call her the next day.

When he emerged from his bedroom, the table was cleared of dishes. Beth had put the remains of his supper in the refrigerator, he knew, but he didn't feel like eating now. She was sitting, watching television and drinking another beer. She turned toward him as he entered the living area.

"Who was so important that you couldn't eat your supper like a civilized man, but had to stay on the phone with for a whole hour?" she chided.

"Pardon?" he said, not prepared to do battle with her.

"Was that the woman in California, the one whose book you read and raved about?"

He didn't blink. It was time Beth knew. "Yes," he said quietly. She was drunk. He could see that.

"And you left me in the middle of an important conver-sa-shun," she said, her words slurred, "to go off and dally with someone you've never even met?"

"I don't think we should talk about this right now, Beth." Ellis turned to go back into the bedroom. Beth followed.

Her mood suddenly changed. "Oh, El," she said in a teasing, placating tone, "you know I didn't mean to upset you." She reached for him, stumbling forward, pushing him onto the bed and falling on top of him.

Beth laughed. "See, we are lovers again. Remember? Do you remember that time . . ." She paused, lifting herself on one elbow and, moving her slim hips lightly over his torso, made a pass to kiss him on the lips. He turned his head, repulsed by the smell of beer on her breath. He put his hands on her shoulders and forcefully pushed her off him and got up.

"Where are you going, lover man?" she purred, slurring her words.

"You are drunk, lady," he told her.

"Ha!" she snorted. "Pot calling kettle," she taunted.

"Not this time, Beth. Not in a long, long time." He was referring to his staunch resolve to stay sober. The thought crossed his mind that it would indeed be a long, long time before he'd ever again want sex with Beth. Part of him felt sorry for the woman. She needed so much more than he was now able or wanted to give.

Beth passed out. He pulled a blanket over her before leaving the bedroom to sleep on the sofa. It had been a long day.

Chapter Twenty

Funny thing, when it comes time to return to Houston from my lovely retreat in Fayette County I have a sense of dread and foreboding, Ellis confessed to Carol upon his return from the country. **Coming back to this place of ugliness and meanness depresses me.** With its polluted air aggravating his already compromised lungs, Houston had lost its original charm. **I feel an unwitting prisoner in a scenario of my own making; I may never find freedom.**

It was easier to tell her about his depression than to discuss the uncertain relationship with Beth and the continuing responsibility of Joanne. **Negative feelings are muted by time spent in the country, but rise again when I return to my gilded cage in the city. The saving grace is I know that there are other worlds.** He was referring to his love for Carol, but kept the message cryptic. *How would he ever be able to break free from chains of his own making, and if he did, would she want him?*

She answered with a long email, sharing insights from her own experience of depression and her training as a therapist. **It is obvious that you feel trapped by your current situation and believe there is no honorable way to escape it, which makes your depression worse. First of all, realize that you *do* have a choice. The choice you have made is to stay with the situation until it resolves itself. Thinking in terms of making**

choices should help you feel less depressed. Accepting that you have made choices and are capable of making other choices opens the door for you to choose to go in a different direction. *Obviously, she assumed he was raising his dilemma of living with an estranged and increasingly irrational wife. She didn't know much about Beth.* He shook his head slowly, contemplating his truth.

She suggested involvement in a group, perhaps an Alzheimer's support group, and taking on more volunteer work. He smiled when he read her suggestions. *If only it were that easy!* He had been in groups before when he was a steady churchgoer, but none where feelings were expressed. He was essentially a private person. Perhaps that's what kept him in situations he longed to escape. No one gave him feedback because, until Carol came into his life, he was unwilling to reveal himself to anyone.

You need loving human contact. I think that is why you enjoy our interactions. Not only do you get something out of them, but you are able to offer something useful and welcome to me. Perhaps, it is the same with Beth, only on a more available basis. *Hmm, so she is thinking about Beth.*

He picked up the phone and autodialed her number.

"What are you doing today, love?" he asked.

"Laundry," Carol answered. "You?"

"Nothing much. I usually do the laundry around here. She doesn't do laundry anymore, though I can sometimes get her to put away her stuff."

"El?" Carol found the courage to ask the question that had long puzzled her.

"Yes?"

"You said a while back I could ask you anything."

"Yes, I did. Ask away." Her request made him unexpectedly nervous.

"I don't know if you are conscious of this or not, but you always refer to your wife as 'she' or 'the woman' when you talk to me. Do you mind telling me her name?"

Anger flared, but he controlled it so Carol wouldn't think his anger directed at her. *When did he stop using Joanne's name?* He wasn't at all sure. Carol heard him swallow.

"Her name is Joanne," he said, as softly as he could.

Carol picked up the change of tone, but restricted her comments. "Hmm. Nice name. How long have you two been married?"

"Fifty-five years."

"A long time," she said casually.

"Yes." He was unsure where this conversation was going. He didn't want to make any awkward mistakes, yet he had told Carol he would answer honestly any question she might ask. He braced himself for her next question, but when it came, he nearly laughed with relief.

"Why did you marry Joanne in the first place?"

"Hormones, my dear. I was young." He was on safe ground now. "I saw her. I wanted her."

"You met in college?"

"Yes. We waited until she graduated. She is three years younger than I. I did grunt work before I was offered a real job looking for oil. However, you remember the Cold War and our initial involvement in the Vietnam mess? The draft was still active then, and as I was about to get called up, I joined the Navy and postponed my career in oil exploration. Coincidentally, I was stationed at The Naval Ammunition and Net Depot at Seal Beach near the place where they were building the first offshore oil rig. Though my job at the base was physical, loading ammunition aboard ships, I had enough time off to explore the beauty of the California coast there.

"Did Joanne go with you?"

"Yes, we were assigned housing and lived there through my time in the Navy. Then we landed in Houston, where I was able to get a job with a large oil company and go looking for new oil fields in Texas and other states. I wasn't home much."

"Tell me if I'm prying."

"No, I want you to know me." It felt good to open up to her. Though it was impossible to see through the phone lines, he could hear the smile in her voice. "That pleases me," she said. "Did you get accomplished all that you planned on your retreat in Fayette County?" she asked, changing the subject.

"Hmm, yes and no," he began. He wasn't ready to discuss Beth's problematic behavior with Carol, though he wanted to. The morning after her drunken advances, Beth met him in the kitchen, poured herself a bowl of cereal, and ate without a word of explanation. He wondered whether she remembered what had happened. They spent the rest of the ten-day retreat in the trailer, talking pleasantries. He began to relax, and once again, they were able to talk about the television shows they watched or the books they were reading, reminding him of the good times he had shared with her. Unwilling to reconsider more than a close friendship, he hoped Beth understood that question was settled. It troubled him that her drinking brought out an apparent sexual desire for him.

He turned his attention back to Carol's question. "I oversaw the pasture shredding and mowing of the grass acreage, as usual, but I'm concerned about the refrigerator. It's making noises that concern me, yet it seems to be running okay."

"Ellis?" She asked her question in a hesitant voice.

"Yes?"

"I want to tell you something. I'm a little timid about this because, well, this may not be an appropriate topic, but we've been telling one another about our activities."

"Don't be hesitant, love. You can tell me anything." He was half alarmed. "You haven't found someone else, have you? Not that I'd be surprised. It's a wonder those men in California aren't beating down your door."

"And what would you do if they were?" She couldn't resist teasing him.

"I'd come out there with my baseball bat and beat them off."

They both laughed before she said breathlessly, "Oh, El, there's not another man in my life. Only you." Her answer pleased him immensely but he, too, could tease.

"Me?" he said in mock surprise.

"Yes, you," she said, euphoric with her own certainty.

Surely, the time had come. "Let me say it first," he ventured. "I love you, Carol."

"And I love you, El." The soft declarations filled them both with magical exhilaration. Neither could speak. Sighs of longing, soft and sweet murmurings in the language of the spirit, flowed through the phone connection. When he finally broke the silence, he stunned her with his solemn revelation: "I've loved you ever since I read your book. Gal, I'm crazy about you. I thank God you came into my life."

"I thank God for you too," she said wondrously. "At our ages, truly our love is a gift from God."

"You think?" he said, delight ringing in his voice.

"We're crazy, though, you know," she said, a twinkle in her tone.

"Why do you say that?" He felt anything *but* crazy.

"I don't know," she answered. "It's just really incredible. Two old folks playing bridge online, deciding to message one another and then finding a way through bureaucratic nonsense to exchange emails. Now, phone calls . . . and, suddenly, we're in love!"

"Not suddenly for me, dear. And don't say *old.* We're mature, remember? Not old." He laughed to let her know he wasn't really reprimanding her, just claiming the great feeling of being young again, young and in love. "There was something about you in those online card rooms—the way you bid and played your hands, the willingness to chat with our opponents, your openness. I was intrigued from the beginning. Your new book had just come out, remember? You were telling our bridge buddies about it, and I knew, even then, I had to meet you."

"That early?" She was pleasantly surprised.

"Yes, ma'am." He was absolutely sure.

"But I offered to talk to you about your loneliness when you told the room your wife has Alzheimer's, and you didn't take me up on the offer," she told him, puzzled. "In fact, you suddenly disappeared from the card room."

"Yes, I know, and I regret that. I didn't quite know what to do with what you were offering. No one has ever shown such loving concern for me before. I was blown away. I would have responded except I was not feeling physically well at the time. I went to the doctor and didn't get to go home—I was whisked off to the hospital."

"That was a hard time for me," Carol told him. "I had no right to feel as I did, but I felt lost without you, cheated almost, because you were there, you were interesting, and then you weren't there."

"Let me tell you something, love. I'm here for you now. If you want me, you can have me—whatever's left of me, that is—though I think this 81-year-old just might surprise you."

She burst out in a mighty gale of laughter, the emotional intensity of the moment shaking her normal aplomb. He could imagine what the effort of fighting for control cost her. She gulped for breath and then, with laughter still edging her voice, told him, "See, I told you we are crazy."

"Crazy in love," he countered. His smile of enjoyment was huge.

"Yes," she agreed. "I don't understand this yet, but I am reveling in this glorious feeling. Oh, God, I'm not sure I've ever felt so loved and so loving in my whole life."

"And I as well," he said.

Again, they were silent, except for deep breaths and sighs.

Finally, he said, "You were about to tell me something about some kind of activity."

"Was I? Oh yes," Carol remembered. "I'm glad you can't see my face right now; despite being so happy, I'm blushing."

"I like blushing."

"Well, my women friends and I are having a discussion about seeing a new movie called *Hysteria*." We read about it recently, and we're very curious about how they shot it. You probably know that hysteria in the nineteenth century was considered a woman's ailment.

"I seem to recall reading that the word *hysteria* is related to the word *uterus*." He wondered: *Were they back to an intellectual discussion now?*

"Yes, you're right and, of course, hysteria was seen as a disease. Seems like throughout most of history anything to do with women and sex was seen as either unclean or diseased. Anyway, this movie is very interesting. It's based on a real doctor's experience in the late nineteenth century of treating hysteria in women by stimulation."

"Stimulation?" He was suddenly very curious.

"Yes, El, stimulation, and if you are thinking that what is being stimulated is . . . well, *that*, you're right. Don't make me say it. I'm blushing again." Carol sensed his amusement, but still couldn't spar with him on this; what he thought of her was too important to her. Would he think her too forward? *Oh, God, here's that teenager feeling again in a 78-year-old body!*

183

"You say they made a movie out of this?" He was trying to make the telling easier for her, but he couldn't help himself. "How do they handle the . . . uh . . . stimulation part?"

Carol was looking for words to describe a simple object without naming it. She started to giggle nervously. "The doctors who perform the stimulation get carpal tunnel syndrome."

He laughed heartily then—a huge, honest laugh with waves of genuine pleasure. *Thank God, Carol. You are as wild and alive as I imagined!*

His laugh gave her confidence, but she rushed her words anyway. "And so one of the doctors invents a machine that does the job for them."

"Hmm," he said. "No more carpal tunnel?" He expected her to duel a bit with him—be witty about the vibrator—and so he paused, waiting for her comeback. When she didn't engage, he gave her room to retreat behind her intellect by asking, "What did the women think?"

"Oh, El, I don't know," she said, relieved. "I haven't seen the movie yet. It's not out until May."

"Hmm," he mused again. "I think I'd like to see this movie."

"Well, come along," she said.

"I wish I could." He groaned, ending with a verbal "Grrr." *What an interesting way to express frustration with the vast mileage between us,* she thought. She was delighted with the sexiness of their banter, but even more so with the flush of pleasure she felt knowing *he really does love me.*

"So, are you going to see this movie because you are curious about its making, or do you hope to learn something?" She had opened doors to places he wanted to explore.

"You rascal. That's exactly why I'm blushing." *Why had she brought up* Hysteria *in the first place?* she asked herself, but she knew the answer: she had planned to use the movie as a ploy to fish for an admission of his feelings for her. Now, she was dangerously close to being forced to admit to a practice that everybody indulged in, but few talked about. *Oh how deep and tangled are the roots of sexual repression!* Embarrassing or not, she was glad she'd brought up the subject.

Another thought seized her. *This man has just told me he loves me, and I immediately get into a sexually suggestive conversation with him.* Her feelings were bouncing all over the place.

Part of him was shocked that she had been so open, yet El knew Carol hadn't been entirely forthcoming. Well, neither had he, for he let her squirm in her own playful naughtiness without admitting his own strong sexual urges and remedies. *This woman is a dazzling sensuous being, struggling to come out,* he thought. *And, yes, yes, yes! I do love her.*

"I want you to know something, lady." He had thought of a way to make her feel comfortable.

"What?"

"My legs are crossed." His voice was as serious as he could make it.

The laugh that thundered out of her was a robust, but sweet, the sound of satisfied pleasure.

"Okay," he said, letting her off the hook. "We'll talk more about this later. No sense storming all the battlements at once."

"Agreed," she said in a flutter. "We've been talking for over an hour!" She was suddenly all business. "I have to get back to my laundry. See you tomorrow?"

"You bet," he said. "Before you go, though, please remember what I said."

"I will," she said in a low, tender voice.

"I love you," he repeated.

"And I, you." Then knowing it wasn't enough, she added," I love you."

He moved from his wing chair to the couch in the living room, lying down and thinking: *Now if only I can get better. Please, God, make me better.*

Chapter Twenty-One

"What happened here?" he asked his wife as he and Joanne were about to step into the car to drive to Jake's for supper.

"What?" she asked, her eyes following his arm gesture. Seeing the dented bumper and broken headlight on the Lexus, she gasped. "I didn't do that!"

"Well, who else and where did this happen?" he asked her. "It wasn't there this morning when I filled it with gas." Joanne blanched. She had gone out to lunch with her friends that day.

"I...I don't know," she stammered. He could see how frightened she was. Anger flared, but he tamped it down. Now he'd have to report an accident for which he couldn't account. *How do I do that?* he wondered, wearily.

"We have to go back upstairs," he patiently told her. "We can't drive this car at night, and I need to report this to our insurance company right away. Are you sure you don't know how this happened?"

"I don't know," she said indifferently. Already she had distanced herself from the problem, but she trailed after him to the garage elevator.

In the condo, he dialed the insurance company and began to tell his story, hanging onto the chair by the phone with one hand and firing frustrated kicks to one of the chair's thick legs.

"Was that the accident Mrs. Thompson reported at one-thirty today? Lexus, headlight broken, fender damaged?" The revelation shocked him. He gasped, pulled the chair toward him, and flopped down in it.

"*She* reported the accident?" He was amazed at her action and the accuracy of the details.

"Yes. Seems she rear-ended another car at a traffic light." He could hear the agent manipulating computer keys. "Says here in the notes that a friend of hers provided specifics."

"Oh, my!" he exclaimed. "Was anyone hurt?" He leaned forward, praying for good news.

"No injuries reported."

"That's a relief." His shoulder slumped as he took a deep breath.

"Coincidentally, the other driver is insured with us as well. We should be able to handle everything for you, Mr. Thompson. The police were called, but didn't respond, as the accident was described by both parties as minor. Someone will need to file an official report, however."

Ellis wondered how to do that. He thought of Joanne's luncheon friends. Surely, one of them could supply enough details for the police report. "I'll take care of that," he said to the agent before ending the call.

"That's it!" His voice was firm as he stood and turned to Joanne. "No more driving for you." He wanted to shout at her, berate her for creating so much trouble and anxiety for him, but he knew that losing his temper was pointless. Her mind, imprisoned by her dementia, seemed free only when obsessing on her own needs and wants. Would she care or even know how to care? God, he wanted desperately to pick up and run away from it all. He wanted out, but instead, here was a new problem to handle.

"I can't drive," Joanne said in the flat tone she frequently used. He was never sure if she was asking a question or attempting to understand what was being said. Either way, he had to repeat himself.

"No, Ma'am, you cannot drive. Not anymore." Unexpectedly, he felt sad. What if the roles were reversed and he was the one losing his independence?

Joanne looked at him, quizzically. "Did we eat?" she asked.

He groaned. He wasn't hungry, but perhaps it would be good for them to go to dinner. "No, we haven't. I guess we'd better take my truck."

"Okay," she agreed and walked to the front door. This time it was Ellis who followed.

At home after supper, Ellis settled down beside his computer. It was nearly nine o'clock; he was tired. He made a note to call either Hilda or Floyd, Joanne's luncheon buddies, and ask one of them about the accident. He wanted to phone Carol, not to explain his wife's problem, but just to be near her. Today had been so special. Sadly, there had been no time for him to revel in his good fortune: she loved him. *She told me so*, he thought happily, *right after I told her I love her.* No phone call, he decided. *This needs to be in writing.*

You have become a bright star in my life. Since I don't believe in happenstance, I know we have been destined to cross paths. I believe that God has a gentle way of finding creatures that need love in their lives and offering them just that, something exceptionally valuable. He paused, savoring the warm gladness in his heart.

Those who are in tune with such spiritual offerings receive them. *Ain't that the truth?* he thought. **I have learned to live with this mystery and to expect the unexpected. There are many things in this world we can't begin to understand. Case in point: you and I fall in love with only our words as**

**builders of that love. No sweet kisses, except in imagina-
tion, and yet, the warmth and deliciousness of those imagined kisses fan the fires of passion in us.** *Indeed they do!* He
thought of someday meeting her and actually kissing her. **I believe
in miracles.** *You* **are my miracle, Carol, and I thank God for
you. I treasure your presence in my life. I love you. El**

Satisfied, he headed for bed, hopefully to dream about his love.
Joanne's accident was successfully purged for the time being.

Carol heard the click on her computer and read El's email. She
also didn't believe in happenstance, though she couldn't accept everything as predetermined, either. She thought of raising a discussion of paradoxes, but she was a little tired, yet still exhilarated by
all the love she felt coming to her and going out to him. Yawning
and stretching, she headed for bed, taking the pleasure of being his
"treasure" with her.

The next day, still feeling euphoric, she resisted the urge to
shower him in endearments, though she wanted to. Reluctantly, she
chose to be discreet, but not entirely discreet. Would Joanne read her
emails? Love at a distance with an estranged wife in the house was *so*
difficult! Outmoded standards of moral conduct learned in Sunday
school kept nagging her. She knew he and his wife were not in a loving relationship, but they *were* in a legal one. Does legal status count
more than love? Who knew what to think anymore? She trusted her
intuition. Sunday school hadn't taught her to ask for knowledge of
God's will for her; AA had. She knew she didn't actually know the
will of God, but had developed a trust that it was there for her.

So she wrote: **El, dearest, I do so look forward to your
messages whether they are accounts of your activities or
gems from your marvelous brain. God has been good in
bringing us together. When you are out of range, and I
have to wait for you, I feel deprived and irritable. Even**

though I know you go on retreat because it is necessary refreshment for you, I miss you. Kind of crazy, huh? You are there, yet you aren't. Another paradox, I suppose. He had been back from Fayette County for several days, but she knew he would soon seek respite from the strain of living with Joanne and go off again with Beth.

Later, I'm picking up Evelyn and Stella to meet with Jennifer, Sophie, and Dana. Our group sessions are usually held Wednesday mornings, but today Sophie and Dana are attending a seminar on classical music, so the group is doing lunch instead.

There are many aspects to my friendship with Evelyn. As she has become frail and harder to handle with her heavy walker, I have been very un-Christian in my attitude. I haven't wanted to take her anywhere, yet I find myself doing it anyway. Sunday, for instance, I will take her to see a play. We have season's tickets, and I can hardly wait for the season to end.

Now, I tell God —tell God, ha! — that I'm doing this not because I'm a good person, but because "I hear you, God and, yes, I will do what you ask." Things turn out fine when I accept what I've been asked to do. I suppose I'm supposed to learn something from all of this, but what I'm to learn is a mystery to me.

The truth was that Carol was already mourning the loss of the woman she knew as Evelyn. Seeing her friend's abilities dwindle reminded her of Mario's last days. She didn't want to be reminded of Mario now that El had come into her life. Besides the mental stress, manhandling Evelyn's heavy walker in and out of the car was almost impossible for Carol. Caregiving for someone at the stage of needing a professional caregiver was grueling work. She resented being responsible for someone else's family member. The strain made her all too conscious of her own limitations. Flustered, she decided to finish the email and get on with her day.

I hope that there will be some time to play bridge together this afternoon. I'll be home about 1:30 and will look for you.

Later, my dear. Love you too, Carol

When Ellis woke that day, he knew the time had come to talk to his sons about their mother. He called Henry and George and arranged to meet them for supper. Then he called both Hilda and Floyd and found that they had indeed been in the car with Joanne when she failed to stop for the light and plowed into the car in front of her.

"Not much damage to either car," Floyd said. "It was an accident. She was distracted, I think, by a horn blowing behind her. Probably thought she should move out of the way."

"Hmm," Ellis said. "Thanks for calling the insurance company. Could you drop by tonight and take Joanne to supper? I have an appointment."

"Sure thing, Ellis. I'll see if I can borrow my brother's car. Don't worry; I'll take care of our gal."

Ellis cringed when he heard the *our*.

"Thanks a lot," he said, dismissing Floyd. He didn't look forward to the conversation with his sons, but it felt like the right thing to do. He spent the day filling out the police report and sending it to their local station.

Later, he met his sons at the Salty Sea Restaurant, a new seafood place a few miles from his condo. After eating and small talk, he leaned back in his chair, said a silent prayer, and began to speak. "You know I haven't been in the best of health lately."

"Oh, come on, Dad, you're a strong guy," Henry began, but Ellis lifted his hand. George listened, stone faced. Ellis knew this was not going to be an easy conversation, particularly since the older son was so close to his mother. Henry, he thought, might more readily see him as a mere mortal, but George? Doubtful. The boys had always been so different: George, serious; Henry, devil-may-care.

"It's time to talk about your mother," Ellis said pointblank.

"What about Mom?" George asked in a crisp, no-nonsense voice.

"You both have noticed. . . "Ellis began and then hesitated. He hoped this would not be too hard on them. He tried again. "I know you have noticed that her cognitive powers have weakened considerably."

"Not all that much," George leaped to Joanne's defense. "She's still able to drive to her hairdressers, the gym, and out to lunch with her buddies." He ticked off the places on his fingers. Ellis decided not to tell them about the accident, not yet.

"Drive, hmm . . . well, yes," Ellis admitted, "but has either of you been in the car with her lately?" Silence. "She drifts out of her lane and overcorrects if I say anything. She has a lead foot, which might be okay, except she tailgates. Her reaction time is compromised by a declining ability to think straight." Ellis shook his head sadly. "Sometimes I wonder whether she thinks at all. Last week she nearly creamed the car ahead of us when she decided to run the light in making a left turn."

"Good grief, Dad, that's serious," Henry said.

"You bet. I warned her to slow down and pay attention, but—and you know this already—she'll agree to anything, yet I seriously doubt that she retains much of what I say to her. I catch her staring at the calendar in the kitchen and then asking me if a particular day is her doctor's appointment. When I tell her it is, she walks away, but then she goes right back to the calendar, stares at it, and repeats her question. She does this over and over. It drives me crazy." Both sons, disconcerted and self-conscious, stared at their feet as Ellis talked. *It's hard for them to face this,* he thought. *Hard or not, it must be faced.*

"Oh, she can get up, get dressed, and get her own breakfast and lunch but, beyond daily routine, she's like a deer in the headlights. She freezes. I've been with her to her doctor's. He'll explain a problem she's having, say a bladder infection, and she won't even answer his questions fully. She looks to me. Frankly, I don't know what to say. I haven't been involved with her illnesses for years."

"Yes, I *know*," George's answer had a bite to it.

Ellis heaved a sigh, "Okay, George, say your piece."

Confronted, George settled down and softened his tone. "I'm sorry, Dad, I just get frustrated. Mom calls me for most of her doctors' appointments now, and I'm strapped for time. I know you two have basically lived separate lives under the same roof for years."

Ellis nodded. "Thirty, I think."

"That was okay," George continued, "until she developed this dementia situation."

Ellis lifted his eyes, surprised that George would acknowledge his mother's condition.

"No, no," his son said, in answer to the look his father gave him, "we've known about this for quite some time, Dad." He turned his gaze on his brother, "Haven't we, Henry?" He paused. "It's just that . . ."

"Go ahead," Ellis urged. He wanted to make George's moment of truth easier, but all he could do was sit and listen.

"It's just that you've been involved so long with Beth and going to the country so often with her that I've always felt—not that it has been any of my business, mind you—I've always felt that . . . well, this is so hard . . ." George shook his head.

Henry spoke up. "Not that you mean to, Dad, but it looks as if you've abandoned Mom when she needs you most."

"On the contrary," Ellis said, anger creating a crisp, controlled voice. "Your mother abandoned me long ago, fellows. I'm not about to explain myself to you." He blew out a weak breath and spoke again, this time with cold acceptance. "Suffice it to say, you probably remember when your mother first began to complain about her various pains. Illness after illness snowballed on her until the person she once was got lost. What was left was a woman focused almost entirely on her physical problems. Let me tell you this," Ellis wagged a finger for emphasis, "I tried to help. I tried to be close to her . . ." he paused again for breath, "but she wanted none of it." He finally managed a deep breath, coughed, and stopped talking.

"Yeah." George stretched the word, contemplating the risk in exposing his long-held resentment. He could see his father wasn't feeling well, but he decided to go for it anyway. "We know the rest of the story," he said in a low voice. "Those drinking years of yours were hard on all of us. I'm astounded you two didn't divorce."

"Frankly, so am I," Ellis admitted. Father and son stared steadily at one another, neither giving an inch. It was Henry who broke the silence. "Dad, we're grown men. Each of us has had our own relationship problems, not to mention our forays into destructive behavior. I think we can cut you a little slack here." He looked at George who stuck out his lower lip and bobbled his head. After all, their father was sober now—had been for a long time.

Ellis leaned toward his sons and extended a hand to each, saying impishly, "Wouldn't make much difference if you didn't, you know. I've always been an independent sort, as you so well know, but it really is nice to have your support." He gave his sons a big smile before steering the conversation back to his main point. "What I wanted to discuss with you is a plan to take care of your mother should my own health decline further or, God forbid, should I die anytime soon."

"You're indestructible," Henry quickly retorted.

"Let's hope," Ellis replied, "but I've been in the hospital. I'm still taking these damned antibiotics for that bacterial invasion I had." He coughed again, this time covering his mouth with his handkerchief. "Life is full of uncertainties," he said, moving the handkerchief. "What I want to do is make sure your mother is in a place where she can be taken care of should I no longer be able to see to it."

"We can help. I'm already helping," George said. He wanted desperately to stave off the inevitable.

"Yes, I know, but are you willing to take her into your home in the event that I am no longer here?" Ellis let the question hang, forcing an answer from George.

"Well, no, I hadn't thought about that. Not seriously, anyway. I'd have to talk it over with Ellen." George cupped his lips, his tongue tut-tutting against the roof of his mouth. "I think I know what she'd say. Caring for Mom in her condition would put my marriage in jeopardy."

"Exactly," Ellis said. "And you, Henry?"

"Sorry, Dad, I'd like to help out, but I'm barely making it with two jobs. The strain would put me over the edge, I'm sure. What *can* we do to help?"

"Listen—for now. I plan to investigate care facilities, and make some decisions about what will be best for her. I want you to be aware of this and in on every step, so that you can take over should I become incapacitated."

"You wouldn't go into independent living with her?" George asked.

"No, I wouldn't." Ellis was adamant.

"What would you do, Dad? Rattle around in that condo by yourself?"

"Nope. I'd sell the condo and move to California."

"Move to California?" Both sons exclaimed simultaneously.

"Yeah, my doctor told me years ago that the pollution in Houston would kill me. She actually suggested moving to California."

"But what would you do there? How would you live?"

"Oh, I have resources." His eyes twinkled.

"It's that woman in California, the writer you've been talking about, isn't it?" Henry said, pleased that for all the talk of illness and dying, his father had an entirely different plan in mind.

Ellis's smile was broad. "Yes, Henry, it is Carol Bradley. We've become really close."

George just shook his head. "I don't know whether to be surprised or awed. At your age, Dad, who would have thought?" He put out his hand. Ellis shook it. "You know, Dad, I think I'm happy for you, but I'm very sad for Mom."

"I know, Son. Alzheimer's is a stinking disease. I'm sorry she's afflicted, but I think if we find her a place where she can have some kind of life with people trained to help her, it may be best for her."

He paused. "I didn't tell you this when we first started the conversation because I wanted us all to be calm and see things rationally."

"What, Dad?" George asked while Henry looked at his father intently.

"She had an accident yesterday. Fairly minor, but I've decided she can't drive anymore."

"Is she okay?" Henry asked.

"Yes, no one was hurt. The Lexus lost a headlight and has a dented fender, all fixable."

"How will she get around?" George wanted to know.

"We'll have to work on that," Ellis told them. "I'll need your help in figuring out just what we can do."

Chapter Twenty-Two

They fell into the habit of calling each another daily, sometimes two or three times a day.

"I can't believe this is happening," he said. "It feels like magic."

"Precisely," she replied. "What are the odds of two old people . . . ?"

"Don't say 'old,'" he cautioned. "Mature, remember?"

"Ah, yes, you told me that before." She laughed.

"Astronomical," he said.

"What?" Carol, thinking about El's views on aging, was caught off guard.

"The odds that we'd meet playing bridge in an online game room and fall in love," he explained willingly.

"It boggles the mind," she agreed.

They never tired of talking about this. Both of them knew how unlikely it was to be blessed with a serious love relationship in the twilight of their lives. To credit God with matchmaking seemed natural, though they chortled a lot about His sense of humor: "Seriously, God? Now?" Still, they moved forward together in gratitude, sensing their love a reflection of God's great love for them.

"We'll just take it one day at a time," she'd say, and he'd repeat the same words the next day.

Carol was still troubled by the fact that he was married and told him so.

"I know," he said simply.

"If your marriage died 30 years ago, why didn't you get a divorce?" she asked.

"I really don't know, Love," he said. "I've asked myself that so many times. I did make up my mind once to file for divorce, but then we went into counseling . . ." He paused, leaving dead air on the line between them.

Her heart sank. Would he tell her that divorcing a woman he didn't love was impossible because deep down he really *does* love her? A cold sweat numbed her. She waited as long as she could before asking. "El?" She needed to know.

"I'm sorry," he said. "I'm still trying to make sense of it for myself." He struggled for words. His excuse seemed so inadequate, yet he was exactly the man he was about to describe. Carol, however, was holding her breath, expecting the worse. "You see,' he said in a voice made steady by his beliefs, "I was brought up to honor my commitments. The word *duty* still means something to me as does *civility* and *kindness*. My mother drilled those principles into me. She wanted me to grow up to be a Southern gentleman and," he ventured a laugh, "I guess she got her wish."

Carol almost giggled her relief, but there was more to learn. "Did the counselor convince you to stay with her?"

"No. I think I convinced myself. Even then, she seemed incapable of processing the significance of what I was feeling." Carol noticed that El still referred to Joanne using a pronoun rather than her name. She wondered if he were deliberately or unconsciously distancing himself from his wife. Underneath his professed civility and kindness, she sensed a smoldering anger. El kept his voice casual. "She wouldn't talk about it, not even with the counselor. In the end, I just couldn't abandon her. She was chronically ill. Who would take care of her?" He sighed. "I just decided it best for me to stay with her and build a life of my own."

"So, did you seek comfort in other women?" The question felt intrusive, but not asking it wasn't an option.

"Yes." His straightforward answer spoke volumes. It gave her confidence to trust him now.

"But none that you wanted to be with all the time?" She hoped for a negative answer.

"No. It's a long story, and I will tell you all about it sometime if you want to hear it. Suffice it to say, for now, that none of those ventures were noble." *That admission must have cost,* she guessed.

"What about Beth? Have you slept with her?"

"Yes." Carol flinched; her quality of life from now on depended on his answer to her next question: "And now?" Her heart was in her throat.

"No. I love Beth. I've known her for a long time." *Quiet straightforward answers again.* "She's been a companion to me, but she isn't able to fully give herself to a permanent relationship with me. I don't know why, except she is so involved with the problems of her grown children, she seems to ignore her own needs. Through the years, we just became good friends. I never got a sense of her loving me like you do." He seemed lost in thought for a moment but then, unexpectedly, he gave way to joy: "Oh, gal, you really do know how to love!"

"You should try me in person," she suggested, laughing now with genuine relief.

"Now that's an invitation I heartily accept." His voice shifted to match her sudden playfulness. *A relief to him too,* she guessed.

Days, weeks, and finally, months passed as their daily phone calls built a sturdy relationship from the details of their lives. He shared with her his frustrations with Joanne's slowly progressing

Alzheimer's. "George and Henry keep finding rides for her to lunch with her friends or go to the hairdresser's, and George takes her to her medical appointments. It's a real intrusion on their lives. We may have to put her in a continuing care situation, but my sons seem to think she isn't yet ready for that. I don't want to take away whatever life she is able to enjoy right now."

"Did you ever think providing a safe and secure place where she can participate in ongoing activities might give her a greater enjoyment in life?"

"Yes." His voice was strong, but she knew it carried the burden of decision. "I just don't think it is time yet."

After talking to him, Carol felt guilty. Her comment about Joanne's welfare was partly willing her own wishes true. Her intention was not to prompt Joanne's physical separation from her home, but to figure out when she and El could be together. *Life is short*, she reminded herself, *especially now*. Lord, would she have to wait for a meeting in eternity? She laughed as she imagined him carrying out his often-stated fantasy: *When, oh God, when will this man actually drive up to my door in his much-loved white pickup?* She felt downright silly thinking this, but then she thought, *why not?* Impulsively seeking the CD player in the living room, she put in a favorite disc, closed her eyes, and begin slowly and carefully dancing and singing as if to El. *"There's a place for us, a time and place for us . . ."* Hugging herself, she could feel his arms around her. When the music stopped, she sat for a moment before getting up to find something to eat in the kitchen.

Carol kept El current with her many activities in church, her groups, and with her friends. She had formed the habit of talking about these things as if he already knew the people involved. Soon, he seemed a member of her community.

In time he sent her pictures he had taken especially for her. She sent him photos of herself, alone and with family and friends—even photos with Mario.

They talked now about his coming to see her. "If this is the last thing on earth I do, I want to see you," he told her. His cough interrupted him.

"Are you okay?"

"Just this chronic bronchitis, I hope. Not the mycobacterium returning."

"You're still taking antibiotics for that, aren't you?"

"Yep, and I'll be taking them for another year or so, I'm told."

"Oh no."

"That's okay, Love. Antibiotics or no, I'm coming to Santa Bella where I can get a breath of fresh air."

"Isn't the air ever fresh in Houston?"

"Not very often. Maybe after a Nor'easter washes it clean. There's just too much industry here. My doctor told me long ago that unless I get out of Houston, the air here will kill me."

"That's terrible." *Another worry. He might die before anything is settled!*

"Yes, she seriously advised me to move to California." He chuckled. "I know what you're thinking and no, she didn't *just* tell me. She told me to do that *years* before I met you."

"Did you ever tell Joanne that living in Houston will kill you?"

"Yes."

"And suggested you and she should move?"

"Yes."

"And?"

"She'd have none of it."

"Oh, Ellis, I'm so sorry. It's your life that's in danger." Carol was shocked that a wife, even an estranged wife, would not act in the best interests of her husband's health. What she was about to say felt absolutely right to her, and so she told him: "Come live with me."

"Yes," Ellis said. She was surprised by his quick agreement. She had expected a *perhaps* or a *we'll see*, but his *yes* was spontaneous and firm.

"*Will* you come live with me?" Carol repeated. Her eyes were wide with excitement.

"Yes, I will." Again, no hesitation from him.

"Oh, Ellis," she whispered, "this is a commitment, you know."

"Yes, I know." She loved it. Loved the idea of his coming, loved the strength of his commitment to her, the willingness to leave everything behind and be with her forever.

They were giddy with making plans. Their conversation roamed from the closet where he'd keep his things to the food they would eat, the people she'd introduce him to, the sights they would see, the vacations they'd take and, finally, which side of the bed he'd sleep on.

She couldn't help being practical. "You know, my dear, you'd be giving up so much of your life."

"Yes, and I am ready to do that," he declared.

"You'd have to leave friends and family and doctors . . ." *Was he truly willing to give up everything for her?*

"The airplanes still fly from Texas to California. They can come to see me." He coughed again, and she realized, sadly, that a move to California might not yet be possible with the uncertainty of his health.

"You know, Ellis, we've known one another for nine months now, but we haven't really seen one another. You've seen me talking on You Tube presentations, but we don't Skype, so we don't read one another's body language. Not that living together won't work for us—it will, I'm sure—but maybe it would be best to start with a visit, say, two weeks?"

"Yes, that's probably a good idea, my love. Give me a little time to get this coughing under control, will you?"

"Of course."

Carol was astounded. Asking Ellis to come live with her had so freely flowed from her, she wondered if it were another gift from God, particularly since she had no second thoughts. It felt right. She wanted Ellis to be sure, because he was giving up so much to be with her, while she would stay in her own home with her own life intact. Adding a sweet, loving man to her life seemed easy. She was ready for anything, even to take care of him if that were necessary. She knew the depth of that commitment and told Ellis.

"Oh, no," he said. "You won't ever have to be my caregiver," he stubbornly asserted.

"But I would, Sweetheart. I would take care of you," she insisted.

"No, I won't have it. You've been through that once already, and I won't put you through it again." He didn't suggest an alternative, and she was afraid to ask; she didn't want to think about separating before they even had a chance to be together.

Clearly overwhelmed by her generosity of spirit, he nearly choked as he told her softly, "I have never in my life been so loved, my dearest. You love me . . ." he fought for control, "unconditionally."

"As you love me," she said, near tears.

She decided to lighten the conversation. "Oh, by the way, I've purchased one."

"What?" he asked. *What now?* was what he wondered.

She laughed. "I think you know. I'll tell you about it tomorrow when I've had a chance to explore a little."

"I can hardly wait."

Having seen the movie *Hysteria,* Carol and her friends talked about it for days. At the time she felt like a schoolgirl discovering naughty and nice, and though she teased when she told Ellis about the movie, she felt inhibited and didn't fully explain her reaction. She'd grown braver since then.

As promised, she called him the next day.

"Remember that purchase I said I made?"

"Yes."

"I used it." There. It was out.

He laughed heartily. "Oh, so you did, did you?" She imagined amusement spreading over his face.

"Oh, yes. And guess what?" She paused for effect. "I wonder why it took me so long to get one of those!" She was delighted with her own boldness, but blushed anyway. She could tell by nuanced changes in his breathing that he was as excited as she. The mere thought of being together stimulated deep orgasmic promise.

"Have you crossed your legs yet?" she asked, a naughty tease to her voice.

"Honey, I've had them crossed ever since you asked me to remember that purchase you made."

"El?"

"Yes?" The suspense was unbearable.

"I didn't know I still had it in me," Carol exclaimed. "It was all there. I felt it, El and, afterwards . . . She almost lost her nerve. "Afterwards, I was ready—sensitized and ready—for a real one." She didn't say *I was ready for you.*

He knew, though. She imagined a mischievous happy crinkle at the corner of his eyes as he told her, "I see what we are going to be doing a good deal of the time."

"Hurry, Roadrunner, hurry."

Both fell into a silence bathed in a longing so deep that neither had the words to express it. The feelings, however, permeated the air that had contained the words that lit the passion in them. Their sighs were almost simultaneous.

No laughter now. The reality was he couldn't come to her. They knew they had to settle for phone conversations or snatches of communication in Instant Messaging or a running chat at the virtual bridge tables.

He spoke tenderly. "Thank you, Sweetheart, for sharing this with me. I find I, too, need a way to relieve tensions within me." Both had been brought up not to mention the reality of any sexual act, let alone one which was a lone affair. Though they were educated people, neither felt free enough to utter the clinical term, sensing perhaps that movement in that direction would scatter the magic of the moment.

She did, however, venture into an intellectual discussion. "As children we were taught boundaries—forbidden territory—that are hard to cross as adults. Yet, those who do cross those scary lines find freedom, excitement, and satisfaction."

"Yes, I feel sorry for people who cling to old ideas. They are missing out on living fully."

"Amen," she said. The sacred word often ended their deeper discussions. She reluctantly let him go.

Chapter Twenty-Three

"*E*velyn died this morning," Sophie said softly after Carol answered the phone.

The fall from joy to sorrow was swift. Carol had been expecting this phone call for a long time. Still, losing a friend was sad. No amount of joy counters life's ending; all that one is, all that one achieves, and all that one has and cherishes is given up in one last breath. She thought of El—*his* struggle to breathe and, lately, his incessant coughing. Somehow, the thought comforted her for, despite his infirmities, he was very much alive, very much in love with her, and very determined to be a physical presence in her life.

"Did she go peacefully?" Why was that knowledge so important? Would knowing that passing from life is serene ward off suffering and pain? Carol suspected not, but still thinking of death as serene was oddly reassuring.

"Yes," Sophie supplied the hoped-for answer. "She died in her sleep."

When they met as a group the next day, the women raised their coffee cups in a tribute to their fallen friend. At this point, there wasn't much they could do for Evelyn except make charitable donations in her name, since her large family sought no help from them in planning the funeral.

"She was one smart lady, you know," Dana said. "Always concerned with children."

"Yes," Sophie agreed. "Remember how she made her idea for a home for delinquent youth happen?"

"Ah, yes," Stella laughed with the pleasure of memory. "We were in on all the plans and frustrations."

"She didn't know when to quit," Carol offered. "She was always volunteering: feeding the hungry, helping the homeless, or finding clothes for disadvantage women looking for jobs. Even when she could barely walk, she felt guilty for no longer being able to volunteer her services."

"Sounds like she was a classy lady," Jennifer said. "I'm sorry I didn't know her sooner than I did."

"Ah, well . . . "Sophie's voice dwindled into heavy silence threatening gloom. Squaring her shoulders, she brought them back. "Let's talk about us," she suggested and, turning to Jennifer, asked, "Are you doing okay?"

"Oh sure," Jennifer said. "Nothing new with Peter. He still drinks periodically. I stay out of his way."

"No more guns in the house, I hope," Carol said.

"No, none that I know of, and I'm pretty good at ferreting out these things now. I have no compunction at all about looking through his things when he's out."

"I can't say I blame you," Sophie granted. "Do you feel in any danger?"

"Not really. I guess I'm resigned to having no real relationship with this man," Jennifer reluctantly admitted. "I don't think he even likes me, but he won't talk about divorce, and I'm not about to stir him up."

"Must be hard to live that way," Stella said.

"It is. I feel so damned lonely."

"I know what that means," Carol offered. "Before El came into my life, I was going crazy with loneliness."

"But you had us, all your outside interests and friends in church! And you were still lonely?" Stella asked. Her husband was still a vital part of her life.

"It's different, Stella. Not that I don't appreciate all that I have. I do. But I need what you have—intimacy in my life, one special person to love me and care enough about everything I do to listen and be there for me."

"Hmm." Stella wasn't convinced.

Jennifer spoke up, her voice vibrant with nervous reaction. "I know exactly what Carol is talking about. Even though I have a man in the house. I feel all alone. I want—I need— someone to see me as a person: someone to care whether I'm hungry, sick, or healthy; someone who listens and appreciates my jokes; someone who talks to me about his feelings and cares what I think and then folds me in his arms and makes love to me."

"Uh . . . uh . . . okay," Stella drew in her breath. "I guess I haven't thought much about intimacy these days with the Parkinson's taking up so much of our time and energy. Then, too, Ralph hasn't been feeling well, though he does seem to have energy for his weekly golf games."

"How are *you* feeling?" Sophie asked.

"Aw, I'm okay," Stella replied. "Having a chronic and progressive disease gets old, that's all." Stella was uncharacteristically sarcastic. In all the years the group had met, she seldom voiced anything but optimism about her health and well being. "Maybe losing Evelyn made me a little melancholy," she confessed. "I'm the youngest one here!"

"Don't you worry, Honey," Carol said. "None of us is going to get out alive. In the meantime, let me tell you something. You are my role model. You have fought this disease for many years without giving into it. You've done what you've needed to do; you even had brain surgery, for God's sake. You gallantly resisted every attempt the disease has made to take you down. But more than that: you've *lived* through it. You've gone on trips, you pay attention to your family, and you still cook and do chores. You are one amazing lady. I admire you."

"Thank you," Stella said simply, "but Parkinson's still sucks."

They laughed then, knowing that's what Stella wanted them to do. Sophie reached out to hold Stella's hand before asking, "Anybody got some good news?"

"I do," Carol volunteered.

"Tell us," Jennifer eagerly coaxed. "I bet it's about that man of yours."

"It is." Carol's face glowed with pleasure. "I've invited him to come and live with me."

"You did what?" Dana was shocked.

"Are you sure that's what you want?" Sophie cautioned.

"Yep. I'm absolutely sure," Carol said. "We made a commitment to one another. If he stays in Houston, the air there will kill him. His doctor told him so."

"But you don't know him!" Stella exclaimed. Then seeing the puzzled look in Carol's eyes, she softened her approach. "I mean, you haven't even met yet. Besides . . ." Stella then asked the question that truly bothered her, "what would he do with his wife?"

"I don't know, Stella." Carol told her truthfully. "I just know that she doesn't care enough about his living or dying to move to California with him. If she did, I'd take care of them both."

"You would? You're crazy," Dana blurted out, her hands and arms shaking air in frustration. "Do you realize what an impossible job that would be——moving an Alzheimer's patient across the country and helping her adjust to new circumstances?" She paused for emphasis. "It's just plain nuts."

Carol laughed. "Hold on, Dana . . . Everybody hold on. None of this is going to happen anytime soon. Ellis's own health is still too tentative for an airplane ride. Besides, he has already talked to his sons about their mother, and they all agree that she will need to be placed in a care facility."

"Before he moves in with you, presumably," Sophie added sardonically. *Was she jealous of her?* Carol wondered. She decided to ignore Sophie's cutting tongue and explain rather than argue.

"I don't know," Carol said. "I do know that his sons know about me, and seem okay with the situation. They realized that their parents have not had a real marriage for a long, long time, and appreciate that their dad hung in with their mother because of her illnesses. They thanked him for doing that."

"Do they know he is coming to live with you?" Sophie was not placated.

"I don't think so but, Sophie, they *do know* he is coming to see me. That's what we have decided: that it is best for both of us to see how the relationship goes during a visit before making any permanent arrangements."

"Well, thank God. I think that is sensible," Sophie admitted.

Throughout the conversation, Carol felt self-assured and calm. She was awash in the glow of loving and being loved. Logically, she knew their relationship was built on intimacy needs being met for both of them. Lonely for far too long, Ellis and she were willing to take any risks to be together. She felt capable and strong. Without a doubt, she knew that having Ellis in her home was the right thing for them both.

As for his wife, she felt sorry for Joanne, sorry that she was saddled with an ever-progressing memory loss, a brain that was dying. She finally understood that Ellis's intimate relationship with Joanne was over. Without Ellis, Joanne would need another caregiver. Right now, their sons had stepped up to help out, but eventually, even if Ellis were there, Joanne would need placement.

Now, among her friends, Carol decided not to do any more explaining. They needed time to digest what she had told them. "That's about the size of it," she said.

"It's really quite remarkable, isn't it?" Jennifer began. "Here we are, late in life, and we are still working on feeling loved and loving someone else."

"Speaking of which," Carol pointed at Jennifer, "maybe you should go online, play a little bridge, and find some someone to care for you."

"Fat chance," Jennifer stammered. "In the first place, I don't play bridge and, secondly, who would want me?"

"You'd be surprised, my dear." Carol said.

"That's not a bad idea, Jennifer," Stella said. "Peter doesn't deserve you. It looks like your marriage is, well . . . not so much alive anymore."

"You think?" Jennifer laughed. Stella had a valid point, but burying a dead marriage wasn't easy.

Sophie had been listening, one hand under her chin. She suddenly took down her hand, clasped it in her other, and said firmly, "No, really. I agree with Carol and Stella. You are such a vivacious and interesting woman, Jennifer. Why should you be stuck with someone who doesn't love you enough to do something about himself?"

Carol was astounded. *This, coming from Sophie!*

Dana picked up the argument. "You should think about it, Hon." Dana used endearments with her friends to keep their attention. "I don't have a perfect relationship with my Frank." She shook her head, chuckling. "No siree. I have to do the driving and even have to put his socks on for him. His body is wearing out—but, so what? He's with me. He loves me. He jokes with me. We have good times together." She smiled impishly. "And then I send him home."

"You wouldn't have to marry him, you know," Carol told Jennifer, getting back to talking about her. "You'd be in it just to have a good time." She nodded encouragingly. "Why not?"

"Hmm. Maybe I should." Jennifer put a hand to her mouth to hide a snicker. "You really think I have it in me?" The women all nodded vigorously. Jennifer flushed with pleasure, "Does anyone have any prospects for me?"

"Not at the moment, but you never know," Sophie said. She paused before springing the idea on them: "All this talk makes me think I should get in the game as well."

"Oh, Sophie," Carol was beyond surprise. Sophie had grieved Nathan so long that her friends had lost sight of her intimacy needs. "Go for it."

Sophie giggled. "Maybe. We'll see."

On Saturday they attended Evelyn's funeral. They were surprised to see such a large turnout for a 97-year-old woman. Every agency that Evelyn had graced with her presence and devotion had someone there. Family members and former colleagues stepped to the podium and eulogized Evelyn's stellar qualities. Even some students from a long-ago high school experience were there to credit their former counselor for their life successes. No one in the women's group spoke.

"Wow," Carol said as the group gathered after the services. "Were they talking about our Evelyn?"

"It was moving and a bit overwhelming, wasn't it?" Stella said. "Wonder what people will say about me when I die."

"Well, if I'm there, I'll tell them what a great human being you were," Dana offered.

"Yes, but it won't bring me back, will it?" Stella murmured with a sly smile.

"No, I guess not," Jennifer said. "What was it that Thomas Gray said: "The paths of glory . . . ?"

"Lead but to the grave," Carol finished. "Speaking of which, is anyone going to the graveside service?"

Each of the women begged off with excuses. "Okay, I'll represent the group," Carol offered. Somehow, it seemed important to her to accompany Evelyn on this last leg of the journey. Strange, in preparing to do so, she was reminded of the many times she had given Evelyn a ride to the theater.

The religious service at the graveside was short. When the pastor was done, and clumps of dirt and flowers were tossed on the lowered casket, the family stepped forward with shovels and began to vigorously scoop soil on the casket; Carol had never seen this done before. She looked at Evelyn's daughter, who said simply, "It's a family tradition. Want to help?"

Carol took a shovel, lifted dirt, and gently threw it on the casket. Her eyes were brimming with tears, yet she felt a strange comfort in doing this last service for her friend. It was as if she couldn't leave without tucking Evelyn in for the night. *For the long, long night ahead,* Carol thought. She tackled another shovelful of dirt and then another and another until, with all hands working nonstop, there was a pleasant mound on Evelyn's grave, lovingly patted and shaped by those who cared the most about her. "Rest in peace, my friend," Carol whispered, "rest in peace."

Chapter Twenty-Four

At first, Ellis had been reluctant to take Beth with him to the Fayette County retreat after the unpleasantness of their January stay. However, he reconsidered when he realized he really shouldn't be alone in such an isolated environment. Then too, she seemed completely her old self again. After the wild and unwelcome pass she made at him, she managed the rest of the stay without drinking any alcohol, at least not in front of him. They didn't talk about the incident; he thought it best not to embarrass her. Truth was, he had to admit, he didn't *want* to discuss it. He wanted to forget how much her drunken advances repelled him, to remember instead only the Beth he had known and, yes, loved for so many years.

Since that trying time there had been no objectionable behavior in the four monthly trips Beth and he had made. At the deli stop on the way, she bought only single six-packs of beer. Odd that he couldn't recall seeing her drinking them. *Maybe when she watched late night television without him? Stop it!* he sternly scolded himself. *What difference does it make?* He decided that as long as her drinking didn't affect him, he wouldn't ask her about it.

He was tired, unjustly so, he thought, for he had slept well. His coughing had worsened, though. It was a wicked summer for pollution in Houston, a good reason to get out of town and into the country where the air was sweeter.

His long fight with bacteria in his lungs reminded him he lived from one lab test to another. Though results indicated his particular bacterium conquered, a cautious medical team kept him chomping pills he'd grown to hate. His morose mood spilled over into the email to Carol: **The thing that bothers me is managing a life that has survived into antiquity while forced to accept the inevitability of a malfunctioning body. A further torment is to be obsessed with the results of medical tests. Besides, we who have reached a certain maturity tend to become invisible to others. I see this wasteful indifference in my volunteer work for Christian ministries. So many of the delightful older women I drive to medical appointments are alone, living lives of emotional exile.**

Was *Carol in an emotional exile before we started corresponding?* he wondered. Trapped by her acute sense of loss after Mario's passing, she seemed fragile to him despite the many coping activities she adopted to waylay the loneliness she felt. He marveled at her energy. She appeared in good health, though she used oxygen at night and coughed, too—though not as relentlessly as he did. *Please, God,* he prayed, *keep her well, make me well, and give us time.*

We seniors often find ourselves viewed as hangers-on and non-contributors in a society that dotes on youth. Nonsense! You and I, my dear, are very much present to life. My heartbeat quickens when you tell me you care. When you reach out to me, all my senses come alive. To be loved by a mature woman with life experience is the greatest gift a man can receive. To know that you care, and I make a difference in your life is more than enough to keep my passion alive.

Feeling immensely better, he paused. Thinking of Carol did that to him. He reluctantly ended the email to her and reached for the phone to call Beth, intending to invite her to go to Fayette County with him next week. Before he pressed the speed dial, however, a coughing fit seized him. He had to stand up and use his inhaler to catch his breath.

When Carol saw his email, she was struck by its serious tone and answered right away. **Dear El, I'm not sure what you are saying, though I sense a struggle of some sort. Let me tell you what your words mean to me. "Antiquity" suggests being worn and frail—put on the shelf as no longer useful—while "malfunctioning body" and "becoming obsessed" bring me down. If I allow terms like these to sit with me, I develop anxiety, which is more debilitating than any illness I experience! On the other hand, if I reject fear and keep the words, I experience anger.**

She was protesting—vigorously challenging—even the suggestion that El might be old and nearing the end of his life. *She was his hope. Didn't he tell her that in the same email?* No way would she consider an end to this promising relationship, when they hadn't even met or touched one another yet.

When I'm faced with such strong negatives, I find denial a useful tool. I tend to do whatever I can about such a problem, and if I can't solve it, then I just learn to live with it.

In other words, if I can no longer hike up a mountain, I go as far as I can and enjoy the view from there.

I am grateful for what I have and do not bemoan what I've lost. I grieve, yes, but even then, there's a point of acceptance and a forward movement. If not, I would never have bothered to play online bridge or talk to an interesting gentleman who plays with me.

She smiled, knowing that he would be pleased with her writing these particular words.

I try not to spend time with regrets. What has been is done. If I have remorse or guilt about something that cannot be changed, I ask for forgiveness and move on. She thought of Patrick: the long years of estrangement between them and losing contact with her precious grandchildren.

Sure, I have my moods. Sometimes I want to strike out at people who can't seem to get their lives straightened out. Don't they realize that life is precious? We have to live it just as it is, not rail against it. So I *choose* to be happy, positive, and optimistic. Simply by making a choice, as strange as it seems, I get to live while I'm dying. The other option— being negative—means I get to die while I'm living, and who wants that? Love, Carol

When he received this email, El knew he had caused Carol concern. He was sorry; yet he had to be honest with her. He wrote back immediately. **Dear Heart: If you sense that I have paused at this point in our relationship to wonder if my physical impairments might stop me from following my heart, please think otherwise. I don't want you to misinterpret my discouragement. Yes, I confess that I have been depressed lately, but I hate the thought that you might feel, my love, that I would allow my physical state to stop me from following my heart.**

I made a decision, months ago, to make a difference in your life if at all possible. I have known for some time that I loved you—that has not changed. However, I feel compromised by my health; I am not all I wish to be for you. I ask for your patience and understanding while I work to

get better. He bowed his head, knuckles pressed hard in his cheeks. Losing her would be unbearable.

You, above all others, have touched me in ways I have never known before. I love you, Carol. I will not let you go. E.

Anyone who loves that strongly has to be able to overcome his physical limitations, she told herself. She got up to go to the bathroom and caught a glimpse of herself in the mirror. Her blue eyes shone with confidence. *I'm ready for this tall Texan,* she told the excited woman who grinned back at her. *Surely, God will heal him. He'll be with me before I know it.* She winked, laughing just as delightedly as the woman in the mirror.

Just before Ellis was to leave for Fayette County with Beth, he bought a round trip airplane ticket to Santa Bella. He was coming to see her in October, a year and a month to the day they had begun their correspondence with the chicken casserole recipe.

Carol was out of her mind with happiness when he sent her a copy of the ticket, and she called him. "Oh, El, you really *are* coming to see me?"

"Yes, ma'am," he said, glee dancing in his voice. "I'll be there soon."

"You know the Santa Bella Symphony opens its season in October."

"Ah, yes, I do. I hoped we would go to a concert together; I would hold your hand while we listen to beautiful music." She could hear his breathing. "You must know," he said, gravely, "that you are the music, my dear."

"Oh, Ellis. . ." His words flowed through her, generating a glow of heat so intense she swore she could feel his warm body cradling her. She sighed happily. "I'll buy a pair of tickets as soon as we get off the phone. I'm really excited. To think, you will be sitting beside me. We'll be hearing classical melodies we love at the same moment in time!" *No more sitting alone envying the loving couples around her.*

"And I'll lean over and give you a quick little kiss on the neck."

She felt the heat rising again. "Oh, El, you can't do that in public!"

He laughed. "Not to worry, my dear. I'll not embarrass you in public, though you can never count on me to be entirely predictable. Not where you are concerned."

"You are a rascal," she said, now delighting in the electric charges his words continued to light in her body. "Just get here, soon, won't you?"

"You can count on that," he said.

Carol realized how lucky she was to attract a man totally enamored of her, yet, as far as she could see, appreciative of her as she was, without wanting to change anything about her. A flood of gratitude swept over her. "Oh, El, you are such a gentle, sweet, and kind person. I adore you."

He was stunned by her words. "You take my breath away, you know."

She laughed heartily. "Yes, I know. I don't do it deliberately; I just feel that, with you, I can say what's in my heart. I don't have to hide my feelings or be afraid of hurting yours, or of being rejected. I have no fears with you."

"Ah, Honey, I'm thrilled. Listen to me. I want you to know this: you are the woman I love; you are safe with me."

"I'm so glad you love me, El, and that you know how very much I love you. What freedom to love without expectations. What joy!"

"We're free at last, Lord God Almighty, free at last!" Ellis rejoiced. Her words fed his soul and washed away his pent-up resentment toward Joanne. The years he had spent without close, intimate love and caring from another human being had hardened him to some degree, though, Lord knows, he had tried to substitute country air and a companion for what was lost through Joanne's illnesses. None of that loss mattered now. He simply cared for the life he was living now. He was loved, thank God; he was loved.

"Amen," Carol said, so softly that Ellis wondered whether she was reading his thoughts. Her tone brightened. "So now we can stop the serious stuff and let it rest for a while."

He agreed. "I got tired earlier and could not understand why. I seem to be better now," he said with a grin she, of course, could not see, but sensed. "Maybe I needed to eat?" He felt he could give her latitude to be more involved with the details of his life.

"I think you are on to something, particularly with your history of hypoglycemia." She quickly took to nurturing him. "What *did* you eat today?"

"It could well be low blood sugar, though it hasn't shown up in recent lab work," El commented before answering her question. "I had lots of potato salad, cottage cheese, fruit salad, toast, and chocolate chip cookies"

"Sounds good," she said. "I would have added a little chicken salad for more protein for those muscles that you are building, but you did well, my love."

"Thank you." He was buoyed by her concern, her willingness to give him the advice a loving helpmate would. "The spirit is more than willing, but the flesh is often weak."

"I wish I were there to whisper all this in your ear," Carol teased.

"Now that event is something that *I* wish with all my heart," he said, tears stinging his eyes.

"My sweet darling," she said, trying on words that matched her feelings. "Who knows what God has in store for us? I just believe it is something very good."

"That is what I think too," he said.

223

"Wonderful! Remember, I will be there for you, one way or another. You will not waste away with me in your life." She was worried about his health, his tiredness. She had heard him cough too often lately.

"Thank you, love," he said simply.

They chatted then about what was happening in their lives. Carol was getting more invitations to speak about aging and to sell her book. "All this self-promotion is so much work!" she complained.

"Yes, it is, Honey, but you are helping a lot of people."

"I hope so," she said.

He then told her that he was leaving for the trailer in a week.

"Beth going with you again?"

"Yes. She needs the change. Her children are still living with her."

"Well, I'm glad she is going. I don't think it's a good idea for you to be alone out there." How easy it was now to accept Beth's presence in his life.

"Neither do I." He coughed then, and when he had trouble stopping, he asked if she'd mind if they ended their phone conversation.

"Of course not, Darling," she said, quickly. "Take care of yourself. I'll see you later. I love you."

"Love you too," he said, trying to clear his throat.

Carol held the phone close to her heart while she said a silent prayer, consisting of two words—words that Ellis himself often used: *Please, God.*

Chapter Twenty-Five

The nagging cough was getting Ellis down. As he loaded his truck for the trip to the trailer, he noticed he was short of breath and had to rest frequently. He thought of canceling the trip, but all the plans were in place—in fact, Beth expected him to pick her up within an hour. He told himself things would be fine. Beth could drive most of the way.

His cell phone rang.

"Ellis?" The number was familiar, but the voice wasn't.

"Beth?"

"No, this is Lauren. My mother needs your help."

"Lauren, what's going on?" Ellis was suddenly anxious. It was unusual for Lauren to call him, especially on her mother's cell phone.

"It's Mom. She fell in the driveway. I'm afraid it's bad. Her leg is twisted under her."

"Good God, is she still in the driveway?"

"Yes. I didn't know what to do."

"Call 911."

"I did. They're not here. I knew you were on your way, but I just wasn't sure where we'd be when you showed up."

"What happened?"

"Oh, I hate to tell you this, El. She was drinking while she was packing to go with you."

"And?"

"She and I got into an argument. I went to my house last night, thinking Craig was working, to get more clothes and . . ." she paused. "Well, he was there, and he was pissed at me for not being at home with him. I smart-mouthed him. I knew better, but I'm tired of him wanting me to be there cooking and cleaning for him while he screws around with other women. I guess he thought I didn't know. . . "Her voice dropped into a half-sob whisper. Ellis thought of the countless tales he'd endured of this troubled and apparently irresoluble relationship. He was impatient to hear about Beth.

"Lauren, get to the point, please."

"Craig pulled out his gun and pistol-whipped me."

Her words stunned him. "Oh, my God, Lauren!"

"I know. I know." She was near tears, frustrated with the enormity of what had happened to her. "I have some bad bruises, one on my face. I scrambled to my feet and ran for my life. Once in the car, I headed straight for Mom. Craig actually fired a shot at me, trying to hit a tire, I think. It missed. When Mom saw me, she went into a rage against Craig. Said she was going to call the police on him." Lauren's voice broke. She caught her breath. "Oh, God, El, I couldn't let her do that. No telling what Craig would do if I ever turned him in."

"But . . ." Ellis was astounded. What could he say to that insane reasoning? "Tell me, Lauren, what in God's name happened that Beth fell on the driveway?"

"She stumbled, running after me."

"Running after you?" He was incredulous. El couldn't imagine Beth running anywhere unless—he paused, remembering the instance of alcohol-fueled passion in the trailer.

"Yes. I pulled her phone out of the wall and grabbed her cell phone so she couldn't call." Lauren's shame spilled over in her speech. She cried: "I know. I know. Don't scold me, please." She took a deep breath and continued her story. "I headed for my car; I was just going to drive away and come back after you two left for the country, but she ran after me. Because of the drinking, she wasn't too steady on her feet. I got to the car and was about to open the door when I heard her crash down behind me. She screamed and so did I."

"Oh, Lauren, have you done anything for her other than call 911?"

"Yeah. I had a pillow in the car. I put it under her head. Oh, El, it looks bad!"

"Can she talk?"

"Yes."

"Give the phone to her." Lauren handed her mother the phone. Beth's voice was tortured when she responded to El's, "Oh, Beth, what happened to you?"

"El. . . El?" Beth's voice was shaky, barely audible, her breathing terrified gasps. He wasn't sure she knew where she was until anger spurted out: "That son of a bitch!" Now, her voice was thick with fury, pain, and booze. Eerily, El could separate the resonances. "He hurt her bad. This . . . Ooh, ooh," she groaned as pain hit her. Determined, she gulped and, finding the breath she wanted, declared firmly, "This time I won't stand for it!"

"Beth, you're injured!" Ellis stomped one foot, upped his volume and, in clipped tones, demanded, "Listen to me, now."

Beth groaned heavily again, but still found energy to spit out, "That bastard. I'll kill him. I swear I'll kill him."

"Slow down, my dear. Take a deep breath."

"I can't. It hurts too much."

"Forget Craig. Forget Lauren. You need to concentrate on yourself right now. Hush, now." Ellis lowered his voice to soft and soothing. "Try to relax a little. Wait for the ambulance."

"Can you come, Ellis? I need you." Beth strained to get out the words.

"I'll be there. You just do what the doctors tell you. Give the phone back to Lauren, please." He could hear the ambulance sirens in the background.

"Yes?" Lauren said.

"Call me as soon as you know which hospital she's in. I'm on my way."

"Okay. They're here now. I've got to go."

Ellis exhaled wearily. He'd have to camp out at Beth's now, at least until it was decided what to do with her. He was angry, mostly at Lauren for causing Beth's fall, but also at Beth for drinking so early in the day—it was barely ten in the morning—and then getting involved again with her daughter's endless marital dramas. Lauren was never going to leave Craig permanently, not as long as she had her mother to run to. And Beth was always going to be there for her daughter, no matter the cost. The business with the gun was horrifying; Craig's abuse of Lauren was escalating. He couldn't understand her reluctance to have her husband arrested, though he suspected she was both afraid of him and afraid that she would lose her economic security if Craig went to jail and lost his job. Despite her education, she seemed incapable of taking care of herself. Had Beth crippled both her children by continually rescuing them from their plights? And what about himself? Did he enable all of them by being there so often to pick up the pieces?

He finished loading the truck and went upstairs to say goodbye to Joanne, forgetting for a moment that she had gone to her hair appointment. He wrote a note, saying he'd call her later in the day. Sinking into his recliner, he closed his eyes and tried to slow his breathing. He wasn't coughing, which he took as a good sign, but he wasn't at all happy. He really looked forward to going to the country, and now he was stuck in Forest Cove, not as badly polluted as Houston, but still not fresh country air.

He reached for his cell and dialed Carol.

"Oh, hey!" she responded, cheerily. "Aren't you on the road?"

"No, unfortunately, Love, I'm still here in Houston. Beth fell in her driveway this morning and injured her leg. They are taking her to the hospital now."

"Oh, I'm sorry." Carol said, pulling her feet off the couch and sitting up. "How awful! That sure puts a kink in your trip."

"Yep. I need to go see what damage's been done to Beth. I wanted to let you know."

"Well, maybe she's not too badly injured, and you can take the trip anyway."

"Somehow I doubt that. I talked to her before the ambulance came, and she was in a lot of pain."

"How about you, Love? Are you okay?" Carol asked, leaning back into the couch once more.

"Oh, I guess so," he answered. Carol knew he wasn't telling her the whole story.

"Want to tell me about it?" she asked gently. She held the phone as if holding his hand.

He smiled. It always made him feel better to talk to Carol. She had a way of opening him up, letting him drain the toxicity Beth and her family brought to him.

"Well, Honey, it seems that Lauren got beat up again by her husband."

"Oh, no, is she hurt?"

"I don't know. He pistol-whipped her. She said she has bruises."

"That's terrible. She should call the police. This domestic dispute is going in a direction that is bound to be tragic, sooner or later."

"I know," Ellis agreed. "Beth wanted to call the police, but Lauren wouldn't hear of it. They argued. Lauren yanked the landline out of the wall and ran off with her mother's cell. That's why Beth fell. She was running after her."

"God, that's crazy. Why would Beth do such a thing?"

"I don't know. Lauren said her mother was drinking. I guess Beth just went out of her head when she saw her daughter banged up again."

"Sweetheart?" Carol was about to say something he knew he wanted to hear, but knew he couldn't bring himself to do. "I'm afraid for your safety. Don't get mixed up in this."

"Believe me, my darling, I don't want to. I just can't completely abandon Beth. Let me go see what's happened to her. I'll give you a call from her place."

"You'll be staying there?"

"I think so, at least until something is decided." He didn't know what would need to be decided, but knew that these women, irrational as they were for the moment, needed help.

"Okay," she said, reluctantly. She could hardly speak. Her fear of El caught in the middle of a dispute with a gun in the mix nearly paralyzed her. "Please," she begged, uncertain of the effect her pleas would have, "take good care of yourself. Remember I'm here for you, my treasure. I love you." Her obvious concern touched him.

"I love you too," he said, the distance between them tearing at his heart. He longed to hold her in his arms. "Oh God, I really do love you. You are such a help to me."

Carol, reassured, laughed softly. "As it should be, my love. Stay safe."

"I will. Be back soon." He hung up.

When he got to the emergency room of the Kingwood Medical Center, Beth was out having a CAT scan of her leg. She had fractured her shinbone. He was surprised to find Lauren in an examination room. She talked rapidly, nervously. "Mother told them the whole story, including Craig hitting me with the pistol." They insisted on examining me too. X-rays and ultrasound showed nothing broken, but they are worried that I might have some internal bleeding and want to keep me under observation for a day or two. I'm waiting for a bed."

"Well, maybe your mother saved your life by falling and getting you here." El was looking for a way to bring the women together.

"Possibly," Lauren said. "Only I wish she hadn't told them about the gun. Now, the hospital is making a report to the police, and if they go after Craig, I don't know what will happen." Her eyes were wide with fear.

"They'll arrest him and put him in jail; that's what will happen, dear." El tried to sound reassuring. But Lauren started to cry. "I'm really afraid, El."

"Don't be, Lauren," El said, sitting down beside her bed and taking her hand. "This may be the best thing to happen for both of you. He needs treatment, and you need support. The state will step in now and help out."

"But I'm so ashamed." Tears flooded her face. Ellis let her cry, petting her hand, and making soft clucking sounds of sympathetic understanding. When her sobs subsided, he told her, "Don't worry. You'll get through this. Just relax now, and get well."

He stayed with her until Beth came in from her tests. The doctors found the fracture stable, no surgery needed. It was decided to put her in a cast because of her age and admit her for observation. Her blood alcohol, at 0.135, indicated she had drunk the equivalent of five cans of beer. Ellis was shocked, but said nothing as they prepared her cast.

By the time he left the hospital, he was bushed. He decided to go to his own bed and come back to check on the women the next day. Once home, he realized he hadn't eaten at all that day and felt woozy. Joanne met him in the living room and asked if they were going out to eat. She didn't question his coming home after leaving her the note that he was on his way to the trailer.

"No, I'm tired, Joanne." He told her of Beth's accident, leaving out the details of the abuse against Lauren and the struggle for the phone, which caused Beth's fall. Joanne seemed uninterested. She stared at him blankly. He shook his head slowly, pressing his lips together. "So I'm not going to the country. I have to go back to the hospital tomorrow."

She ignored most of what he said and pleaded in a childlike voice, "But can we go to Jake's tonight?"

"Would you mind going out and bringing me back some soup?" he asked. He didn't like sending her out on her own, particularly since he had forbidden her to drive after the accident, but, tonight, he felt he couldn't take another step.

"Okay," she said. She picked up her coat and found her car keys. It amazed him that she knew where he had hidden them after the Lexus was repaired. Without another word, she left him there. He settled into his chair and quickly fell asleep. When he awoke, there was a bowl of soup on the kitchen table, waiting for him.

The next day, after calling Carol and filling her in on the details of his change in plans, Ellis headed back to the hospital. His truck was still packed with supplies for the trip to the country. Again, he noted how tired he was. He was coughing more frequently, and now his head hurt.

He stopped at Lauren's room first. She was in a three-bed ward with two older women.

"The police came," she told him.

"And did you tell them what happened."

"Yes." Ellis could see the fear in Lauren's eyes. He reached for her hand and held it.

"You did the right thing, Lauren," he said softly. "Craig had to be stopped before things got worse. Now, he'll get some help, and you and he can get on with your lives."

"I didn't do this for him, El. I did it because of Mom." Lauren began to cry and El tightened his grip on her hand. She sniffed back her tears. "It's my fault she's hurt. I didn't mean for that to happen."

"Lauren, hear me now. This is neither your fault, nor Beth's. You both went a little nuts over a situation that, up to now, you found impossible to handle." A cough cut through the last word, becoming a frightful spasm of labored noise. Lauren could hear the wheezing as El struggled to clear congestion in his chest. The spasm continued mercilessly; El's face reddened with the effort to regain control and catch his breath.

Alarmed, Lauren reached to locate the call buzzer. "Let me get you some help, El," she said.

Ellis held up his open hand and shook his head. Lauren paused, her hand on the buzzer. El finally spit mucous into his handkerchief and told her, "I'll be okay," though he wasn't at all sure he would. "You are the one in the hospital," he reminded her. "Are you okay?"

"Yes, I think so. They didn't find any internal injuries, just the extensive bruising. They said there were old scars, though: bones with small fractures now healed." She looked away, embarrassed. Pulling herself together, she met El's gaze and said, "I'm going to do whatever it takes to get my life back. I've had more than enough."

"Good girl." Ellis raised a thumb in salute. They talked a bit about finding help for her and Beth after they got out of the hospital. Then Ellis left to visit with Beth who looked tired, old. "How are you feeling today?" he asked. She pulled the covers back to show him her leg cast. "Hmm. That doesn't look bad at all," he said.

"No, not bad," she granted. "Thank God, it was a clean break. I didn't sleep much last night."

"Pain?"

"No, the pills they gave me took care of that." Beth closed her eyes and bit her lip. When she opened her eyes, she looked directly at him. "I really messed up this time, El." He didn't say anything, only kept looking at her, waiting for her to speak again. She did, sighing heavily. "You told me I was enabling my kids. I didn't believe you, but now I do. Lauren could be dead, and it is my fault for interfering with her life."

"No, Beth," he began, but she shook her head.

"Let me finish, please. This is hard enough." She stopped for a while, contemplating what to say next and settled for an explanation. "Lauren's always been contrary. I'd say 'black,' and she'd say 'white.' If I hadn't been so stubborn and interfering, she wouldn't have wanted to prove me wrong by going back to him so many times."

"You don't know that," he said.

"Oh, yes, I do." Beth insisted. "We need help, El. This situation is beyond us."

"Lauren told me that a social worker is coming to help her make a plan."

"Good." Beth's eyes lit up briefly. "But I'm not happy with myself, El." She lowered her eyes and took time to suck in air before speaking again. "I know you think I stopped drinking. I even thought that I had stopped after we had that stupid episode when I tried to force myself on you."

Ellis said nothing. He intended to comfort Beth, but suddenly he had no energy for speech or anything else; he felt that he was going to pass out.

Beth wasn't looking at him. The confession was harder than she thought it would be. She inhaled and then blew out a long breath. "I need help, El," she said and then repeated adamantly, "I need help. I can't stop drinking."

Ellis had waited so long for this confession. He wanted to share with her his own struggle with alcohol and his salvation in finding AA. He wanted her to get well as he had gotten well. He wanted to be glad for her and help her find sobriety and peace. He wanted so much, but instead, he passed out, sliding slowly down the side of her bed and sinking to the floor.

It was Beth who pressed the nurse's call button while shouting for help.

Chapter Twenty-Six

*E*l spent the night in the hospital, wobbled home the next day, and curled up in his recliner like a whipped puppy. Carol and he grieved October; his illness forced cancelation of the trip to Santa Bella. They tolerated Thanksgiving and Christmas and made a nod to New Years without him moving out of his condo.

"I don't know what to do at this point. I'm really discouraged," Carol told the women in her group.

"Don't say that, Honey," Jennifer coaxed. "You've been in love with this guy for so long. Don't give up now."

"I'm still in love with him," Carol stammered, awed by the strength of her feelings, "and he's still in love with me, but he just isn't getting any better." The sparkle in Carol's blue eyes dimmed with sadness and worry. "When he collapsed in the hospital last August, they kept him overnight because of a flare-up in his chronic bronchitis. More antibiotics and steroids were prescribed, as if he needed to add to the pharmacy he's been taking this whole time trying to ward off any return of that ridiculous lung infection."

"Yes," Stella interjected. "You said he got better after that collapse, but wouldn't leave his condo, even after being homebound for five months. That's a long time. Didn't he send his impaired wife out foraging for food for them both?"

"That sounds awful, when you put it that way." Carol winced, sensitive to any mention of Joanne, yet she was resigned to the reality of the situation. "Yes, he relies on her. Alzheimer's or not, it appears good for her to help him for a change. Even though she has to drive the car."

"Scary." Sophie remarked.

"I agree," Carol said, "but I have no control over that situation. He is so depressed—sick and depressed. Taking care of Joanne was one thing, but being knocked off his feet with yet another attack on his lungs must have made life seem impossible. He won't fully admit his depression to me, but I know how serious it is. If he'd only get in that pickup truck he so dearly loves, I believe there's a chance for him to recover. That truck is the only lever I have to pry him from his malaise." Carol's shoulders slumped. "He says he's trying to get well, but I'm not sure."

"Give it time, Honey," Dana said. "You know how men are. If they can't fix something, they either flare up in anger or sit back and brood. I think your man is in the brooding stage right now."

"Really?"

"Yep. He had to cancel that trip to come see you in October. It must have taken the wind right out of his sails. I wouldn't be surprised if he is second-guessing himself now, wondering whether he will be man enough to satisfy you."

Carol laughed uneasily. "Man enough? Good grief. I wonder whether I'll be *woman enough* to satisfy him! I know about erectile dysfunction in men. I'm just not sure about my own ability to have sex at this late stage in life. What do men and women do in bed at our ages?"

"Oh, come off it, Carol," Jennifer teased, an unholy smile on her face. "You're creative and lively. You know you've had a satisfactory relationship with a certain—shall I say it?— *objet de plaisir* we women sometimes use. I think I heard you say you bought one after we saw the movie *Hysteria* and that you were in training for when El gets here."

Carol blushed. "Sometimes I say too much, I see." Everyone burst out laughing. They well remembered thrilling currents coursing through their own bodies watching the drama of the vibrator's invention and the movie's sweet love story. "Oh, well," Carol said, wiping her eyes with her handkerchief. She sat up straight. "Seriously, you think it might be that he *is* worried about not being able to perform? Maybe that's why he's not talking specifics anymore about coming to see me."

"I wouldn't be surprised," Dana said. "Be a little patient."

"Don't give up on him," Sophie spoke up, surprising Carol. Her not-so-subtle cautions about the relationship in the past had made Carol uneasy. She wanted Sophie on her side and, now, surprisingly, she was actually giving encouragement. "I have to say I envy you," Sophie continued. "You and El have been so certain of one another, so happy. Not many people have what you do."

"Thanks, Sophie. No, I won't give up on him. If there is anything I have learned in this past year and a half, it's been patience. It was terribly hard on us both when he had to cancel that airplane ticket. I think he is still mourning that loss and maybe giving up. I try to put disappointment behind me and be optimistic about the future. I wanted El to do so as well, but I think he fears being hopeful and won't tell me about it."

Carol brought up the subject in the next telephone conversation with El. "Our relationship needs a little tender love and care," she began.

"Always does," El agreed, and then quickly added, "as all relationships do." Carol grimaced at the distancing. She wanted openness, but she wasn't getting it. "El, your heart, my love, not your head."

Her attempt may have been too subtle. It didn't work. "Yes, I know," he said mildly. She wanted more.

"Are you holding back for fear of a weak body?" she asked tentatively.

"I'm not aware of holding back."

"Oh?" *How could he not know that? Had she imagined the man who up to now had spoken so freely and had been an open book with her?* "I sense that you aren't quite with me these days. I know you have a lot on your mind, considering what is going on with your health, but I'm feeling a little disconnected."

"I am so sorry," he said. She felt his sincerity and something else. *What was it? Regret? Remorse?* "If it seems I'm preoccupied at times, it is because I am." Ellis had always said he would be honest with Carol, but now he circled the point, fudged a bit, convincing himself it was sufficient to venture toward, rather than wade in with the whole truth. He couldn't stand the thought of losing her. After the disappointment of having to cancel travel to see her because he was sick once again, he indeed was reluctant to engage in any future planning, worried that he'd never be well enough to be of any use to her. He *was* weak. *God, he did not want to tell her that!* The bout with the chronic bronchitis hit hard this time, leaving him with fluid in his lungs that the doctors drained and analyzed. Fortunately, no cancer cells. He sighed. "I have little, if any, defense of these times except to say that I am the same person you have always known. Nothing has changed."

"That may be," she argued, "but there *is* a change." Carol didn't want to lay it all on him. "We are both caught up in some kind of burden, maybe concern for one another. I think we have lost some of our gratitude."

He felt stretched by her words. He wasn't interested in gratitude today. In fact, he was angry: raging at being sick; boiling over with being denied what he most desired—access to the greatest love he had ever felt. His resentment was deep and wide. Triggered long ago by the loss of intimacy so early in his marriage, it flamed old feelings of cold rejection, burned fiercely at humiliating memories in seeking other women for more in life than he was getting, and flickered into a numb acceptance of a passionless companionship with Beth. Then, by the grace of God, came the miracle of Carol and her love; only, so far, he couldn't physically touch her. That denial was maddening. She was right. He had crawled away in shame. *Carol, ah sweet Carol.* He couldn't stand to think he'd never meet her—that he'd turn into a very old, sick man in a cruel, ironic crescendo to his miserably failed life.

It was difficult to soften his tone, but he tried. "Carol, I understand that I am blessed, but know that I have only so much emotional energy to give to myself and others. When that is gone, I have to recharge. If you feel that I might not be grateful enough right now, then I'd like to correct that idea."

She interrupted. "It's just that I miss our talks."

"Oh! I see," he said, his tone crisp and biting. "Well, each of has been very busy with the nitty-gritty of life, and frankly, I view that as a hindrance."

Ouch. As usual, Carol had been busy with all the activities of *her* life, and though she found time to call him most days, the calls were brief and full of chatter about her own doings. "I'm lost for words now," she told him, stinging a little because of his scolding. *Why is he so bitter and removed? What have I done to deserve this?*

He backed off. "The words will come. Don't get overly concerned with all this."

All what? she thought, but didn't ask him. She felt put off, even put down. Why would he tell her not to be overly concerned when her concern was a major component of their relationship? Of course, she was concerned. His holding pattern and no-talk zone made her edgy. Had he stayed in a dead marriage because he and his wife wouldn't talk about it? What did this attitude bode for her chances with him? Should she end this now or wait and see?

"We need to relax," he continued, "and do the best we can in the circumstances we find ourselves."

Carol thought for a moment. *He was the best thing that had ever happened to her. She needed to follow his advice.* "Okay," she agreed. Hoping to throw him a lifeline for his ungracious behavior, she gave him feedback. "I hear you saying back off for a while until you can get yourself into a more comfortable state of health. Am I correct?"

"Not really," he countered, surprising her. "What I am saying is we connect when we can and do the best we can with the restrictions we have just now. If we wait until I recover, we will drift apart, and neither of us wants that."

Carol felt a welcome rush of relief. "Yes, that is my fear," she acknowledged.

"I don't wish to make something hard out of this," he said.

"You aren't," she reassured him. "Whatever the situation is, it simply is." She tried to engage his interest by admitting, "I just don't feel as close to you as I want to feel. Perhaps it's not our fault. Maybe the distance between us becomes a problem when one of us is caught up in dealing with whatever life brings,"

He was silent. Her heart quivered, but she was determined to finish. "I know I'm not saying things very well. I'm just missing our usual energy and loving ways."

This time, Ellis's tone was soft, though still cautious. "I'm sorry. Sometimes, I get a little thick between the ears. I think it might be good for both of us if you would just tell me what your needs are right now, and I will listen and respond as best I can. At times I think that your needs may be more intense than mine are."

"No, I don't think my needs are more intense than yours," she protested. "It is just that since your flare-up with the bronchitis, we have virtually stopped playing bridge together. We've stopped the barrage of emails we used to enjoy. We make shorter phone calls, and can't seem to find the joy we used to experience in them. I'm not criticizing. I'm telling you that I miss that special connection we had when we were caught up in one another. It saddens me that we are not resurrecting that experience at a time when we both obviously need it."

"Ah, I see," he said flatly. "I have every confidence that our special connection is still there. My life is very complicated. I hope you can understand that. Perhaps the intensity is more than I need right now, and with my wife in the mix, I don't want any more drama in my life."

Drama? What did he mean by drama? She had never thought of herself as a woman who makes a theatrical production out of life's minor details. In fact, her friends saw her as easygoing, reasonable, and sensitive: a problem solver, not a problem maker. She felt as if he were shutting her down. *What's going on? What's the problem? His wife?* Carol quickly asked, "Is there something you haven't told me about your wife?"

"No, nothing at all," he said just as quickly, but then added in a strained tone,

"except that I find it more difficult to cope with her now. It saps my energy."

His spontaneous admission resonated with Carol. "I'm truly sorry, my dear," she said, her heart going out to him. She remembered the helpless frustration she felt in dealing with dementia in her friends and was flooded with compassion, but kept her words neutral. "I had hoped I'd be someone you could lean on whenever you needed to, but of course, I can't even begin to imagine how hard it is to cope with her illnesses, and, especially, when you're not in top shape yourself."

She heard Ellis heave a big sigh. He, too, understood and cared. "Listen carefully, please," he pleaded. "You have given so freely of yourself. I feel your love and support, so rest easy on that count. There is work to be done that I must do alone."

"We'll talk more about this later," Carol said, sensing he had had enough of her probing for today; yet, she was determined to leave him with the notion that he didn't have to suffer in silence. "Though there is work for you to do, you can share your struggles and feelings with me. That's what it's all about. I'm no china doll—you know that! I'm a real caring person; I want to be that for you, so never shut me out, please."

"I have not," he said firmly, and then dismissed her. "Okay. I'm going to eat some lunch now."

"Bye, Love," she said.

"Bye." No *love*, no *sweetheart*, no *darling*, no words of endearment from him in his so abrupt sign-off. In fact, no terms of endearment from him and few from her during the entire conversation! Carol swallowed the hurt she felt and switched her mind into giving herself a good professional talking-to. *Okay, gal, you just have to trust that he is not second guessing the relationship, but is truly wrestling with something in his life that he hasn't felt free to share yet.*

Feeling vulnerable, she fell to her knees. "God, take over this problem please. I can't solve it. I don't even understand it."

El called the next day. "Sweetheart, are you all right?" he asked.

"Not really," she said. She had been able to sleep that night, but woke thinking gloomy thoughts about him. "How are you?"

"I'm miserable," he said. "I thought about what you said yesterday, and I couldn't sleep. I've hurt you, haven't I?"

Carol caught El's change from shutdown to apologetic. She didn't know what to say, but heard herself murmur "yes," in a small voice.

Ellis was near tears. "Oh, oh, oh," he moaned. "I'm so very sorry."

Hard-earned wisdom taught her to let her pain go to find what she truly valued. "My dear El," she said, using the phrase to soothe a path between them. "Will you please tell me what is going on with you?"

His silence was palpable. She felt she could hear his pulse drumming anxiously. She strained to speak gently, "You know I am here for you. You can tell me anything. Just be honest with me, El. Whatever it is, I'll survive, and I'll still love you. I know I will."

"I'm so damned angry." The words came out in a rush.

"At me?" Carol wanted to know.

"Oh, no, Love, no, no, no, no, no. I am never angry with you. I'm just up to my gizzard in frustration. I've been yelling at Joanne. That's not me. I don't yell."

"It's understandable. I'm sure *I* couldn't live with someone who is there, but really isn't. When Evelyn was going into dementia, it was so hard to be around her, to be deliberately kind and caring. I don't know how you do it."

"It's not just Joanne," El admitted at last. "When I was feeling better, I could handle her with some degree of kindness because that's how I prefer to be—kind. Yelling at her is . . ." He paused, searching for a word. Not finding one, he confessed to Carol, "I'm disappointed in myself. That's one thing, Carol, but with us, I. . ." An agonized pause engulfed him. "I can't stand the thought of never seeing you. Turning in that ticket last October nearly tore my heart out."

"Shh. Shh," Carol soothed. "You'll see me, my dear. Don't lose hope."

"This being sick shit is so old!" Ellis was on a roll now. "I'm so tired of not being able to do what I want to do. I'm tired of being cooped up with her in this condo. I'm tired of going to doctors and getting nowhere."

"Good," Carol said. "Let it out. Let it all out. I'm glad you're angry. You have plenty to be angry about."

Ellis let out a long-held breath. "I want so much to bring you a healthy, hearty man, but here I am thirty pounds underweight and feeling like I'm never going to be able to be much use to you. I will *not* bring you a sick man to tend to." She imagined him pounding his fist on a counter.

"Hush," she said. "Just come here, my dear one. I love you just the way you are, and I'll love you no matter whom you bring me. I told you before I'd take care of you. I mean that."

"Oh, no, you've been through that with Mario. I won't put you through it again."

"You don't get to decide that, my dear," Carol said, emphatically, claiming her usual independence. "We'll cross that bridge when and *if* we come to it. What I want you to do, now, is to concentrate on getting better. Stop feeling that you can't recover, or you never will recover. You want to see me? Then fight for yourself, and I'll fight with you. Forget the October ticket. We'll work on a new date."

"God, lady, I love you so," Ellis said.

"Feeling better?" Carol asked.

"Yes. Talking to you always makes me feel better."

"You should try it more often." Her own humor lightened her heart.

"I'm thinking, Carol, that I want to be more that I am just now for you. I want to be a whole man. I've been thinking about going into therapy." Ellis spoke with strength now.

"Physical therapy?"

"No, but that's a good idea. I'm thinking that I need to work on my demons and put them at rest. I need to talk to a counselor."

"You have one at the other end of the line," she blurted out, laughing as the remaining tension drained from her. "But you are absolutely right. You can't use me as a psychotherapist. I'm your love, and I'll listen and I'll advise, but I won't give you therapy."

"I know and agree," Ellis chuckled. "I don't want a professional relationship with you, thank you. I want a personal relationship. Very personal, I might add."

"Now, *there's* the Ellis I love," Carol said, happily. "Seriously, the therapist is an excellent idea."

Ellis told her about his deep-seated anger toward Joanne. He confessed that when his wife got ill, her rejection of him and the end of their sex life had nearly done him in. They talked in detail then about his turning to alcohol to relieve the pain, and then to affairs with other women, his long recovery in AA, and his eventual return to a dissatisfying home life, made tolerable by frequent trips to the trailer with Beth.

"I've got my work cut out for me, "he declared." I'll call the doctor tomorrow for a referral to a therapist. Now, as for being cooped up here, I am not steady on my feet so I'm reluctant to go out. I hang onto the walls when I walk in here."

"Oh, El. You have a cane?"

"Several."

"Well, use one of them."

"Okay. Okay. That is a good idea."

"And when you call the doctor, you might ask about some physical therapy as well. You haven't been active in so long, you need to work on getting your strength back."

"I will."

Both of them felt the change. Ellis got profound release with his decision to be completely honest. Carol felt relief that problems, now revealed, could be solved together. They were a couple now, acting in one another's interest, though both experienced an agonizing longing to actually be in one another's arms.

"Our time will come, my darling," Carol sighed.

And, Ellis, sighing too, said simply, "Yes."

Chapter Twenty-Seven

"I hope you haven't tired of waiting, my love," she typed in an Instant Message to El. She knew he'd be waiting at his computer; he wanted to be available to her as much as possible.

"Not at all," he typed.

She had sped to the supermarket and back, wolfing lunch as she put away the groceries. She too wanted every moment possible with him. "I am home and well-fed," she wrote.

"And I am sitting here in my robe," he typed, "showered and smelling like lilac blossoms on a fence in South Georgia. "Take me, I'm yours!" he teased.

"Okay. Come right over," she answered, coyly.

"Aaah!" The intensity of his feelings was unmistakable. At this point in their relationship they could read one another's imaginations.

She moaned, "And so we rest in that thought."

He conceded, knowing that the touch they both wanted so much couldn't travel the Internet. "Yes, we'll rest the thought. Do you want to play?"

"Of course, I want to play." She knew what he meant, but couldn't resist the urge to flirt some more. "But, oh!" she toyed with him, "You mean *bridge*."

"Either or, my dear." She pictured him batting his eyes in a bug-eyed Groucho Marx leer, middle finger rapidly tapping his huge cigar.

"Oh, no! You have made things so hard for me," she wrote, all the while laughing delightedly on her side of the Internet. Was she Pauline in peril or Camille with a fending hand to the forehead? "Let's see, hmm. Bridge or . . . ?" She let the text slide smoothly into another frame. "Okay. I . . . Choose . . . You."

"Oooh whee!" He came to an Internet climax.

"Rascal!" she scolded.

"Caught again," he typed. "By the way, has anyone told you today?"

"Told me what?"

"I love you, Carol." The words always brought overwhelming warmth, sliding down her body, fueling sparkle in her eyes, and igniting arousal in the smile on her lips. The "ooh" that came from her mouth was pure pleasure. If words could do this to her, what would his loving touch do? Her imagination caught fire; she felt his fingers, his lips exploring her body.

She gave him a flustered reply. "How in the world do you expect me to play bridge, now?"

"Give it your best shot, dear," he teased.

"But I've lost all control."

Another "oooh whee" from him.

"Rascal!" she typed. "Watch out. I'll get even."

"Oh sure," he wrote.

"You mean 'yeah, yeah, yeah,' don't you?"

"Maybe."

She turned the subject back to bridge. "You ready?"

"Well, I have on my robe and not much else." It was his turn to tease.

"Whew!" She blushed, though he couldn't see her. Her fingers moved rapidly on the keys. "Whatever you're doing—wearing—not wearing, it's working!" She felt currents of desire making gooseflesh of her skin. "It's hot in here," she wrote. "Very hot. Oh, God," she wrote, suddenly shy, "I'm saying so many things here."

"Are you?" She wondered if he were this adept at lovemaking. In the back of her mind, one of his early emails reminded her he was a "hands on" kind of man.

"Stop it!" she wrote.

"No," he wrote back. She startled at his daring. She knew then, absolutely *knew* he would be more than a match for her own appetite, and longed to really feel his hands on her.

"We'll get booted, you know," she warned.

He went along with her, though their Instant Messages wouldn't show up in the chat of the bridge game room. Besides, there were no others there, unless one counted the robots that played as opponents.

"Alas," he typed. "Had we best behave?"

"Yes," she typed, although she didn't want to. She loved being turned on by him. However, her idea of sex didn't extend to orgasm by Internet, though she had come close to that.

"If you insist," he typed. "It's your turn to bid, you know."

"Oh, yes. I guess you might say I was distracted. Let's play bridge now, Darling." They moved from computerized intercourse and concentrated on the hands dealt to them.

It was September again, two years since they met playing bridge online. Carol and El were entirely comfortable with one another, routinely speaking on the phone about all areas of life. He consulted with her frequently about his medical treatments and therapy sessions, filling the void left by Joanne, who never seemed to comprehend what he was saying. When he spoke about his ailments, Joanne would wander away, a habitual action that irritated him, but not so much now that Carol was in his life.

"She's not hearing you, I suspect," Carol told him. "Her deafness together with her failing brain must complicate communication for her."

"Maybe," he said, "but I don't really care if she hears me anymore. I have you, thank God. You are so good to listen to me. I do pay attention to what you say, you know."

"Well, my advice is there for you to heed or not. Your choice," she said. "I like being your helpmate, for I've noticed, Sweetie, you sure do need one."

"No kidding," he said.

It was Carol who suggested a second opinion about his long-term use of antibiotics. El was advised by the new doctor to "go ahead, discontinue them, and see what happens," but he, to Carol's surprise, was reluctant. His attending physician reiterated that in treating mycobacterium infections, it was protocol for the patient to be on antibiotics for at least a full year after negative lab reports, so El decided to continue taking the antibiotics. At this point, Carol, who had researched the topic, agreed. "You've come this far, El. Stay the course. In the meantime, let's see if we can put some bulk on you. Let's get back some of that weight you lost."

El was bored with eating. Every night, he and Joanne went to Jake's and ate from a menu he had long since memorized. Forays to different restaurants, which Carol suggested, didn't work out. "Why don't you hire a caregiver who cooks?" she proposed.

"And why would I need a caregiver?" he countered, baffled and slightly offended by the idea.

"Not you, Sweetheart. You're fine, except for your skinniness. I'm suggesting a caregiver because if you hire one to come in to cook and freeze meals that can be reheated in the microwave, you can tell Joanne you are hiring this person because you want to gain weight. Basically, you'll kill two birds with one stone," she pointed out. "While she is there, she can also assist Joanne with her medications—sequence them in her pill boxes, or do her laundry for her or maybe stay with her when you are away in the country. Hiring someone now would provide Joanne an opportunity to become accustomed to receiving care from an individual who isn't family, which almost certainly is in her future."

"Hmm," he said, "interesting idea. I *would* like more variety in my meals, and Joanne getting used to a caregiver makes sense."

He hired Belle, an affable widow whose husband had died of Alzheimer's. She knew the disease well. To El's surprise, Joanne took to her right away. She knew how to talk to Joanne with simple language, yet in tones that showed respect and consideration. Belle was also an accomplished cook. After a few weeks of her meals, El gained five pounds.

Surprised, he thanked the caregiver. "I didn't think I'd gain weight while I was still on the meds."

"Honey," Belle replied, "Y'all's been starving yourselves before I got here. There's nothing like Belle's Southern fried chicken to put flesh on skinny bones!" Belle's chicken with mashed potatoes and her special gravy seduced El into second helpings as did her honey baked ham. Both dishes were never frozen, for El wanted them handy for sandwich making.

Carol was busy with yet another project. She had started to research late-life love affairs, thinking she might write another book. The project seemed a natural one to take on, since love had come to Carol late in life. El had once written to her: **I must tell you that love is very powerful and no respecter of age. Love is paradoxical. If we seek deliberately to find it, we will fail. Love finds us.** For them, that principle was unarguable: love to them was a tangible presence with will and purpose. Love had found them; love infused them with grand intentions and made them willing to risk life itself to be together. The question that interested Carol in her research was whether love existed in that particular way for other older couples.

Chatting every day was natural for them now. Besides talking about the happenings in their lives, they loved to reminisce about the beginning of their romance. Laughter was almost always a part of the conversation, for both realized how preposterous some of their ideas were, especially on the topic of late-stage lovemaking. Theirs was no red rose in the teeth, blouse-ripping romance, yet their passion for one another *was* that strong; they were convinced that, given the chance, they could quite adequately satisfy one another.

"I just want to touch you," he growled, bewailing the distance between them.

She shivered. "And I want you to touch me, to hold me, to cuddle with me, to wake up in the mornings with me, so I can reach for you, and . . ."

He interrupted with characteristic humor: "We could lie there and think about it," he said, dryly. She burst out laughing.

"No telling what we'd come up with," he continued.

"Umm," she said, her thighs tingling.

"We *are* creative people, you know," he persisted.

"Oh, God, I wish you were here, so I could hug you and kiss your eyes and nose and lips and explode with my passion for you." She couldn't help herself.

"And I, you," he groaned.

It was time to stop this talk and they knew it. Spontaneously, they laughed: hard, stomach-holding laughter—riotous laughter that distracted them from urgent frustrations of their long-distance loving.

"Seriously," she said, gulping for breath. "Not that we just weren't serious, but, seriously, when are you coming to see me?"

"I don't know," he said, embracing the change in mood. "I've been waiting to be whole once more."

"Didn't we cover this before, my darling?" she argued. "Months ago, it seems. You are better now. What is holding you back?"

"You really want to know?" He took a deep breath. He had hinted at his problem, but hadn't ever come out with it: he feared disappointing her.

"Of course, I want to know," she said.

"What we were just talking about," he said, suddenly sullen. The phone seemed heavy. Had she been too forward, too sensual for him?

She held back her fear. "You mean about having sex?"

"Yes. I haven't had much of an erection for years now. I want to be that man for you, to connect with you meaningfully and strongly, but I'm not sure I can."

"Oh, El, Darling. We've bounced around this subject enough." Her voice was firm and reassuring. "Do you not know I've thought about this already?" She paused, so he could feel the effect of her words. "I'm not expecting caveman virility, my love. I love you. Yes, *you*, just the way you are. There are lots of ways to make love. I know you will satisfy me sexually, my love. You've already told me that."

"Yes, I will," he avowed.

"And I will love you back and give you all the pleasure I can. I am totally yours. I've told you that over and over."

"Yes, you have." He thought of the many times she had signed her emails as "Your Carol."

"I will touch you, caress your body, kiss your lips, and go as far as you want to go or need for me to go, but, mostly, I will respect your needs even if we have to stop in the middle of it all for you to catch your breath," she finished.

"Thank you, Sweetheart," he said. "You don't know how relieved I am."

They shifted into ordinary conversation then. Beth was doing well, having graduated from an alcohol treatment center. "She's learning how to distance herself from the problems of her children," he told Carol, "and that's a good thing. Lauren went back to Craig. Maybe he's better now that he's gone through some anger management and is out on parole. Let's hope so."

"Not our problem, Love," she said.

"No, thank God, it isn't," he said. "Beth's son hasn't settled down yet, though he is still living with the same woman he's been with over a year now. Beth doesn't pay much attention to him anymore. At the advice of her AA sponsor, she doesn't let him stay overnight in her home, though she does invite him and his girlfriend to dinner."

When El got sick and Beth went into residential treatment for alcoholism, the trips they routinely took together to the trailer were suspended. El missed his retreats, particularly since Joanne was more and more dependent. She was often unable to choose which outfit to wear, though she could dress herself still. She'd pile up discarded items and then rail against the mess, not able to see it was a mess of her own making. She'd rifle through the discard pile, putting on the same outfit she had been wearing that day and looking again in her closet for something to wear. Her actions were frustrating to him.

Having an experienced caregiver in the condo three times a week helped. Belle would shoo away Ellis and, turning to Joanne, tell her, "Why, Honey, you look divine in that outfit. How about grabbing those red shoes I see there in the closet, while I hang up these things you don't want just now." Her attention to Joanne provided times of much needed detachment for El. He learned from watching Belle to pleasantly agree with whatever Joanne was saying, even though many of her utterances defied logic. "Yes, I've noticed the dog does track in lots of dirt, and I've been wondering myself what we should do about it," he said one day in response to her. They didn't own a dog, never had. His non-demanding agreement had a calming effect on Joanne. He was genuinely sorry that his wife had to suffer with

Alzheimer's, but he had suffered for many years too. He was glad he had already made the decision to put her in a home when the time came. It made sense that she might even be better off, for such a placement would provide security and reliable help when needed. *More than I could do*, he thought.

Carol and he talked about these things, giving him an outlet for his feelings. The presence of Carol in his life became a new reality for El, one he longed to make permanent. Carol never wavered in her invitation for him to come and live with her, though she suggested a visit first might be in order. He began to talk about coming to Santa Bella.

"When, El?" she asked nearly every day.

"It will happen, my love," he'd say.

Then one day, he made up his mind. He made plans for Joanne's care, called George and Henry, and bought an airplane ticket. He had asked Carol about dates before, so he was pretty sure the one he picked out would suit her. They jostled on the telephone, he teasing her about coming to see her, she pressuring him to decide, before he finally said to her, "I'm sick and tired of being an invalid! I've been going to doctors two years now, waiting for them to tell me I'm better, so I can live. I'm tired of it! I'm going to live *now*, and if I die while I'm living, then I die."

"Good for you," she said. "Does this mean you are coming to see me?"

"Soon," he said, "pretty soon." She heard teasing in his tone, and wasn't about to let him get away with it. She teased back, but he heard the note of seriousness in her voice. "I can start making room in my closet for your clothes?" She demanded an answer and he gave it to her.

"Yes, you can." He was euphoric. She imagined his broad smile and the twinkle in his eyes.

"Oh, El." She let out a long-held breath. "Buy that ticket *now*."

"I already have, my love," he said.

"Thank God, thank God, thank God!"

Carol waited impatiently in the baggage claim area of the airport a few weeks later. She was dressed in the silky royal blue A-line dress he had sent her for her birthday. She wore her red wool jacket over it, as it was cold and rainy that day. She wanted to wear higher heeled shoes in red, but she settled for her best medium-heeled shoes; the last thing she wanted was to fall.

Ellis reluctantly accepted the wheelchair offered him as he came off the plane. Carol had insisted that he accept help "to save energy for more important things, Love." *Some Texan!* he mused. *Riding in on push ring wheels and clunky castors to sweep his love off her feet! Humph!* Nevertheless, he politely thanked the strong, young service attendant and made small talk with her as she pushed him through the long airport passageways. He wondered what Carol would think when she finally saw him, thin as he was and tired from the trip.

People streamed through the door after coming down the escalator into the baggage area, but El was not among them. Carol looked wide-eyed and nervous at the elevators behind her, but none of them seemed active. *He didn't miss the plane. He called me from Houston as he was getting on. Oh, Lord, please, please let everything be all right.*

At that point her prayer was answered; an elevator door slid open. She could see him in a wheelchair: an old man, face drawn with fatigue, his terribly thin body bent forward slightly, a shiny head prominent beneath silver strands of hair combed neatly to each side of his face. She was shocked. He seemed so frail. A moment of doubt seized her. She frowned. *What had they begun?*

Ellis saw her too, but not her facial expression. *How small she was!* The pictures she had sent hadn't accurately reflected her five-foot-two-inch frame. He had thought of her as an exceptionally powerful woman and was ready for someone sturdily built, but Carol seemed more delicate than he expected. *Lord, I love this woman!* His face broke into a huge wide smile and his eyes lit up.

Carol saw the smile and recognized it as the one in pictures taken specifically for her. Her heart beat wildly. The love she had felt these past long years welled up in her. She smiled back. Glee propelled her as she clicked her heels on the tiled floor, eagerly moving toward him.

The attendant barely had time to set the wheelchair brake; Ellis was already gripping the wheel rings. Before her eyes, Carol saw El rise—his tall body unfolding, expanding, and filling the air with the confidence and strength of the magnificent man she had long imagined. The thinness of his body disappeared; he stood solidly before her, deliciously real, her man standing there with open arms inviting her in. Quickly, Carol yielded her body as he cradled her with his long arms.

Tears streamed down both their faces. Lifting her face to his, he kissed her tears and gently whispered, "I love you so." She barely had time to whisper back, "and I love you," before she felt his warm, full lips on hers. With that tender, soft and deep, loving kiss, they said hello to the rest of life.

ABOUT THE AUTHORS

The writing of *Love Comes at Twilight* was a team effort between California author Kay Mehl Miller and Texas geologist Al Francis who, coincidentally, met while playing bridge on the Internet. Both being romantics, they decided to fashion a sweet, but challenging, love story for seniors. Al Francis supplied most of the emails from the male protagonist and valuable feedback and encouragement to writer Kay Mehl Miller. She invented characters, plot and narrative. Dr. Miller is the author of two non-fiction books: Talking it Over: Understanding Sexual Diversity; and Living With the Stranger in Me: An Exploration of Aging.

Made in the USA
San Bernardino, CA
23 March 2014